THE LOCKER ROOM

TIMOTHÉ LE BOUCHER

Life Drawn
By Humanoids

TIMOTHÉ LE BOUCHER
Story & Art

•

MONTANA KANE
Translator

•

AMANDA LUCIDO
US Edition Editor

VINCENT HENRY
Original Edition Editor

JERRY FRISSEN
Senior Art Director

RYAN LEWIS
Junior Designer

MARK WAID
Publisher

Rights and Licensing - licensing@humanoids.com
Press and Social Media - pr@humanoids.com

THE LOCKER ROOM. This title is a publication of Humanoids, Inc. 8033 Sunset Blvd. #628, Los Angeles, CA 90046.

Library of Congress Control Number: 2020903659

Life Drawn is an imprint of Humanoids, Inc.

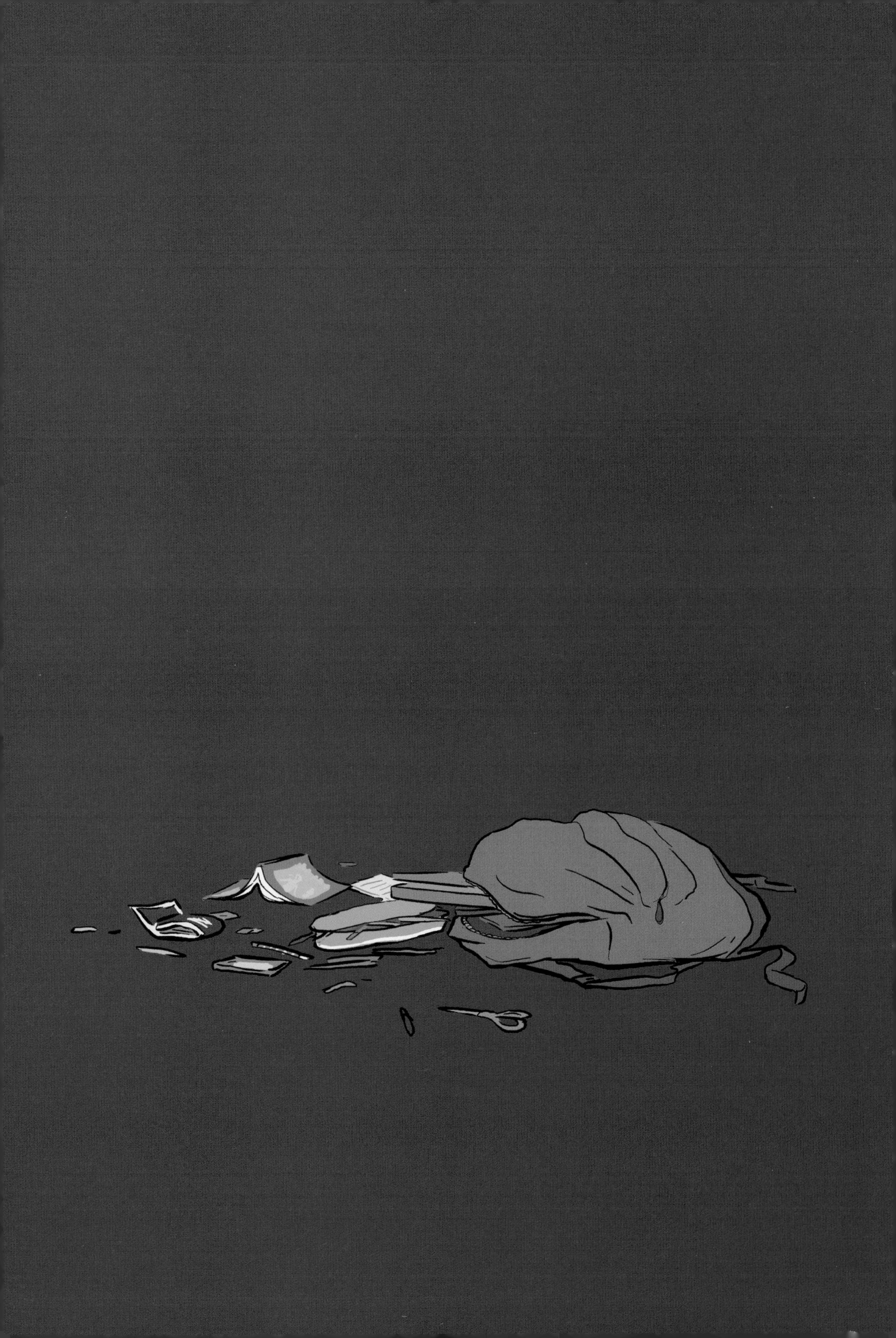

FOREWORD

This is a story about school-based bullying and harassment that, while fictional, was largely inspired by my experiences in middle and high school, with many anecdotes paralleling true, lived events. The locker rooms were a closed space, devoid of any authority figures, where students were left to their own devices. The words were harsh, the violence recurring. Being even slightly different was enough to make you a target.

This story takes place within a game of hierarchical domination, one that is exacerbated by toxic masculinity. This theme, these experiences, this voyeuristic perspective mixed with the claustrophobia of such a confined setting, are the foundation upon which I built *The Locker Room*.

The wounds of the body heal, but those of the spirit live on in me and in these pages.

–Timothé Le Boucher

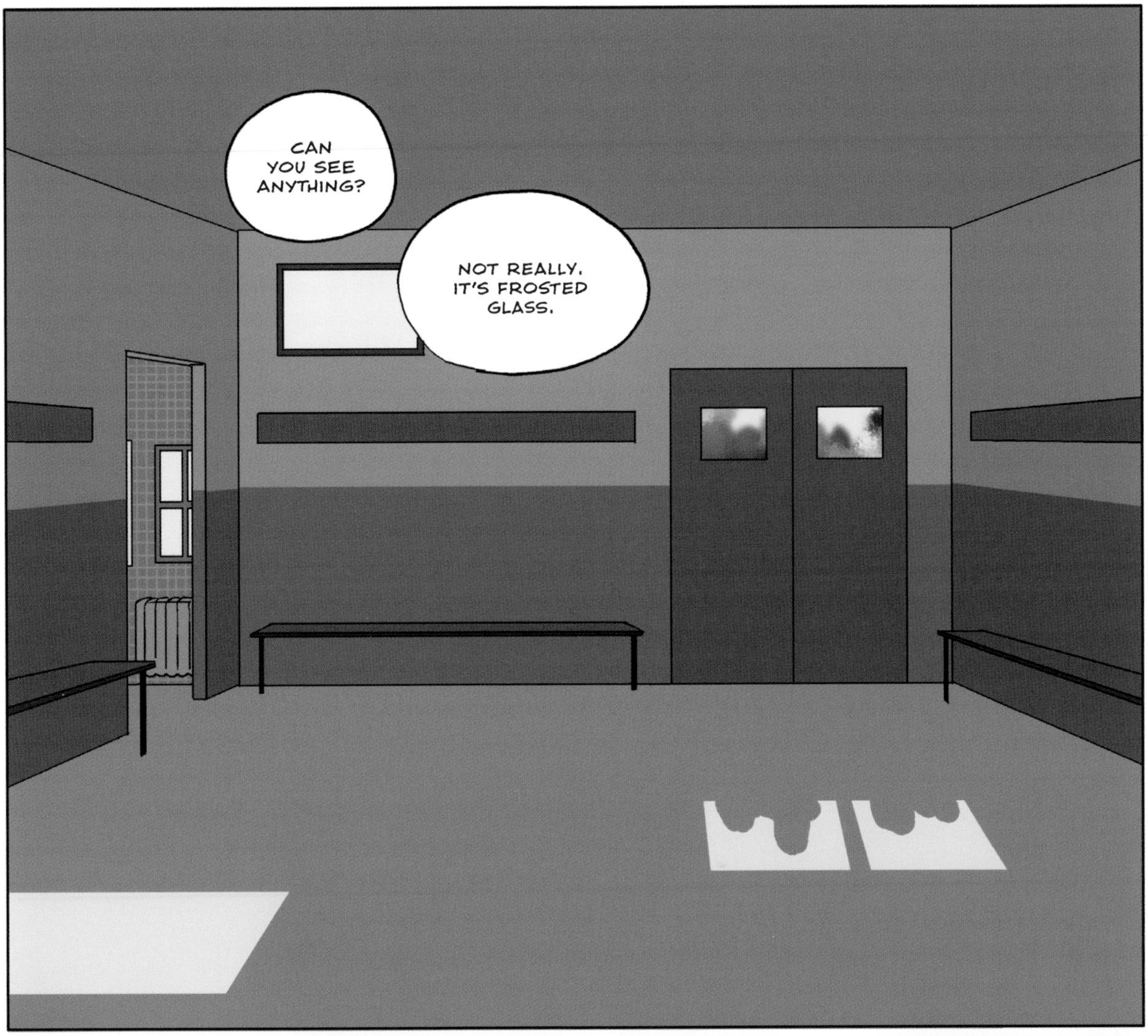
CAN YOU SEE ANYTHING?
NOT REALLY. IT'S FROSTED GLASS.

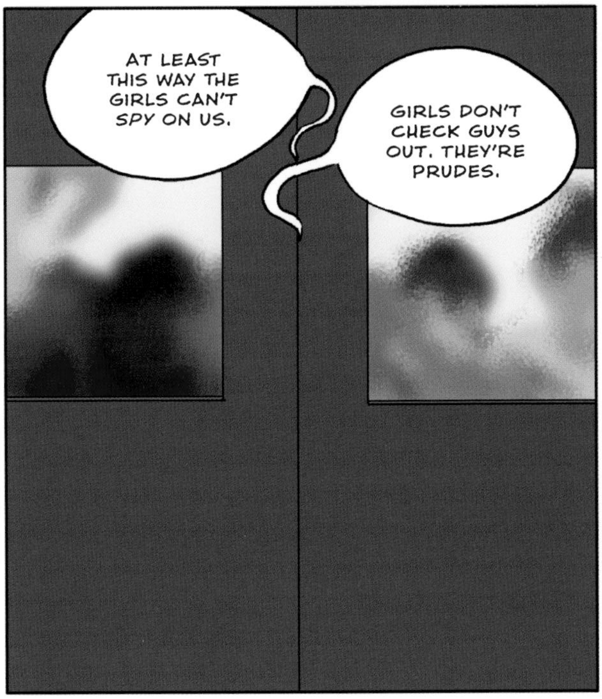
AT LEAST THIS WAY THE GIRLS CAN'T *SPY* ON US.
GIRLS DON'T CHECK GUYS OUT. THEY'RE PRUDES.

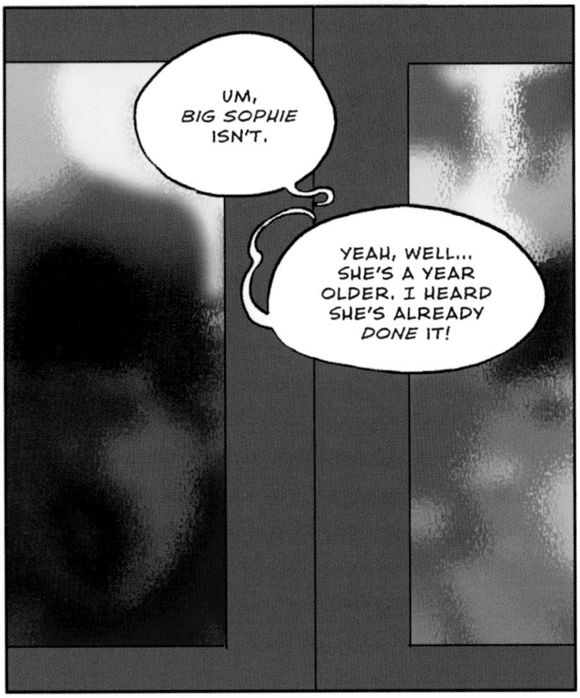
UM, *BIG SOPHIE* ISN'T.
YEAH, WELL... SHE'S A YEAR OLDER. I HEARD SHE'S ALREADY *DONE* IT!

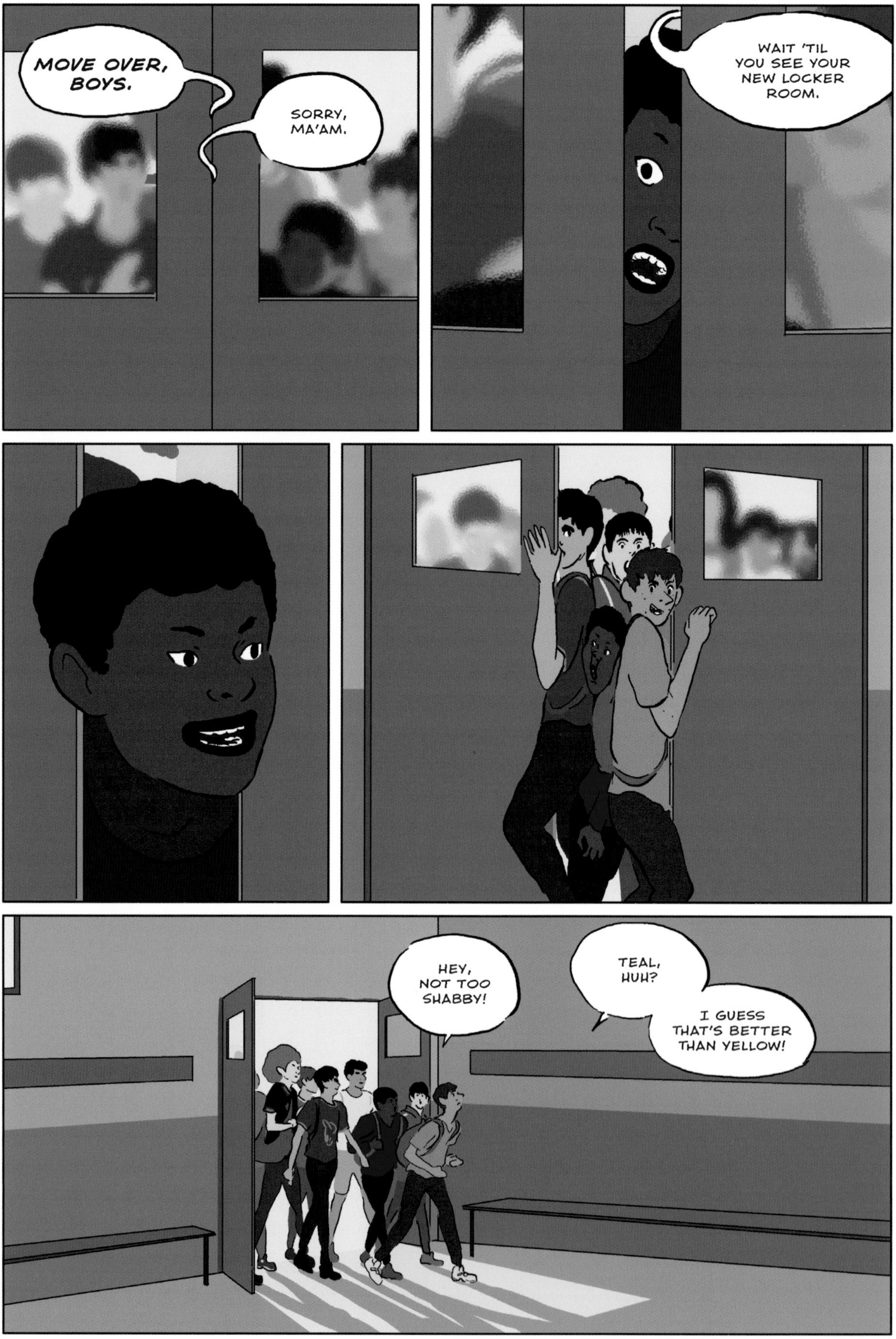
MOVE OVER, BOYS.
SORRY, MA'AM.
WAIT 'TIL YOU SEE YOUR NEW LOCKER ROOM.
HEY, NOT TOO SHABBY!
TEAL, HUH?
I GUESS THAT'S BETTER THAN YELLOW!

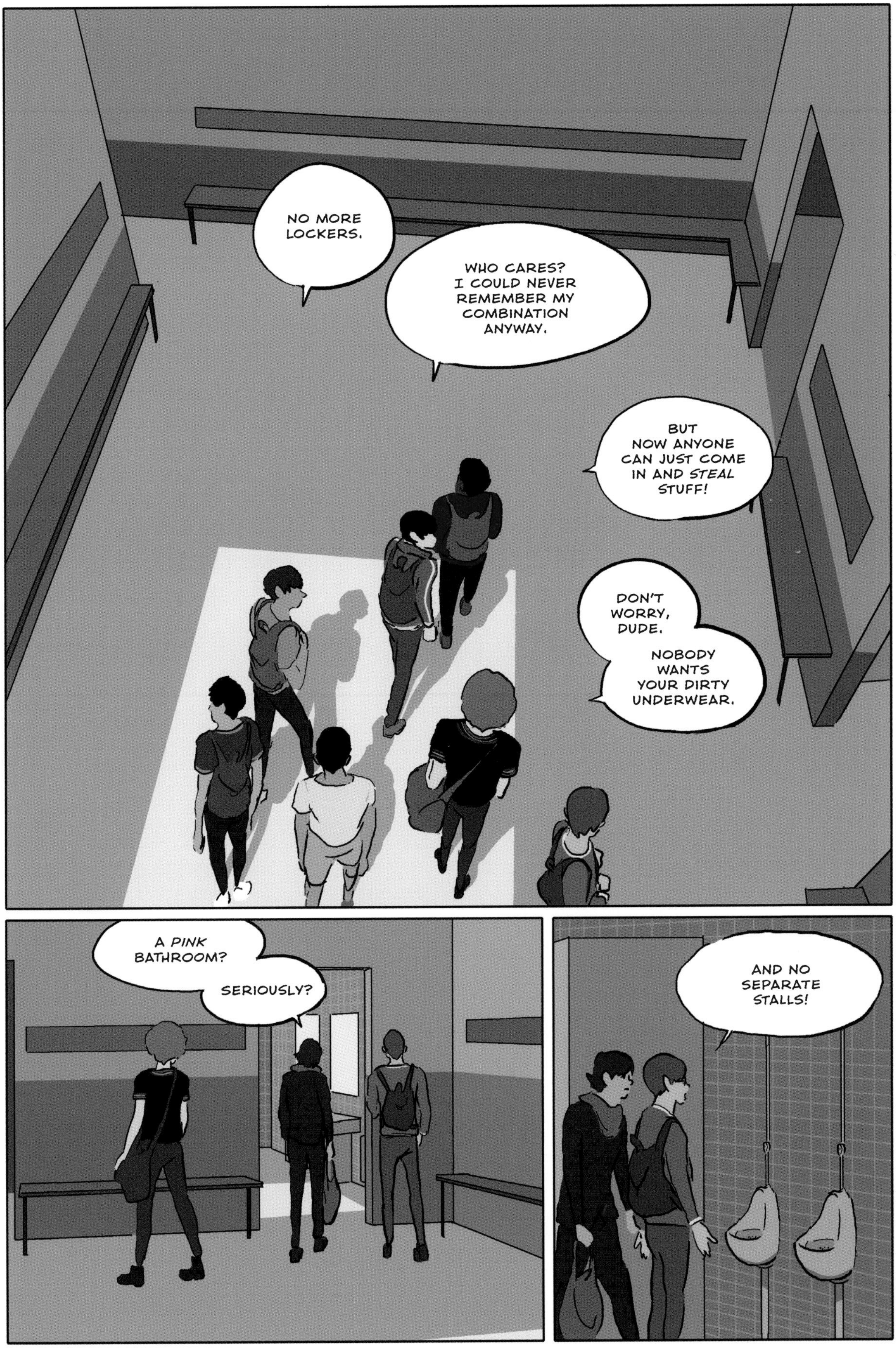
NO MORE LOCKERS.
WHO CARES? I COULD NEVER REMEMBER MY COMBINATION ANYWAY.
BUT NOW ANYONE CAN JUST COME IN AND *STEAL* STUFF!
DON'T WORRY, DUDE.
NOBODY WANTS YOUR DIRTY UNDERWEAR.
A *PINK* BATHROOM?
SERIOUSLY?
AND NO SEPARATE STALLS!

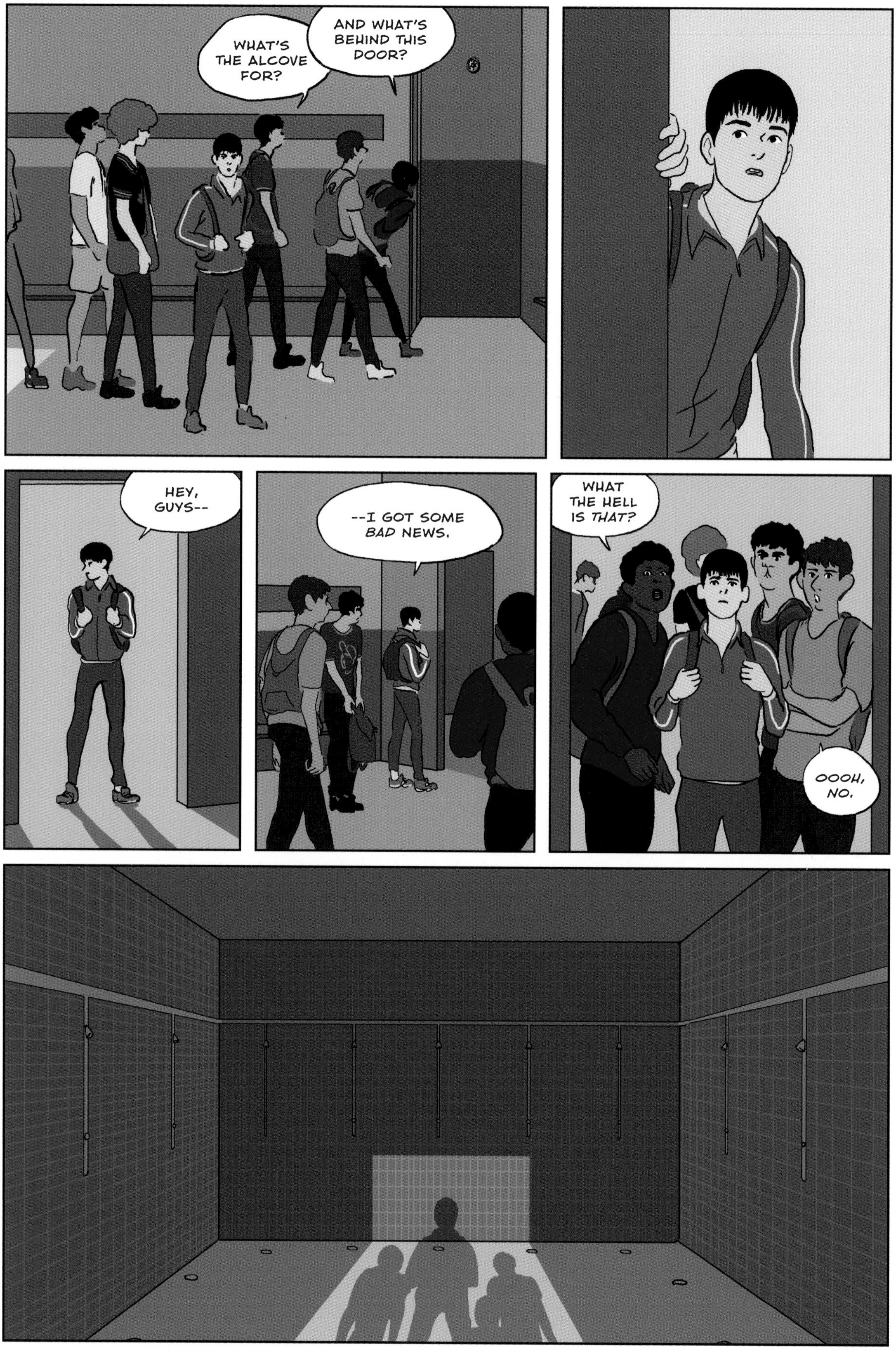
WHAT'S THE ALCOVE FOR?
AND WHAT'S BEHIND THIS DOOR?
HEY, GUYS--
--I GOT SOME *BAD* NEWS.
WHAT THE HELL IS *THAT?*
OOOH, NO.

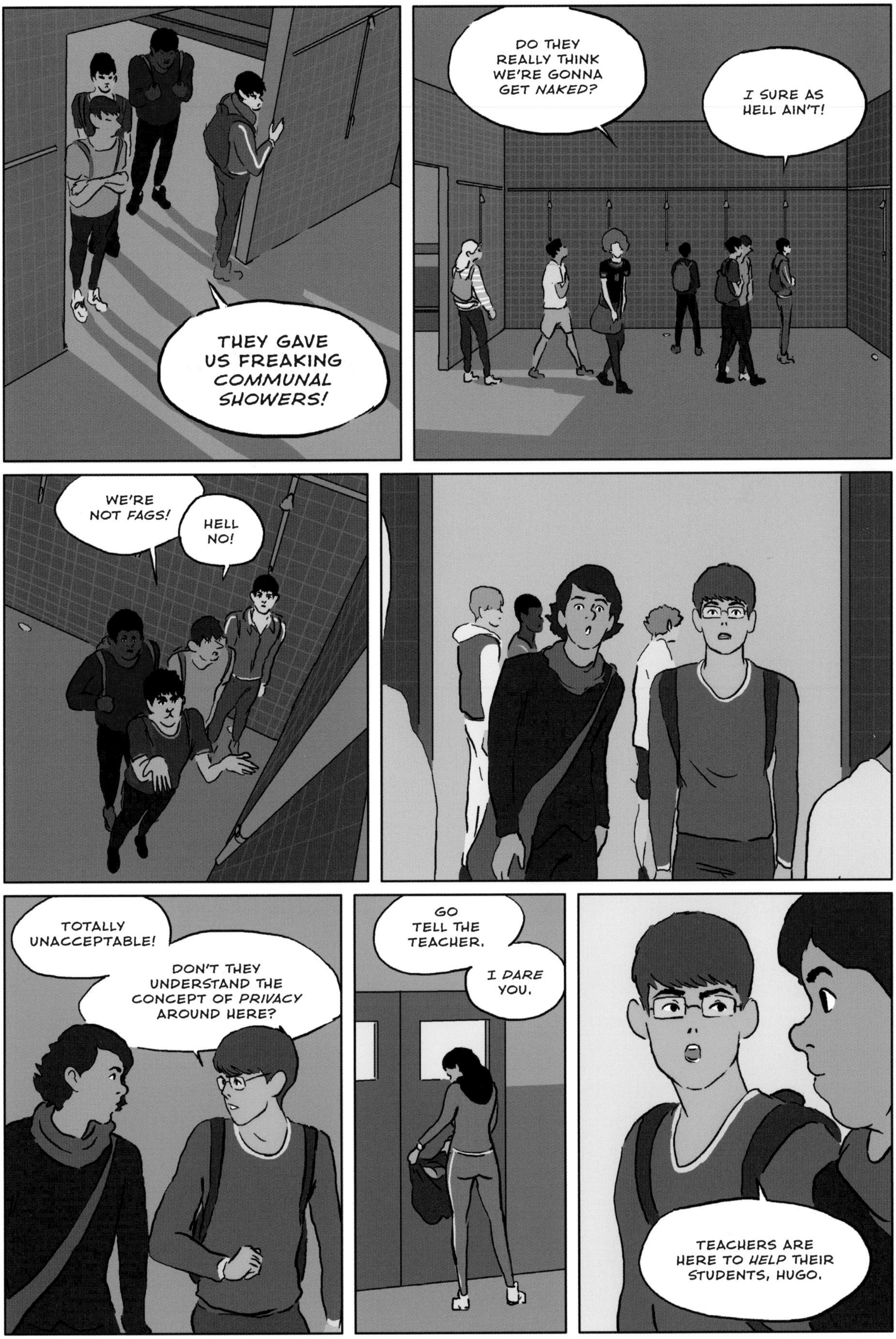
THEY GAVE US FREAKING *COMMUNAL SHOWERS!*
DO THEY REALLY THINK WE'RE GONNA GET *NAKED?*
I SURE AS HELL AIN'T!
WE'RE NOT *FAGS!*
HELL NO!
TOTALLY UNACCEPTABLE!
DON'T THEY UNDERSTAND THE CONCEPT OF *PRIVACY* AROUND HERE?
GO TELL THE TEACHER.
I *DARE* YOU.
TEACHERS ARE HERE TO *HELP* THEIR STUDENTS, HUGO.

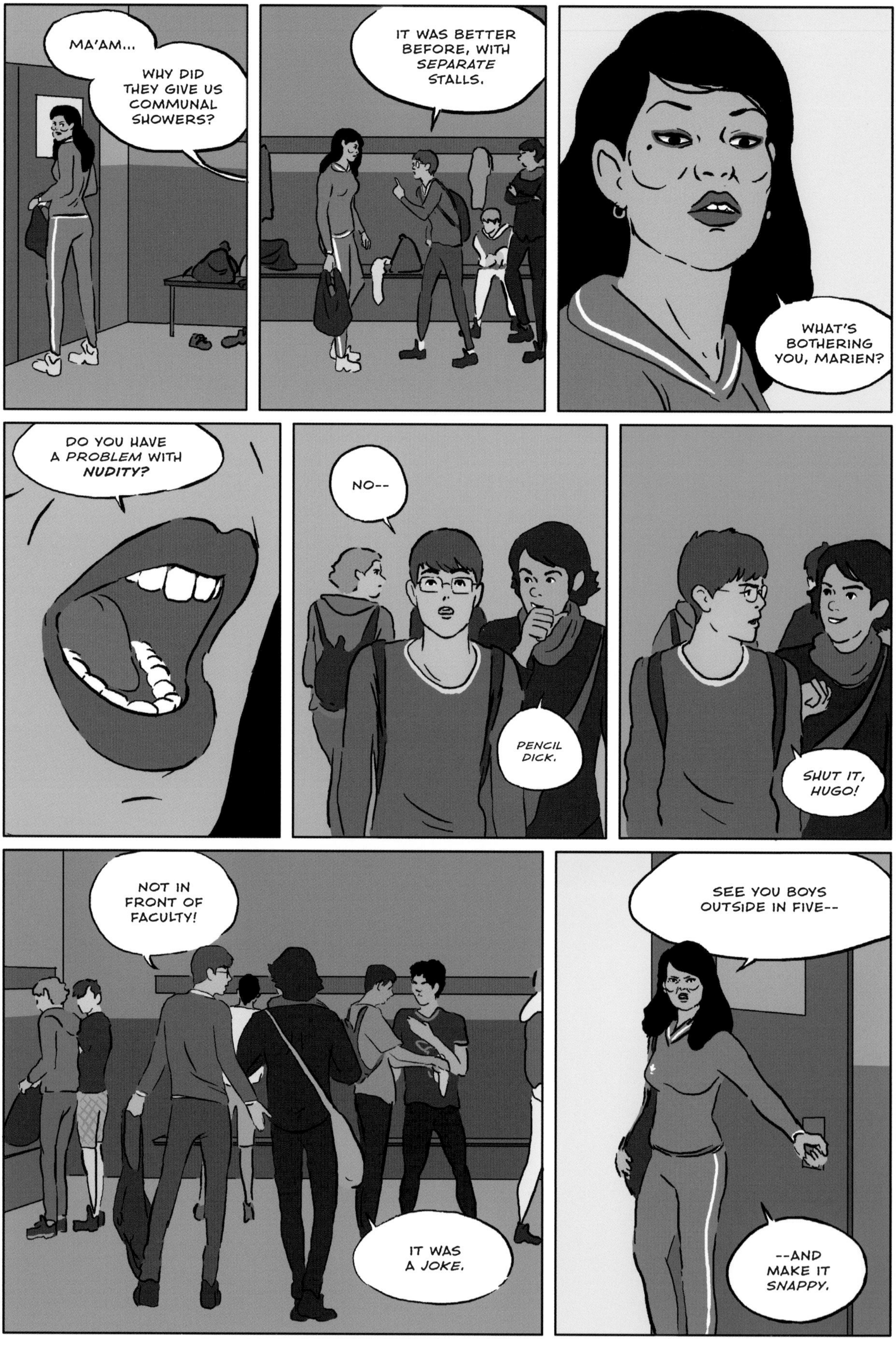
MA'AM...
WHY DID THEY GIVE US COMMUNAL SHOWERS?
IT WAS BETTER BEFORE, WITH SEPARATE STALLS.
WHAT'S BOTHERING YOU, MARIEN?
DO YOU HAVE A PROBLEM WITH NUDITY?
NO--
PENCIL DICK.
SHUT IT, HUGO!
NOT IN FRONT OF FACULTY!
IT WAS A JOKE.
SEE YOU BOYS OUTSIDE IN FIVE--
--AND MAKE IT SNAPPY.

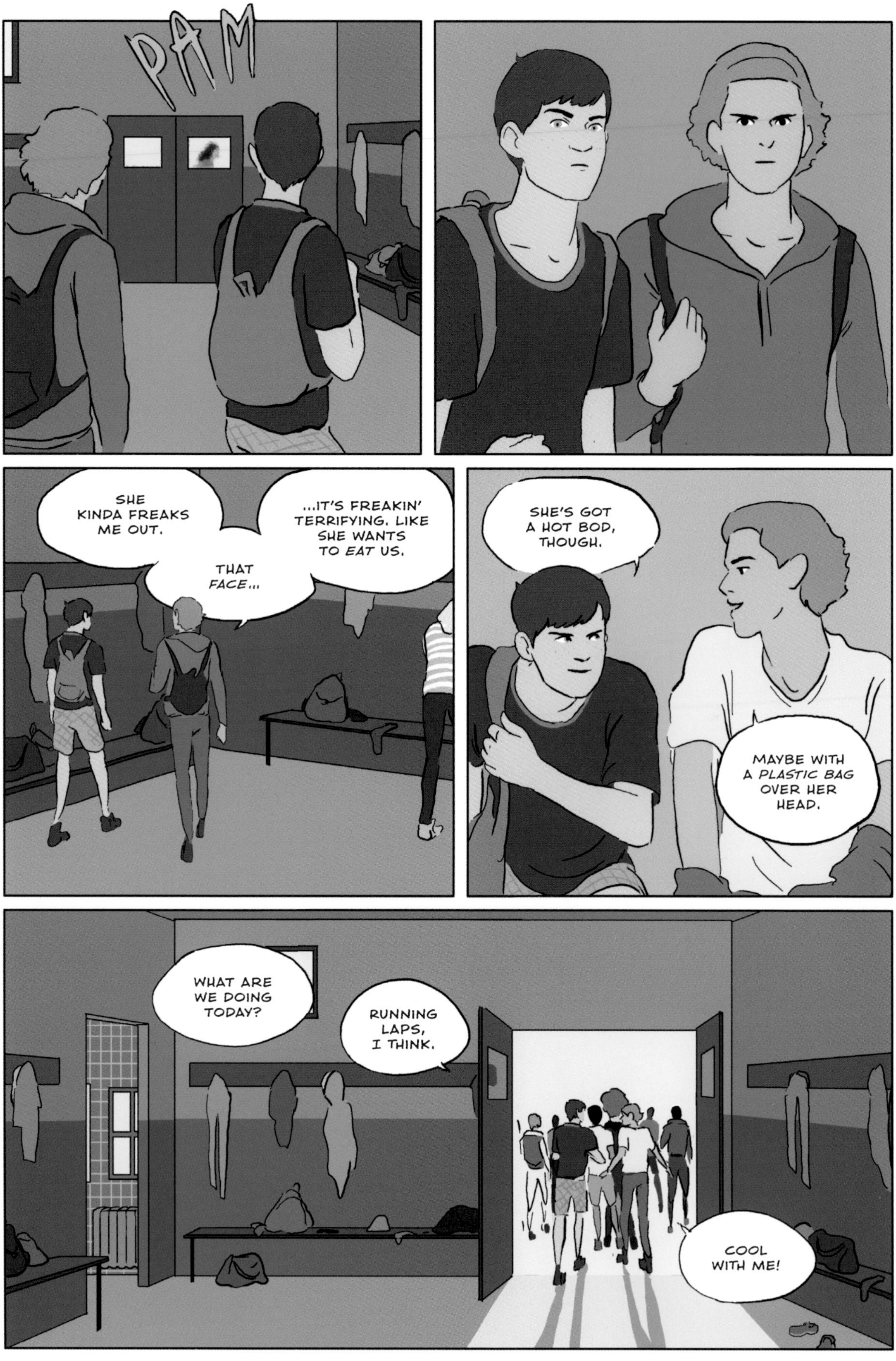
PAM
SHE KINDA FREAKS ME OUT.
THAT *FACE*...
...IT'S FREAKIN' TERRIFYING. LIKE SHE WANTS TO *EAT* US.
SHE'S GOT A HOT BOD, THOUGH.
MAYBE WITH A *PLASTIC BAG* OVER HER HEAD.
WHAT ARE WE DOING TODAY?
RUNNING LAPS, I THINK.
COOL WITH ME!

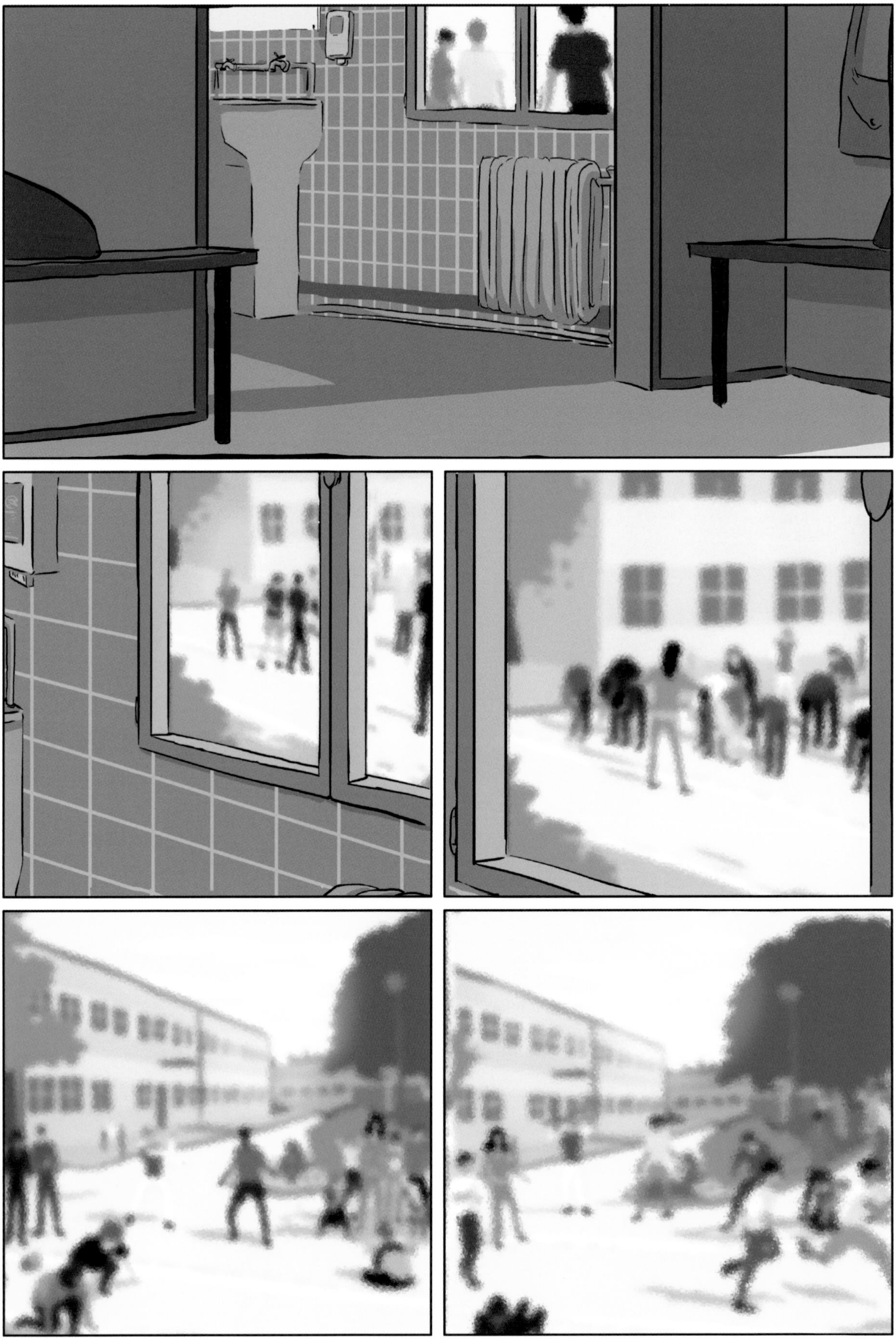

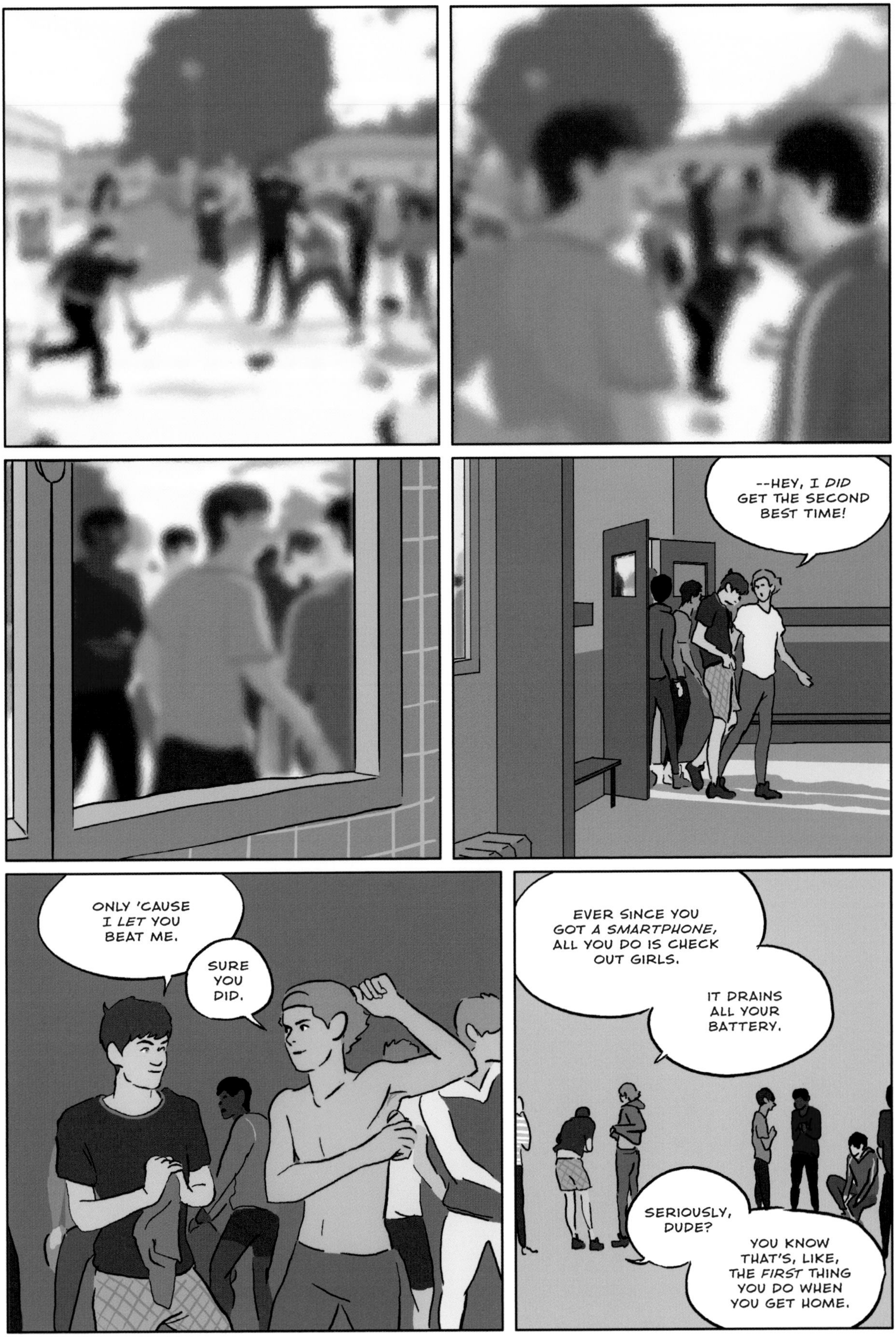
--HEY, I *DID* GET THE SECOND BEST TIME!
ONLY 'CAUSE I *LET* YOU BEAT ME.
SURE YOU DID.
EVER SINCE YOU GOT A *SMARTPHONE*, ALL YOU DO IS CHECK OUT GIRLS.
IT DRAINS ALL YOUR BATTERY.
SERIOUSLY, DUDE?
YOU KNOW THAT'S, LIKE, THE *FIRST* THING YOU DO WHEN YOU GET HOME.

CLOSE THE DOOR, MAN! THE GIRLS'LL SEE US.

SORRY.

GRAT GRAT

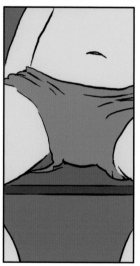

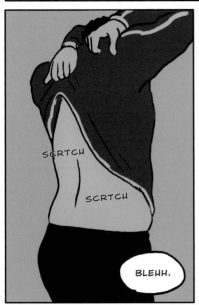

SCRTCH

SCRTCH

BLEHH.

I'M GLAD I'M NOT CORENTIN.

NO KIDDING.

IT'S LIKE *JELLO* WHEN HE MOVES.

LOWER YOUR VOICE, GAUTHIER.

HE CAN'T HEAR ME.

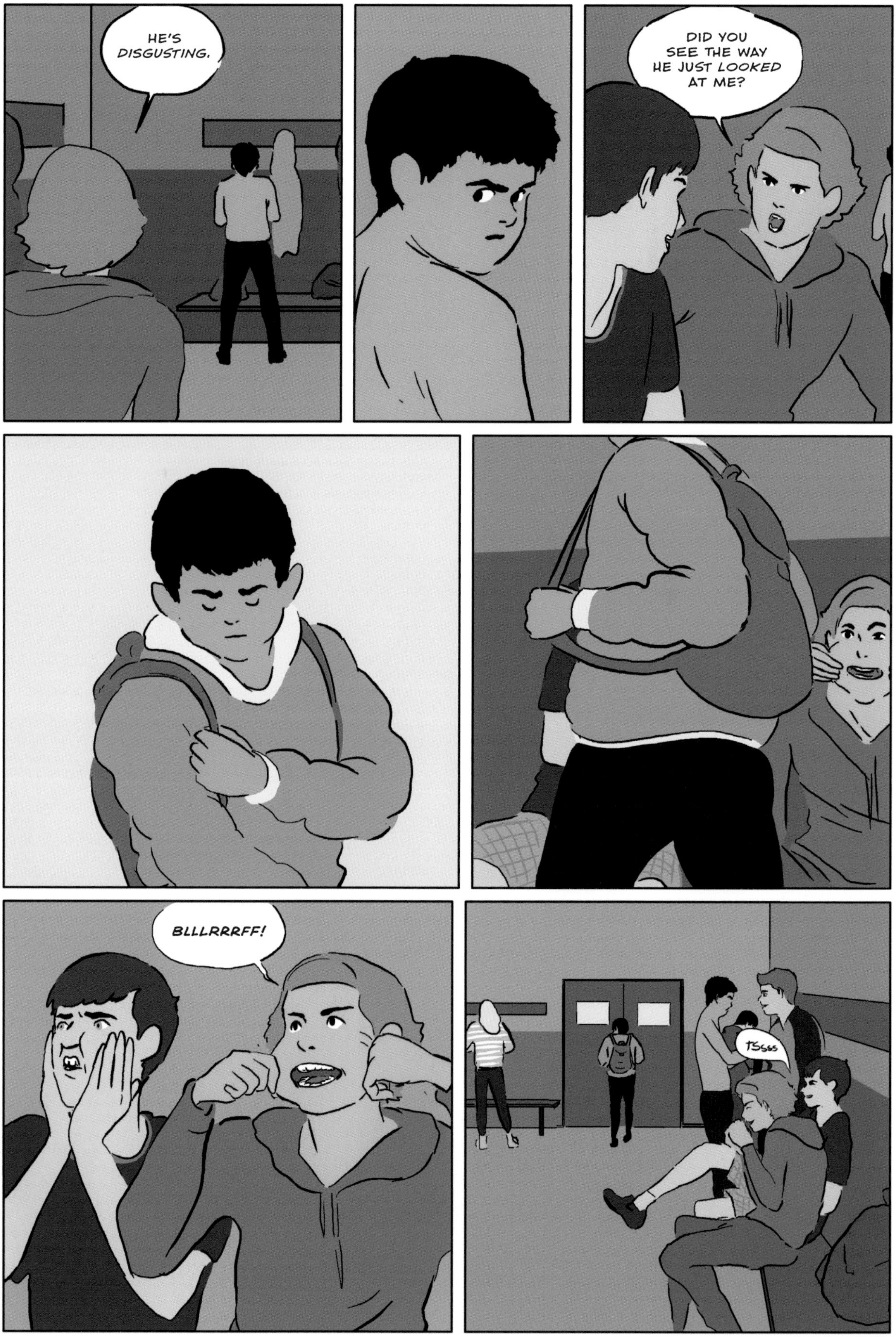
HE'S DISGUSTING.
DID YOU SEE THE WAY HE JUST LOOKED AT ME?
BLLLRRRFF!
TSsss

I NEED WATER.

ME TOO.

AT LEAST IT'S OKAY TO DRINK NOW.

WHAT D'YOU MEAN?

THIS ONE TIME, I WAS DRINKING AND IT HAD A WEIRD TASTE...

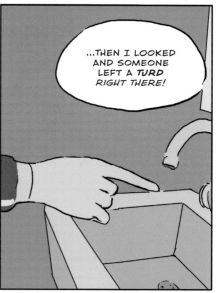

...THEN I LOOKED AND SOMEONE LEFT A TURD RIGHT THERE!

IT WAS ALL DRIED UP AND CONTAMINATING THE WATER.

SO NOW, I ALWAYS CHECK FIRST.

GROSS. GUESS I GOTTA START CHECKING, TOO.

IT FEELS WEIRD TO HAVE CLEAN TOILETS.

I BET THEY WON'T STAY THAT WAY FOR LONG.

ESPECIALLY IF *CORENTIN* USES THEM!

EVERYONE'S GONE.

HURRY OR WE'RE GONNA MISS OUR BREAK.

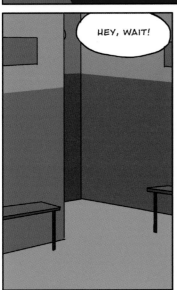

HEY, WAIT!

HELP ME UP HERE!

I WANNA *CHECK* SOMETHING.

YOU GOT ME?

YEAH, GO 'HEAD.

YOU BETTER NOT HAVE ANY *SHIT* ON YOUR SHOES.

YEEESSS!

WHAT ARE YOU BOYS DOING? GET OUT OF HERE. *NOW!*

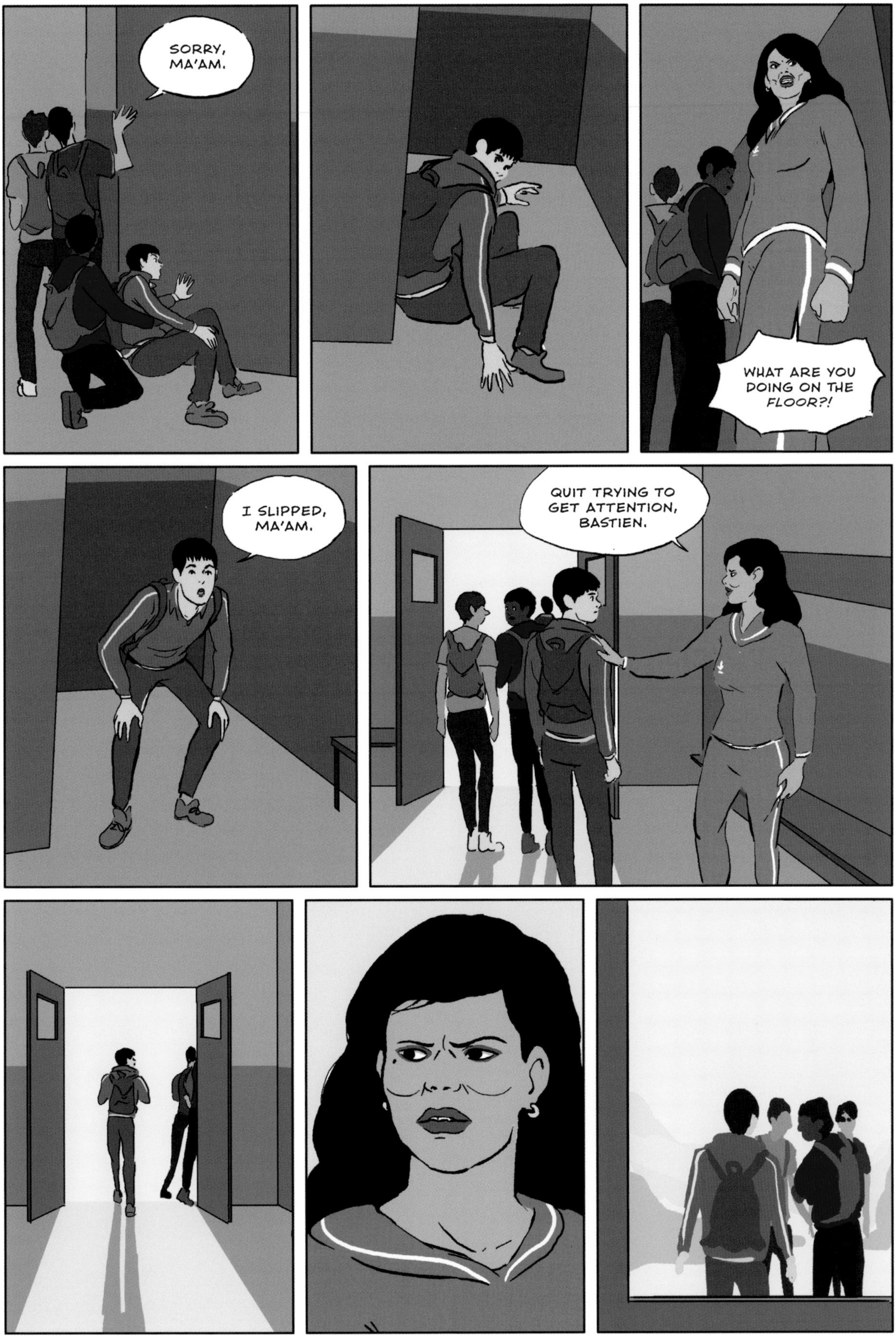
SORRY, MA'AM.
WHAT ARE YOU DOING ON THE *FLOOR?!*
I SLIPPED, MA'AM.
QUIT TRYING TO GET ATTENTION, BASTIEN.

WEEK TWO.

WOO, IT'S WAY TOO HOT OUT THERE.

THE GIRLS SAID NOT SHOWERING IS MAKING US *STINK*.

NAH, A LITTLE DEODORANT AND I'M GOOD TO GO.

THAT ONLY WORKS FOR SO LONG.

IT'S LIKE WHEN YOU TAKE A *DUMP* AND THEN USE *AIR FRESHENER*.

YOU CAN SMELL THE SHIT UNDERNEATH.

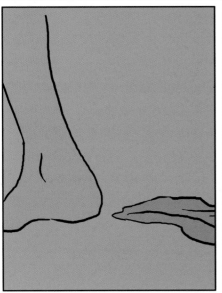

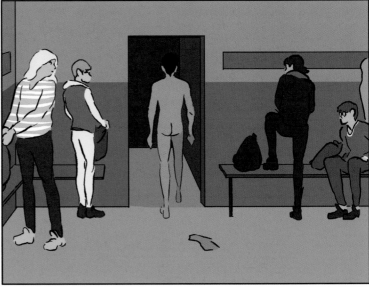

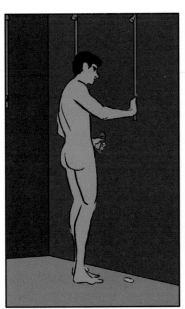

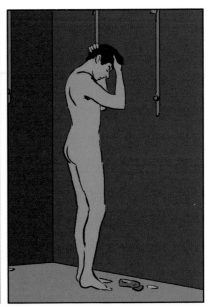

CHECK IT OUT. HE'S TAKING A SHOWER!

THAT IS ONE *HAIRY* DUDE.

THEN AGAIN, HE HAD TO REPEAT A GRADE. *TWICE.*

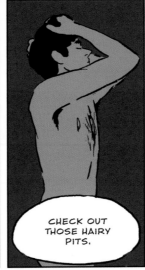

CHECK OUT THOSE HAIRY PITS.

HE'S LIKE A *GORILLA.*

YOU THINK HE'S GOT A BIG DICK?

MEH. AVERAGE.

YOU KNOW, THE DUDE'S TOTALLY RIGHT TO SHOWER.

AT LEAST HE WON'T SMELL.

YEAH.

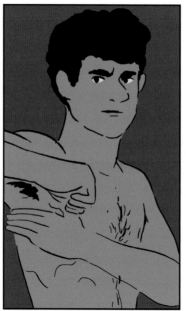

WE NEEDA STOP STARING AT HIM BEFORE PEOPLE START THINKING WE'RE FAGS.

YEP.

YOU KNOW, AT THE RUGBY CLUB I GO TO, *EVERYONE* SHOWERS.

BUT I CAN SEE HOW IT MAKES YOU UNCOMFORTABLE.

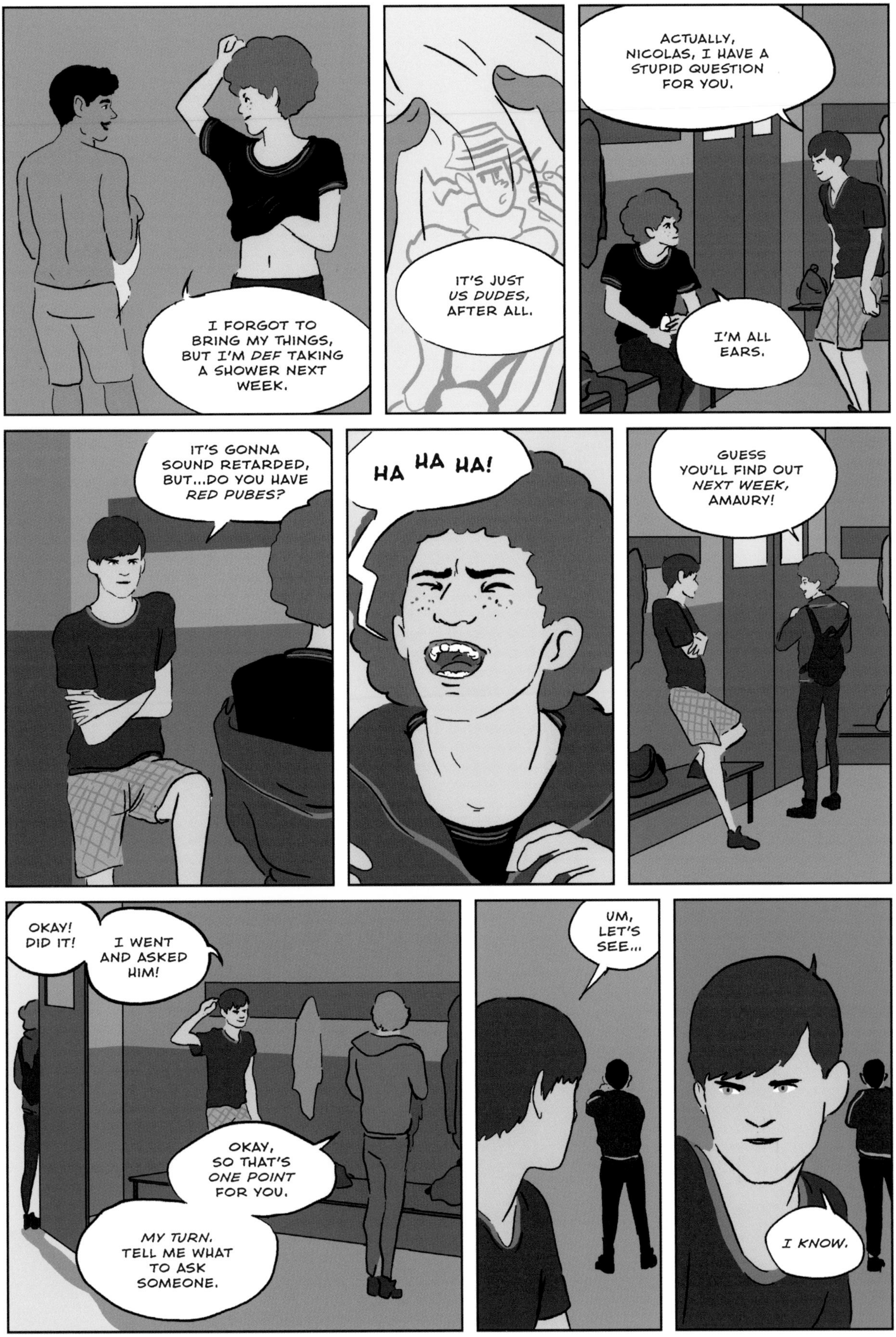
I FORGOT TO BRING MY THINGS, BUT I'M *DEF* TAKING A SHOWER NEXT WEEK.
IT'S JUST *US DUDES,* AFTER ALL.
ACTUALLY, NICOLAS, I HAVE A STUPID QUESTION FOR YOU.
I'M ALL EARS.
IT'S GONNA SOUND RETARDED, BUT...DO YOU HAVE *RED PUBES?*
HA HA HA!
GUESS YOU'LL FIND OUT *NEXT WEEK,* AMAURY!
OKAY! DID IT!
I WENT AND ASKED HIM!
OKAY, SO THAT'S *ONE POINT* FOR YOU.
MY TURN. TELL ME WHAT TO ASK SOMEONE.
UM, LET'S SEE...
I KNOW.

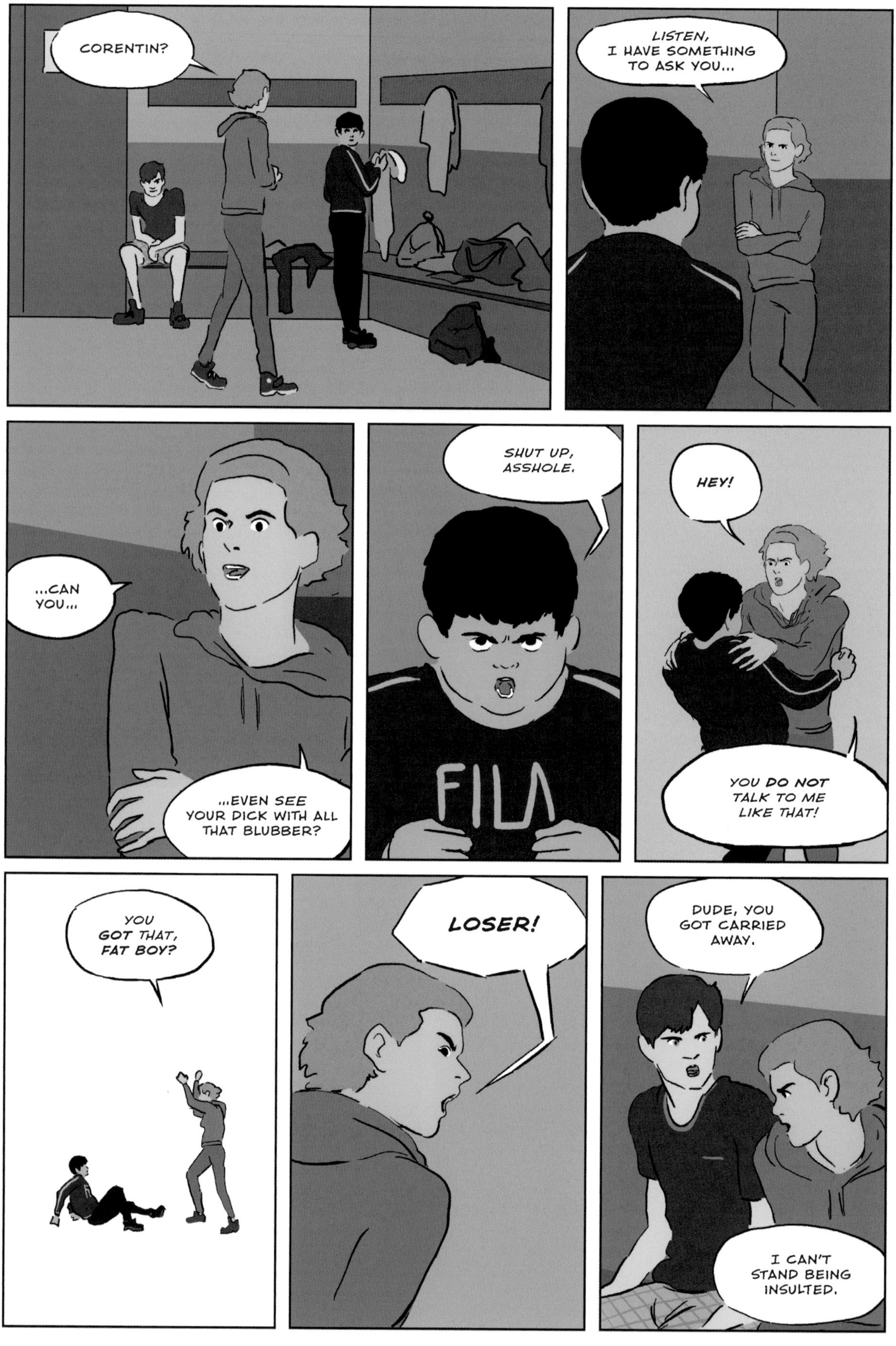
CORENTIN?
LISTEN, I HAVE SOMETHING TO ASK YOU...
...CAN YOU...
...EVEN SEE YOUR DICK WITH ALL THAT BLUBBER?
SHUT UP, ASSHOLE.
HEY!
YOU DO NOT TALK TO ME LIKE THAT!
YOU GOT THAT, FAT BOY?
LOSER!
DUDE, YOU GOT CARRIED AWAY.
I CAN'T STAND BEING INSULTED.
FILA

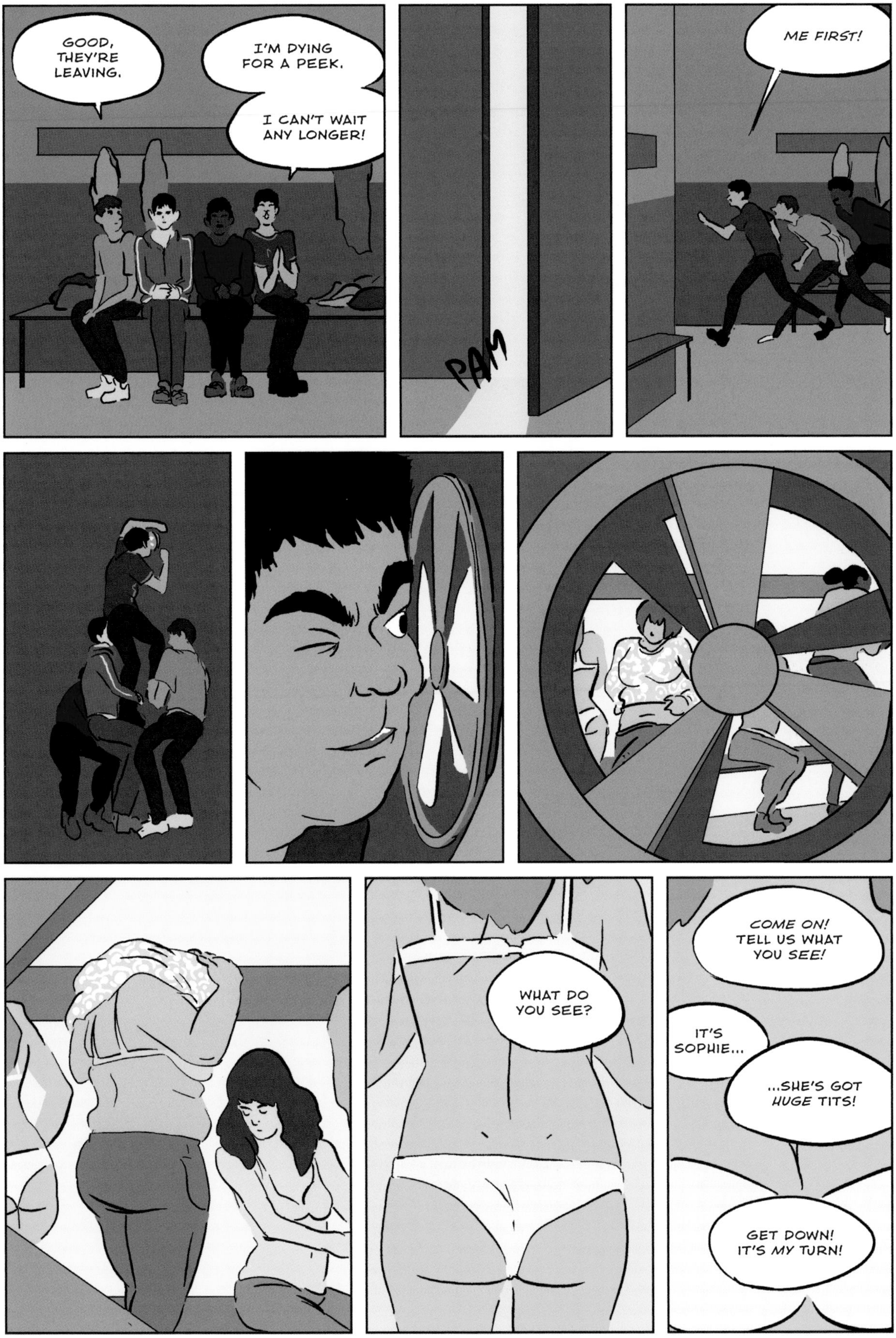
GOOD, THEY'RE LEAVING.
I'M DYING FOR A PEEK.
I CAN'T WAIT ANY LONGER!
PAM
ME FIRST!
WHAT DO YOU SEE?
COME ON! TELL US WHAT YOU SEE!
IT'S SOPHIE...
...SHE'S GOT HUGE TITS!
GET DOWN! IT'S MY TURN!

MAN, THIS IS SO AWESOME!

JUST REMEMBER, GUYS.

THIS IS *OUR* SECRET. YOU CAN'T TELL *ANYONE*.

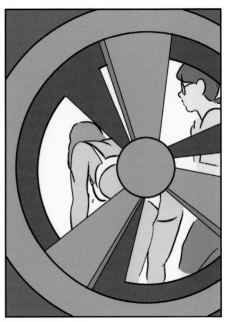

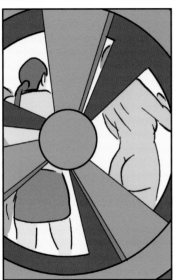

DUDE! YOU HAVE A BONER!

WELL, CAN YOU *BLAME* ME?

WHATEVER! JUST NOT IN MY *FACE*, MAN!

HERE-- I'LL PUT IT SIDEWAYS SO IT DOESN'T SHOW.

FUCK! THE TEACHER!

HURRY UP!

WATCH IT, I'M GONNA FALL!

GET OFF ME!

CAREFUL!

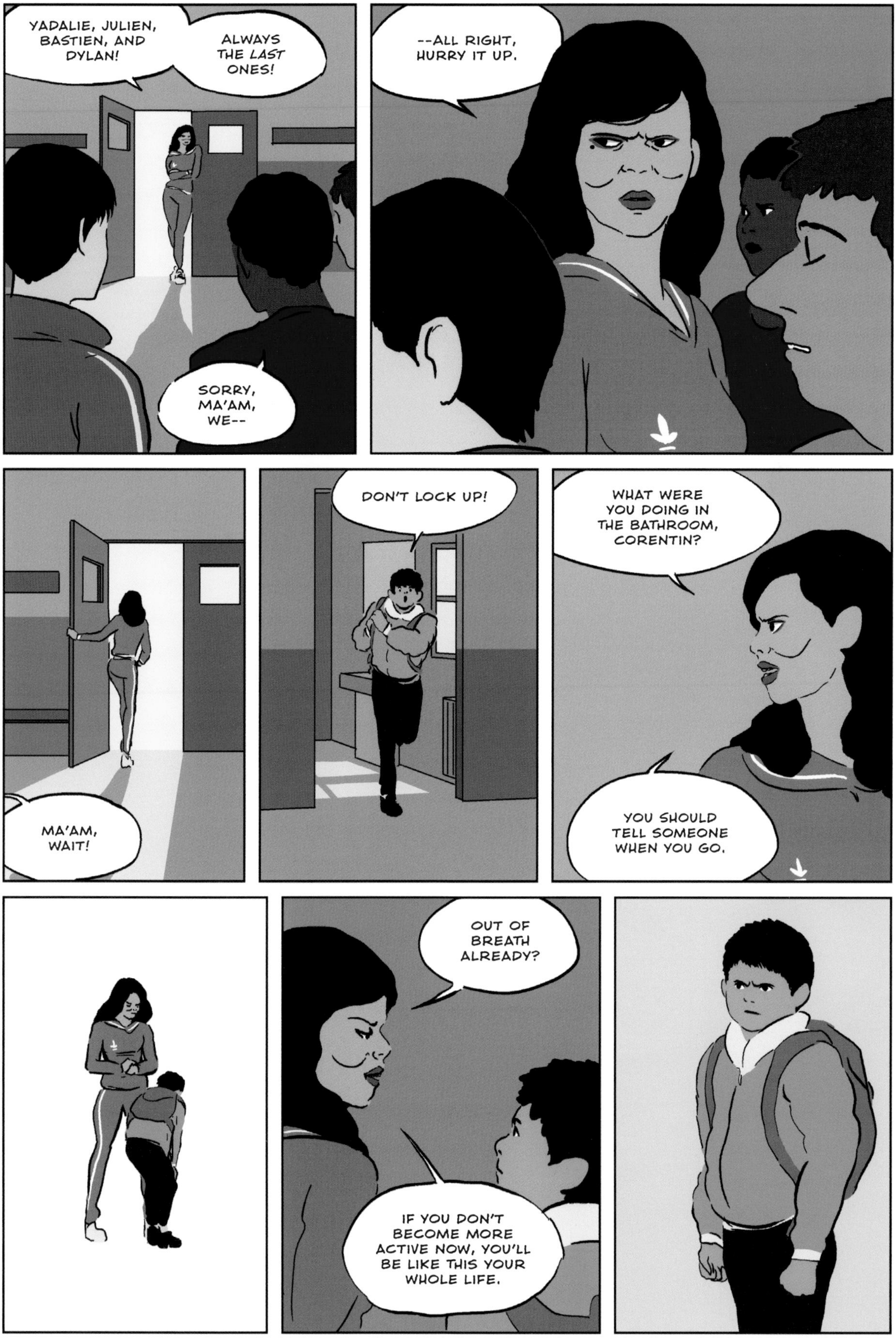
YADALIE, JULIEN, BASTIEN, AND DYLAN!
ALWAYS THE *LAST* ONES!
SORRY, MA'AM, WE--
--ALL RIGHT, HURRY IT UP.
MA'AM, WAIT!
DON'T LOCK UP!
WHAT WERE YOU DOING IN THE BATHROOM, CORENTIN?
YOU SHOULD TELL SOMEONE WHEN YOU GO.
OUT OF BREATH ALREADY?
IF YOU DON'T BECOME MORE ACTIVE NOW, YOU'LL BE LIKE THIS YOUR WHOLE LIFE.

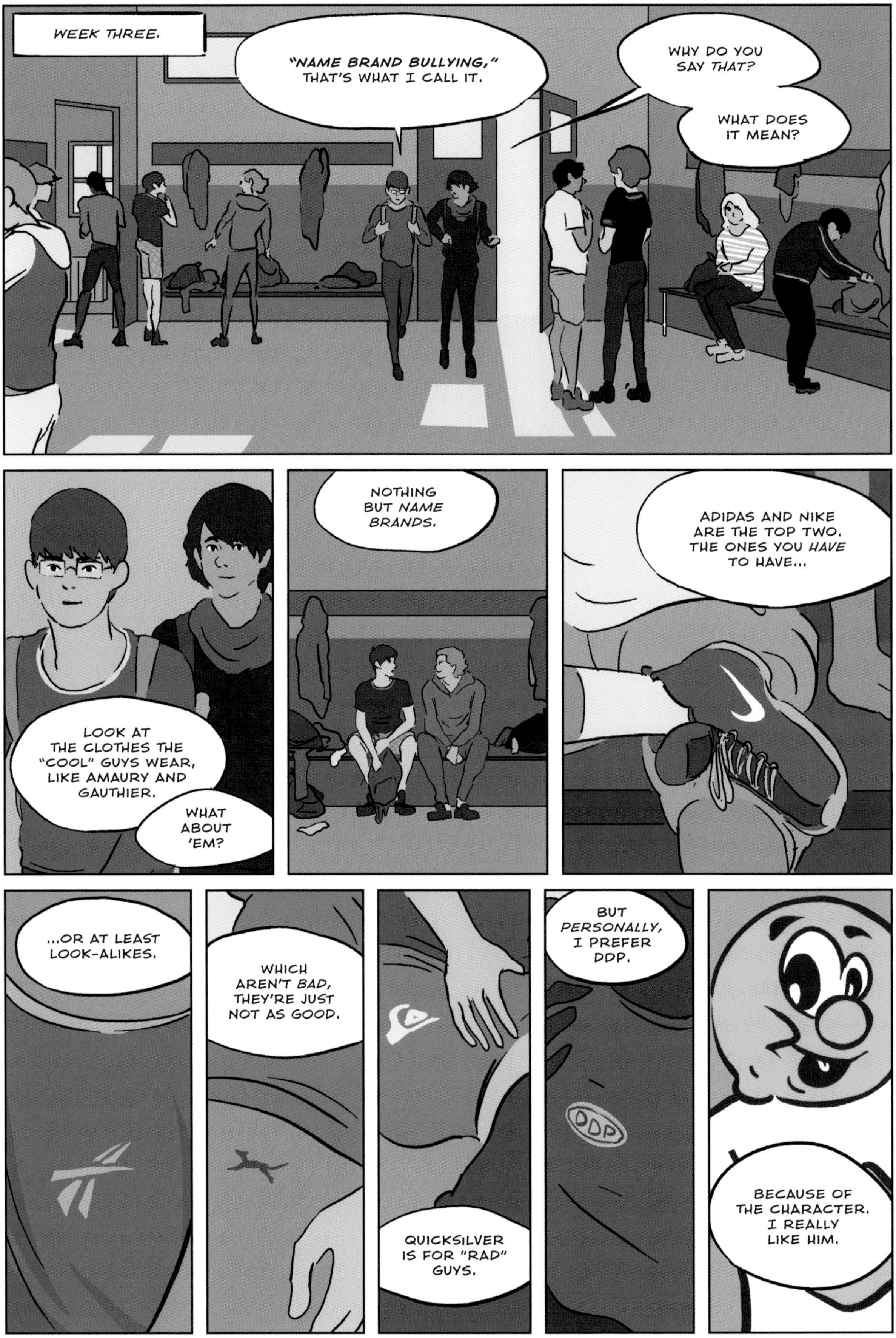
WEEK THREE.
"NAME BRAND BULLYING," THAT'S WHAT I CALL IT.
WHY DO YOU SAY THAT?
WHAT DOES IT MEAN?
LOOK AT THE CLOTHES THE "COOL" GUYS WEAR, LIKE AMAURY AND GAUTHIER.
WHAT ABOUT 'EM?
NOTHING BUT NAME BRANDS.
ADIDAS AND NIKE ARE THE TOP TWO. THE ONES YOU HAVE TO HAVE...
...OR AT LEAST LOOK-ALIKES.
WHICH AREN'T BAD, THEY'RE JUST NOT AS GOOD.
QUICKSILVER IS FOR "RAD" GUYS.
BUT PERSONALLY, I PREFER DDP.
DDP
BECAUSE OF THE CHARACTER. I REALLY LIKE HIM.

IT DOESN'T COME CHEAP...

...BUT THERE ARE *TRICKS*.

FOR EXAMPLE, YOU CAN SEW AN ALLIGATOR ONTO A CHEAP POLO SHIRT.

CHECK IT OUT! MY GRANNY MADE *THIS* ONE.

BUT *DON'T* TELL ANYONE!

PROMISE?

YOU CAN ALSO *BUY* FAKES.

I BROUGHT SOME BACK FROM TUNISIA.

BUT I GOT BUSTED...

...BECAUSE THEY DON'T SPELL THE BRAND NAMES RIGHT.

THE WORST PART, THOUGH, IS THAT EVEN IF YOU WEAR THE BEST BRANDS...

...BUT YOU DON'T KNOW HOW TO DRESS, LIKE CORENTIN, THEN YOU'RE *STILL* A LOSER.

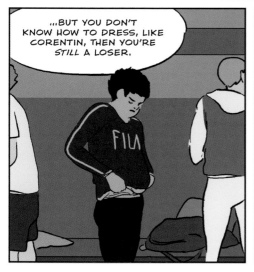

BUT EVERYBODY'S THE SAME *NAKED*, RIGHT?

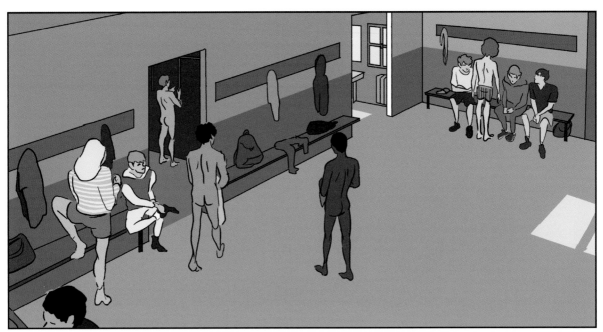

HEY, AMAURY!
TO ANSWER YOUR QUESTION
FROM THE OTHER DAY...

ARE THEY
RED ENOUGH
FOR YOU?!

*DUDE!
GET OUT
OF MY
FACE!*

SERIOUSLY,
GUYS, NEXT TIME,
HIT THE SHOWER.
Y'ALL STINK!

HEY, HAVE YOU SEEN MY BAG?

NOPE.

... HAVE YOU GUYS SEEN MY BAG?

WHO CARES?

GET LOST.

AYE, CORENTIN.

I SAW A LITTLE RED BAG RUNNING TO THE TOILET FOR A *DRINK*.

W-WHAT?

NO!

NO!

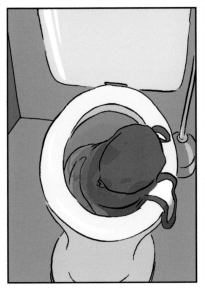

SHOOT!

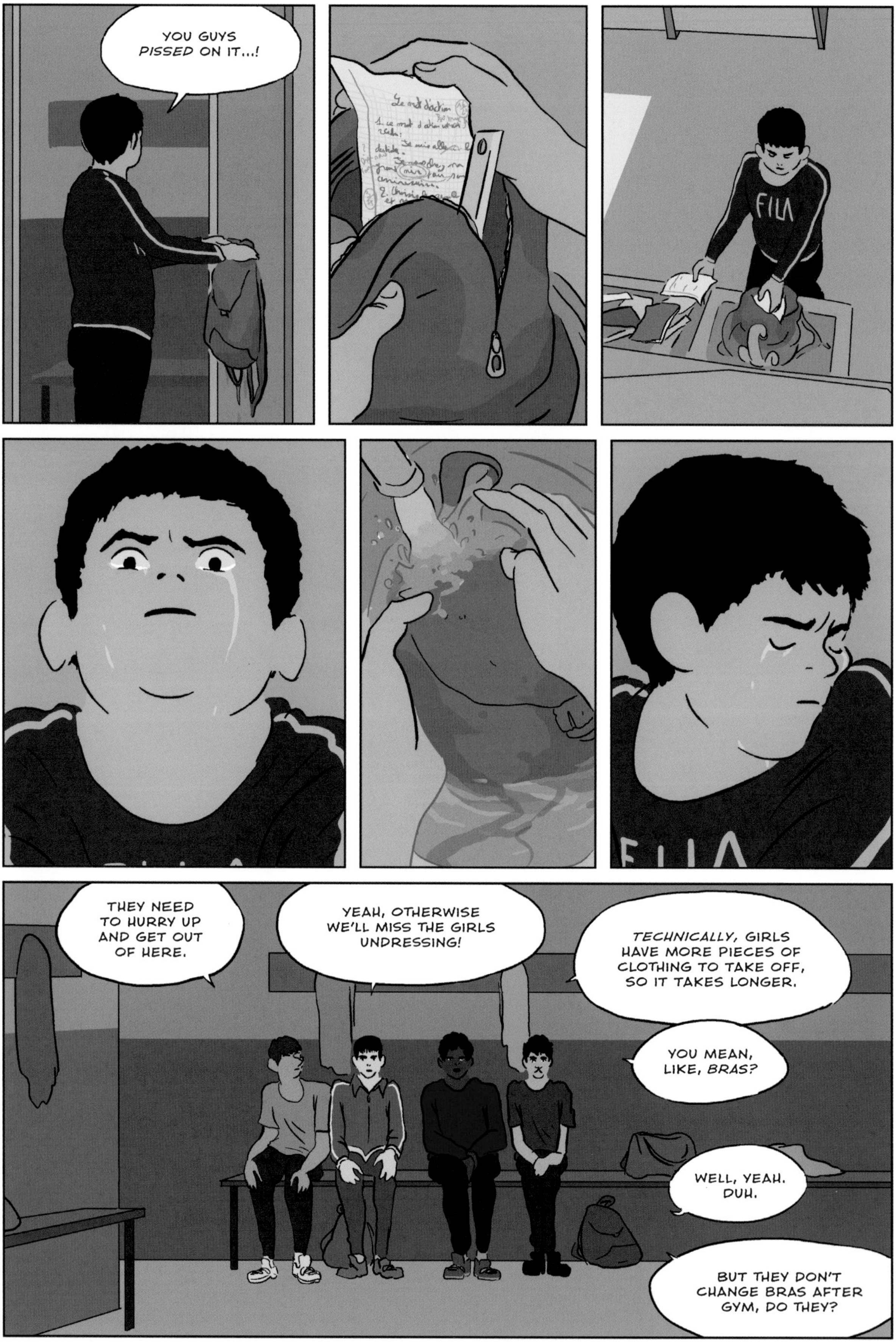
YOU GUYS *PISSED* ON IT...!
FILA
THEY NEED TO HURRY UP AND GET OUT OF HERE.
YEAH, OTHERWISE WE'LL MISS THE GIRLS UNDRESSING!
TECHNICALLY, GIRLS HAVE MORE PIECES OF CLOTHING TO TAKE OFF, SO IT TAKES LONGER.
YOU MEAN, LIKE, *BRAS?*
WELL, YEAH. DUH.
BUT THEY DON'T CHANGE BRAS AFTER GYM, DO THEY?

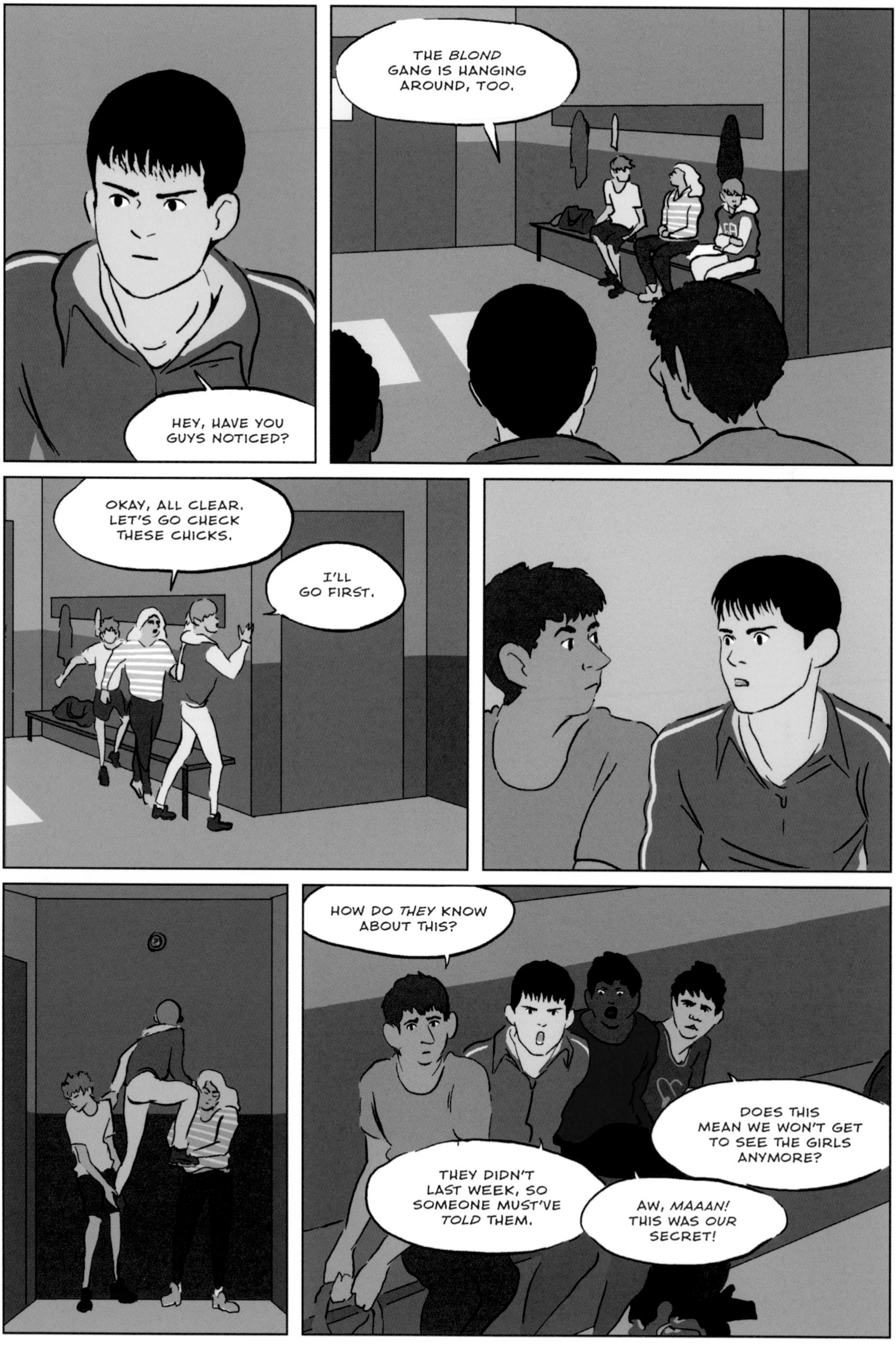
HEY, HAVE YOU GUYS NOTICED?
THE *BLOND* GANG IS HANGING AROUND, TOO.
OKAY, ALL CLEAR. LET'S GO CHECK THESE CHICKS.
I'LL GO FIRST.
HOW DO *THEY* KNOW ABOUT THIS?
THEY DIDN'T LAST WEEK, SO SOMEONE MUST'VE *TOLD* THEM.
DOES THIS MEAN WE WON'T GET TO SEE THE GIRLS ANYMORE?
AW, *MAAAN!* THIS WAS *OUR* SECRET!

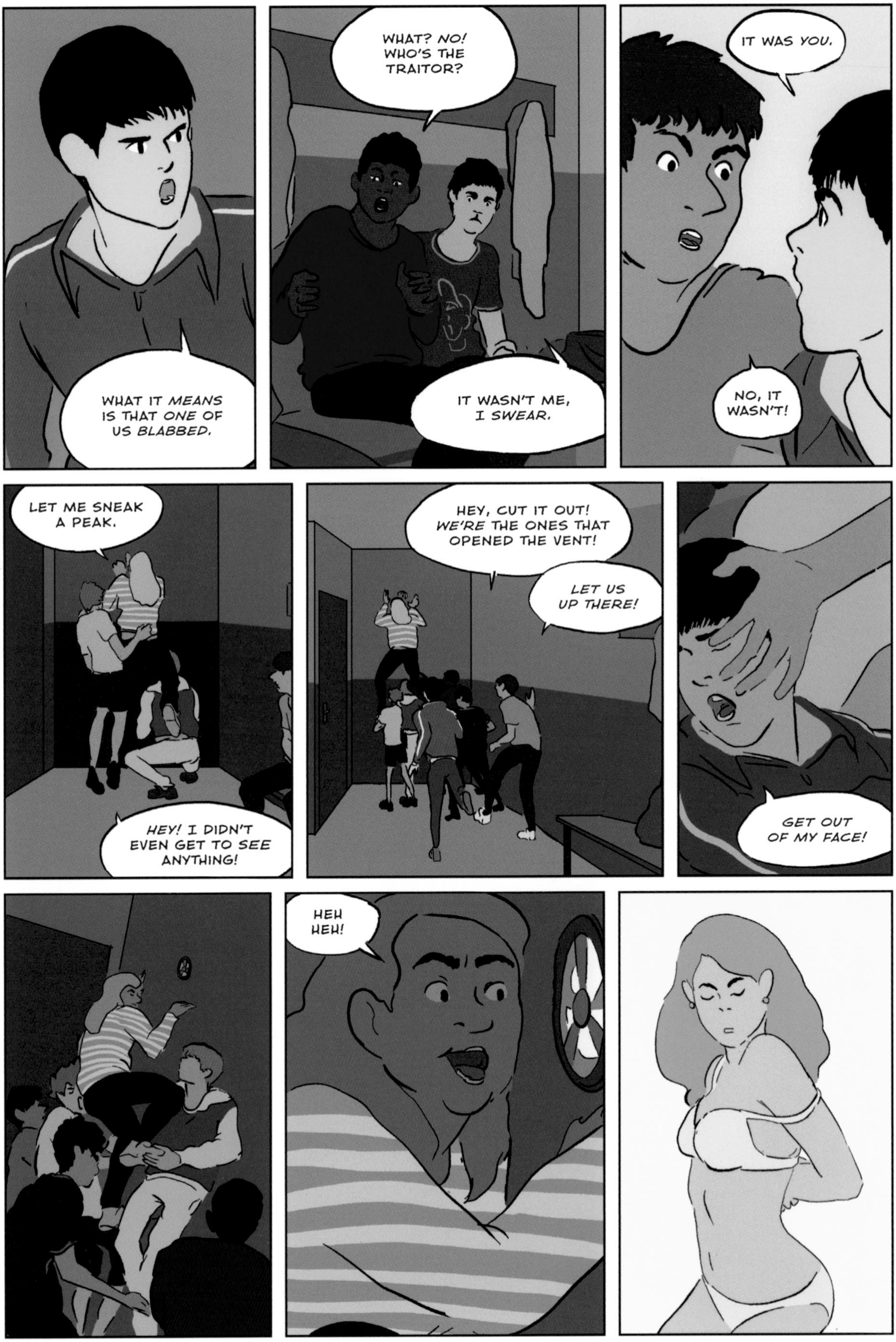
WHAT IT MEANS IS THAT ONE OF US BLABBED.
WHAT? NO! WHO'S THE TRAITOR?
IT WASN'T ME, I SWEAR.
IT WAS YOU.
NO, IT WASN'T!
LET ME SNEAK A PEAK.
HEY! I DIDN'T EVEN GET TO SEE ANYTHING!
HEY, CUT IT OUT! WE'RE THE ONES THAT OPENED THE VENT!
LET US UP THERE!
GET OUT OF MY FACE!
HEH HEH!

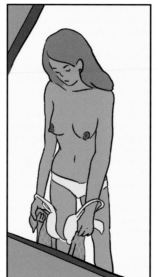

SHIT! I THINK SHE SAW ME!

FOR REAL?

SHE LOOKED *RIGHT* AT ME!

WE'RE OUTTA HERE!

HURRY!

I DON'T WANNA GET CAUGHT.

35

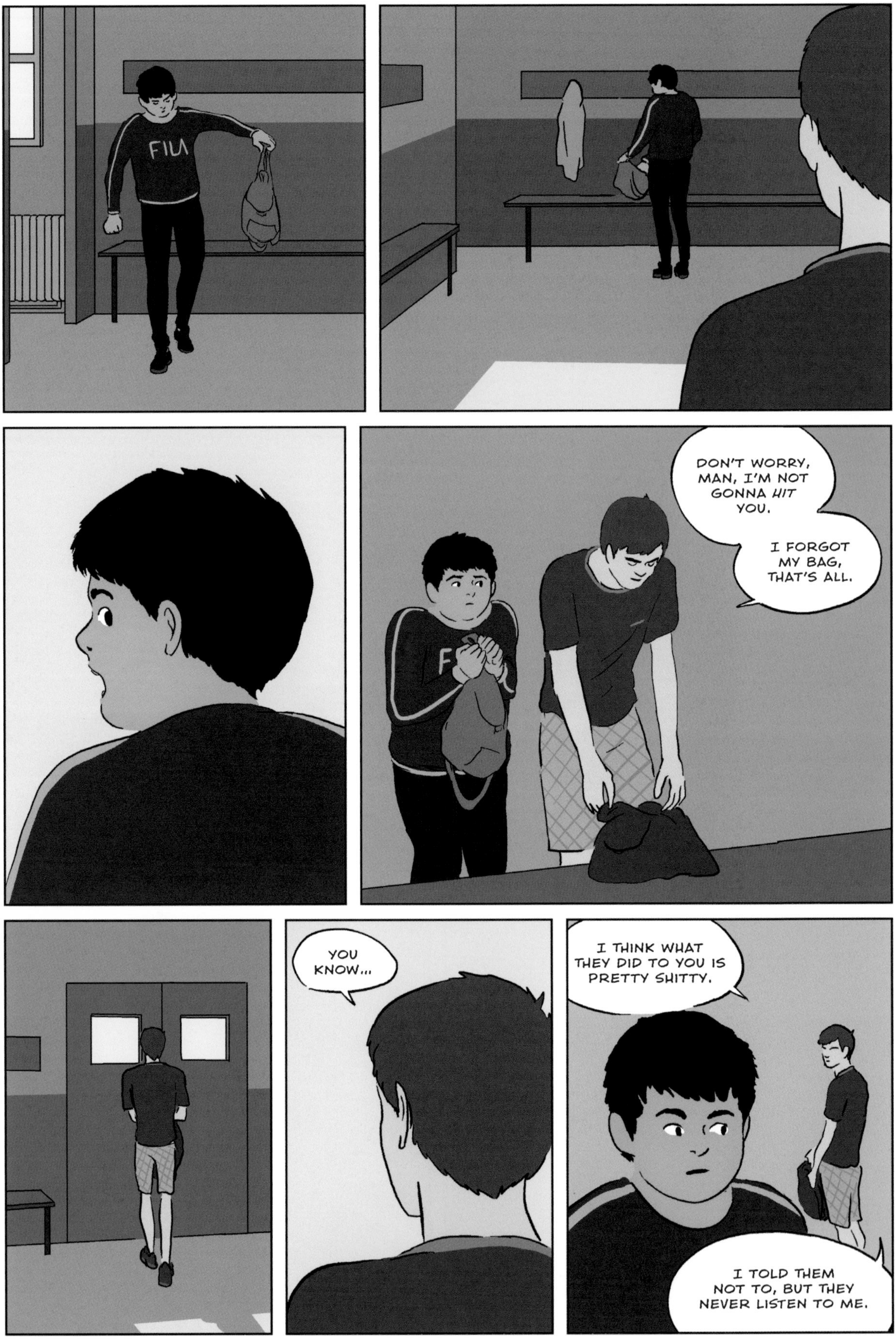
FILA
DON'T WORRY, MAN, I'M NOT GONNA *HIT* YOU.
I FORGOT MY BAG, THAT'S ALL.
YOU KNOW...
I THINK WHAT THEY DID TO YOU IS PRETTY SHITTY.
I TOLD THEM NOT TO, BUT THEY NEVER LISTEN TO ME.

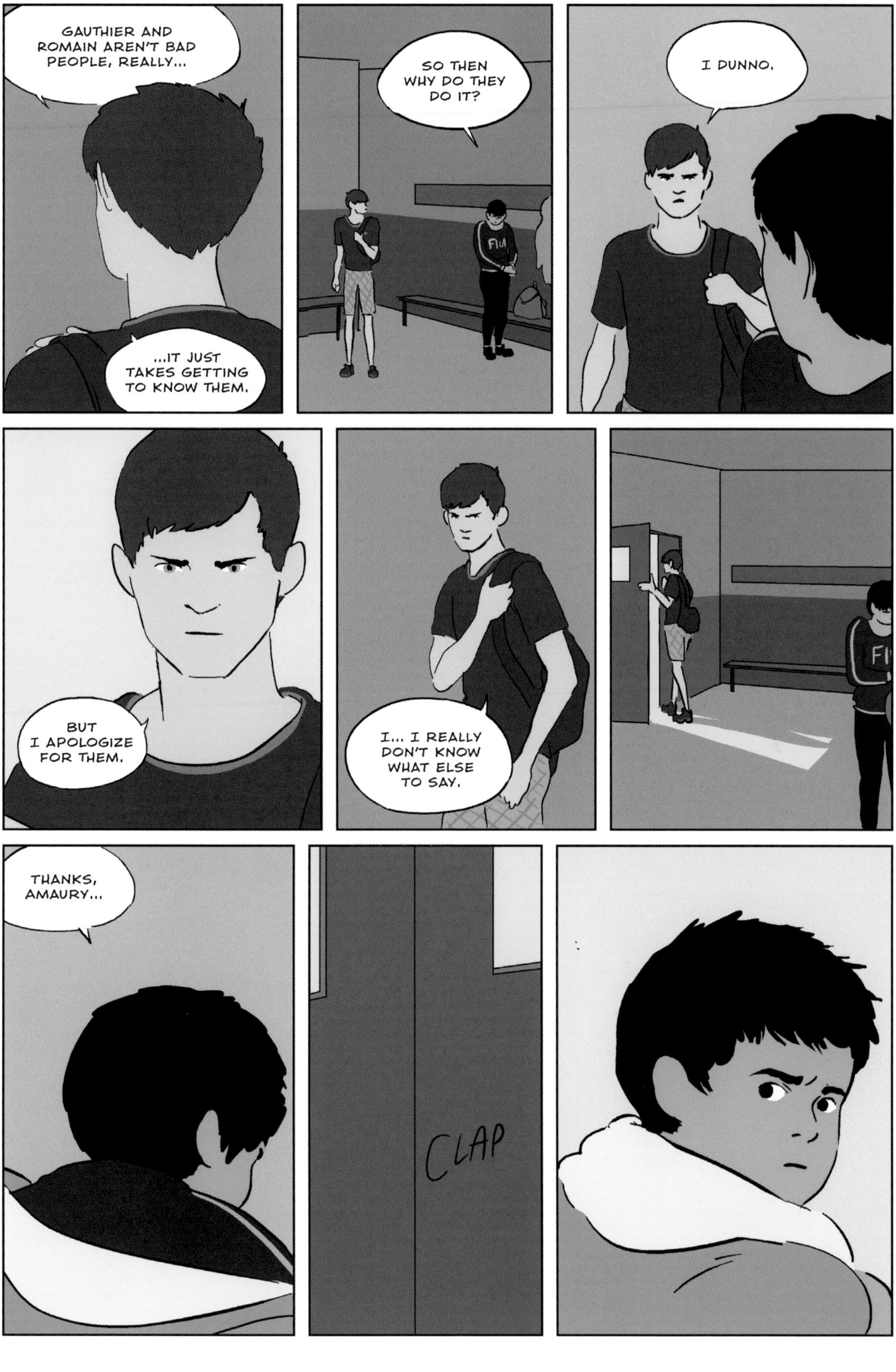
GAUTHIER AND ROMAIN AREN'T BAD PEOPLE, REALLY...
...IT JUST TAKES GETTING TO KNOW THEM.
SO THEN WHY DO THEY DO IT?
FLU
I DUNNO.
BUT I APOLOGIZE FOR THEM.
I... I REALLY DON'T KNOW WHAT ELSE TO SAY.
FLU
THANKS, AMAURY...
CLAP

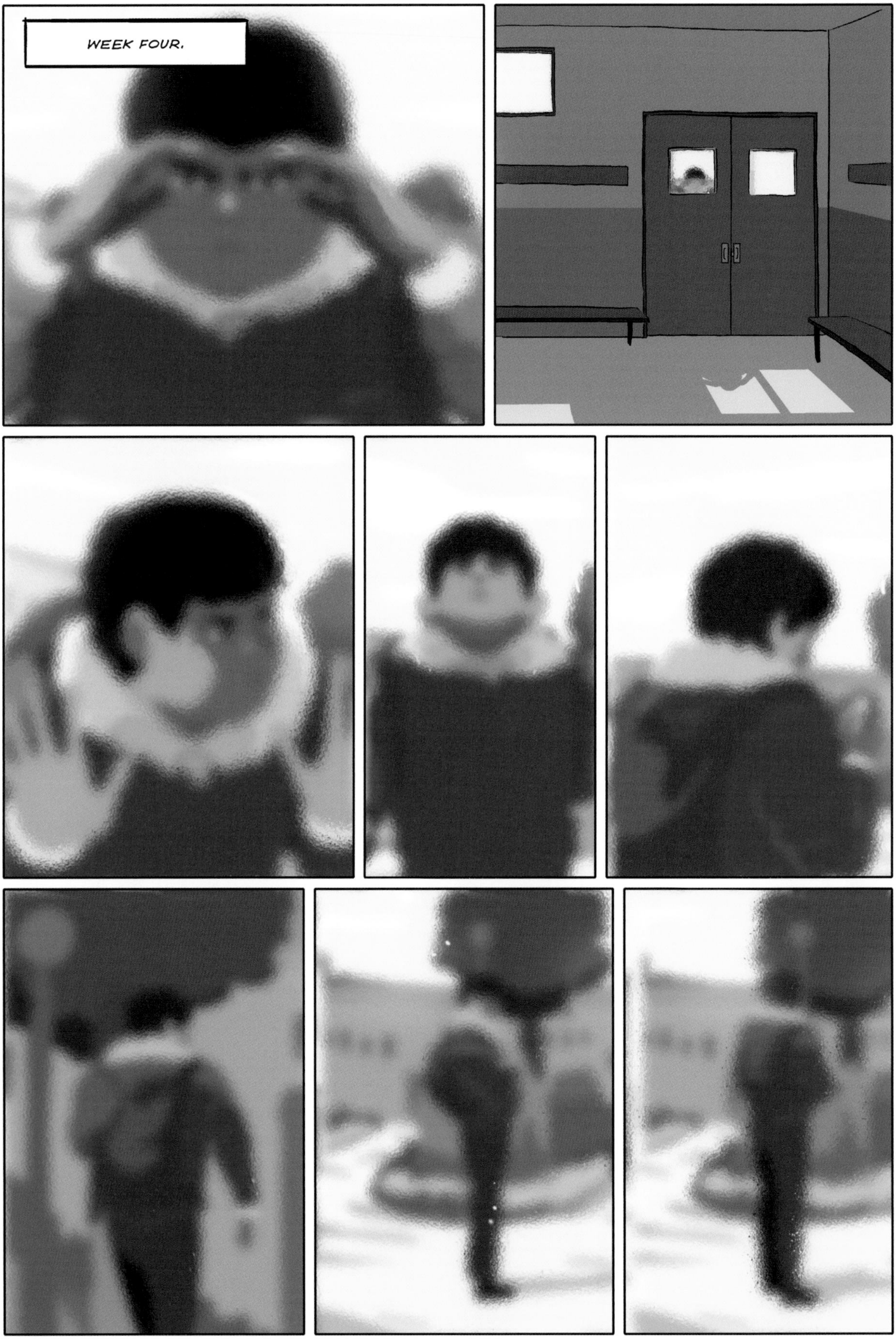
WEEK FOUR.

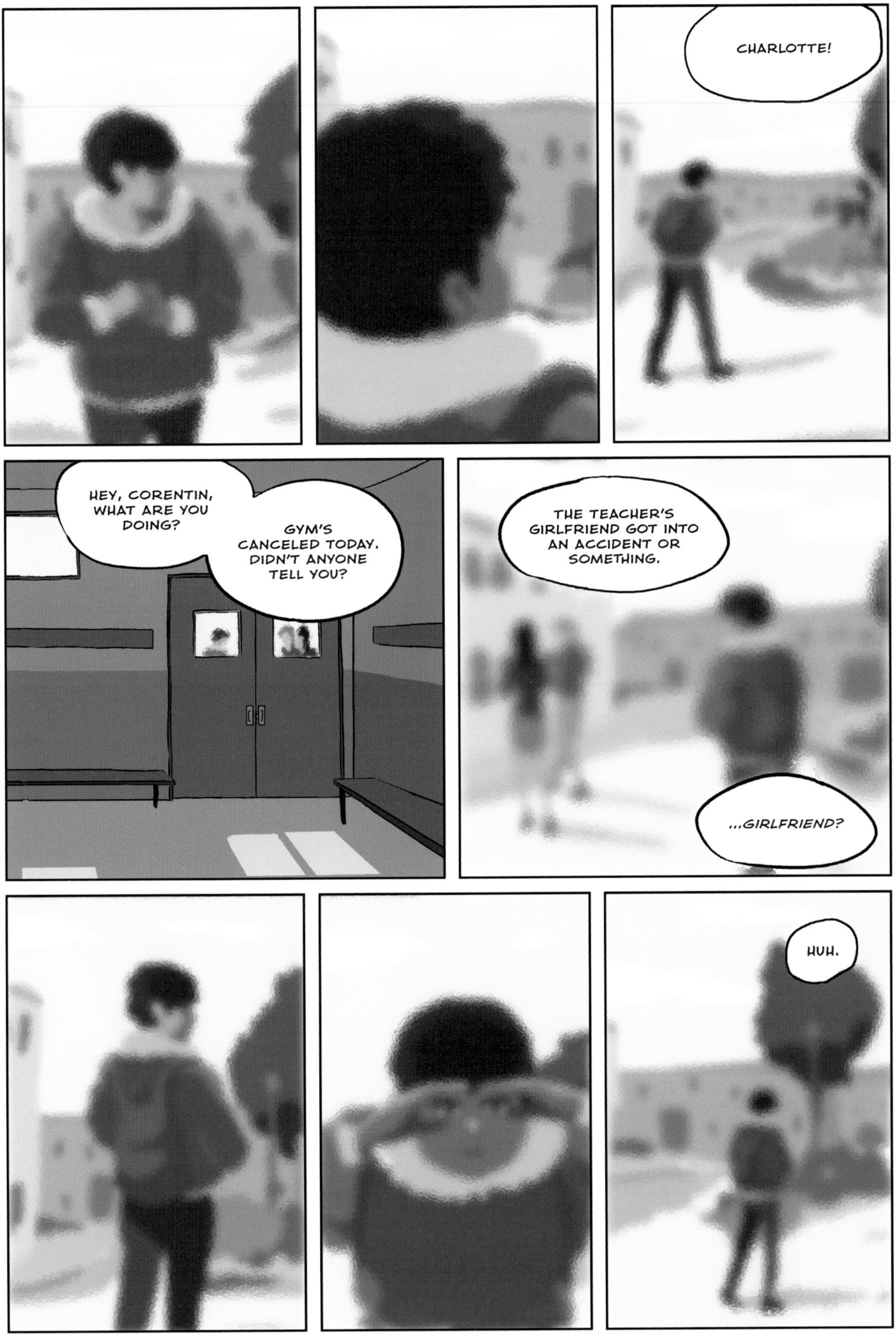
CHARLOTTE!
HEY, CORENTIN, WHAT ARE YOU DOING?
GYM'S CANCELED TODAY. DIDN'T ANYONE TELL YOU?
THE TEACHER'S GIRLFRIEND GOT INTO AN ACCIDENT OR SOMETHING.
...GIRLFRIEND?
HUH.

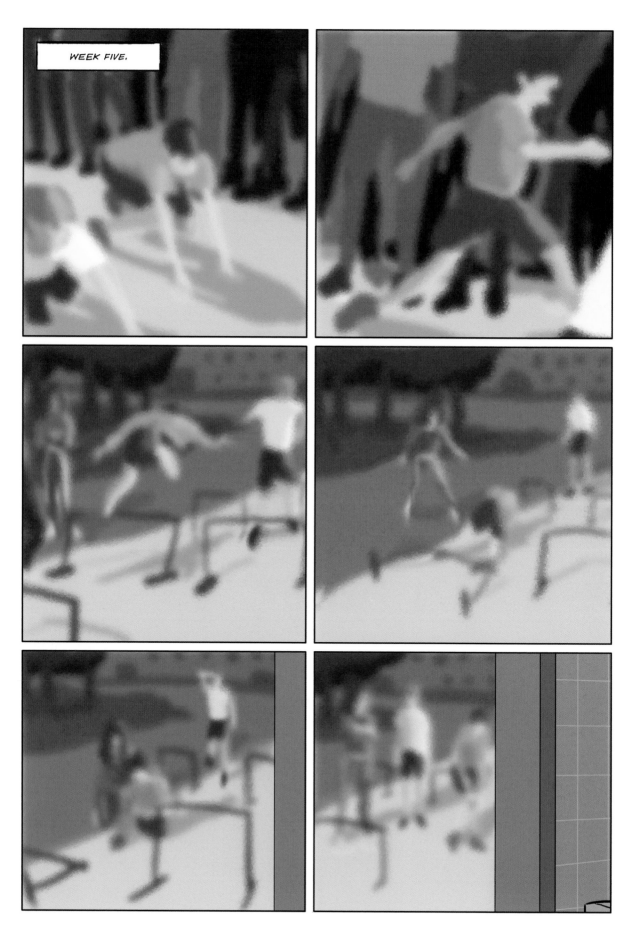

WEEK FIVE.

GET CHANGED
AND THEN YOU
CAN LEAVE.

YES,
MA'AM.

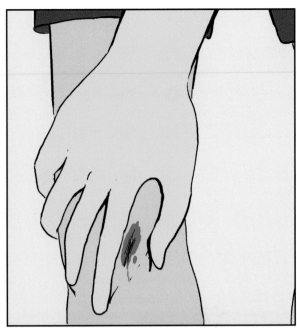

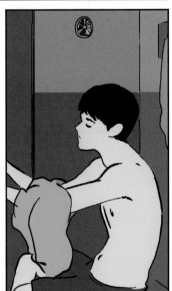

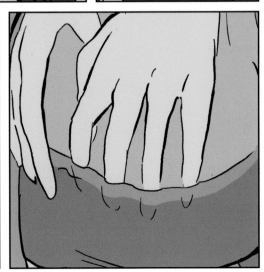

BAAAH
SHIT, SHIT, SHIT.
BITCH!
HOW'S YOUR CUT, BASTIEN?

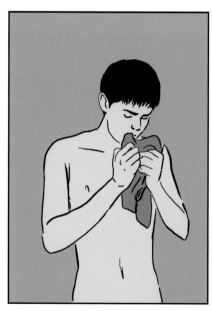

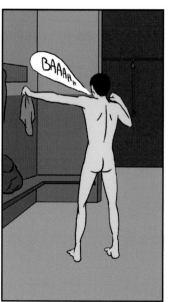

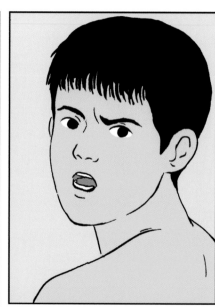

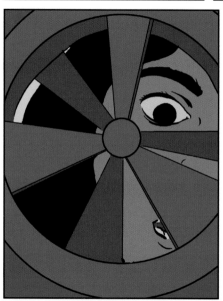

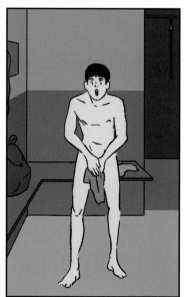

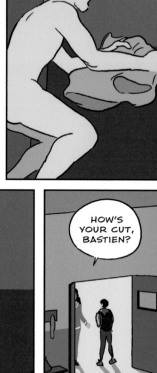

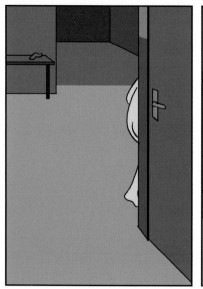

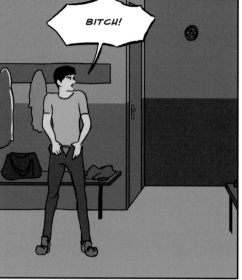

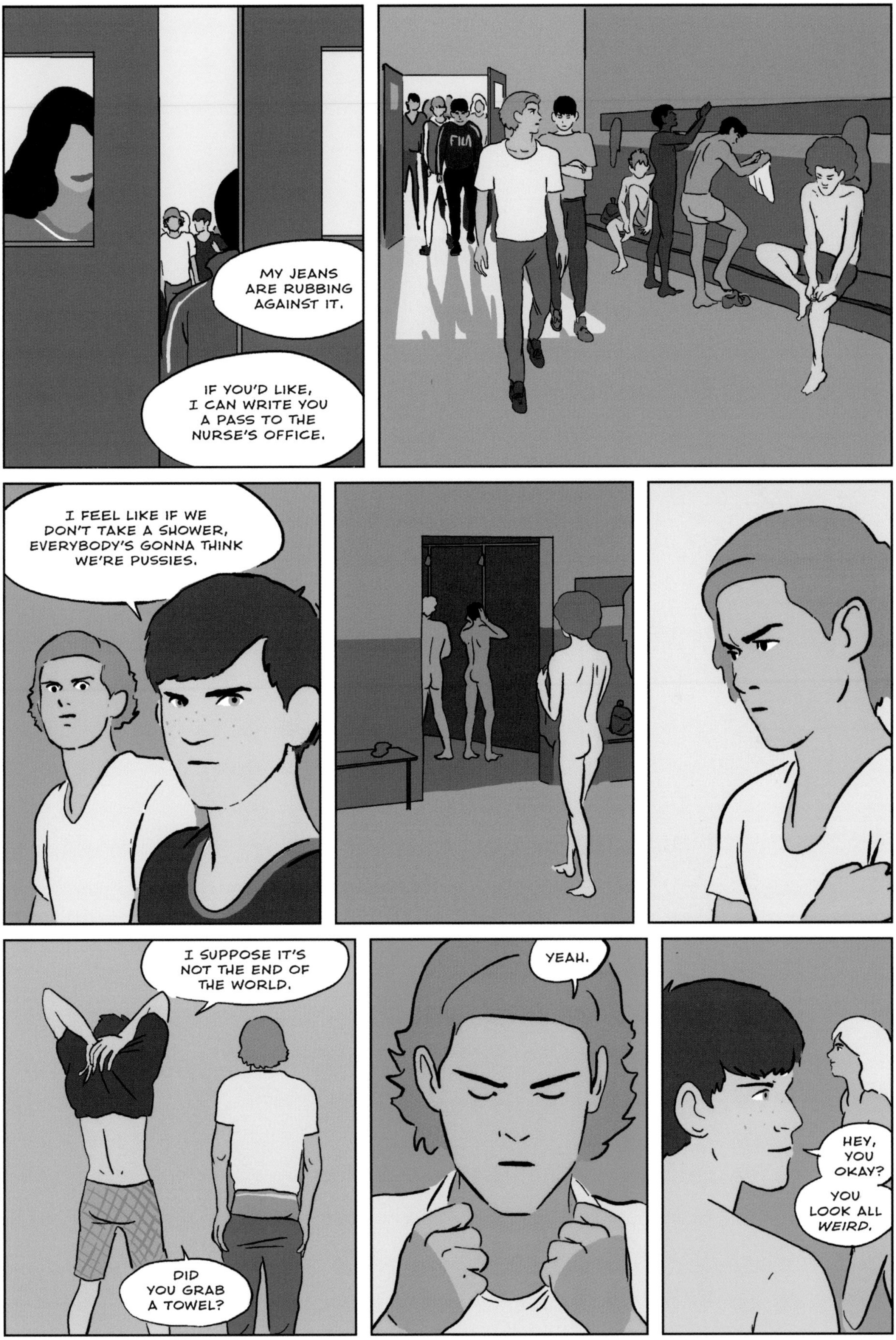

MY JEANS ARE RUBBING AGAINST IT.
IF YOU'D LIKE, I CAN WRITE YOU A PASS TO THE NURSE'S OFFICE.
FILA
I FEEL LIKE IF WE DON'T TAKE A SHOWER, EVERYBODY'S GONNA THINK WE'RE PUSSIES.
I SUPPOSE IT'S NOT THE END OF THE WORLD.
DID YOU GRAB A TOWEL?
YEAH.
HEY, YOU OKAY?
YOU LOOK ALL WEIRD.

YOU AFRAID OF GETTING *NAKEY?*

YEAH, RIGHT. LIKE I GIVE A CRAP!

IF YOU SAY SO!

SEE YOU IN THE SHOWER, GAUTHIER.

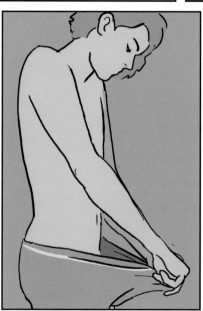

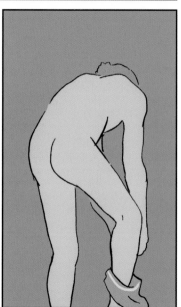

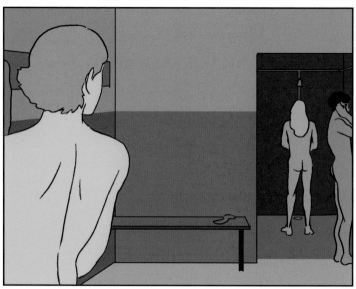

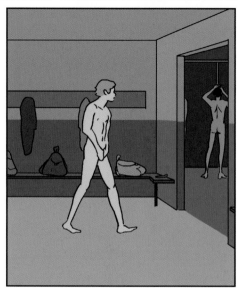

FRUIT
OOPS! SORRY!
SHIT!
PAM
QUICK, YOU IDIOT!
QUIT STARING, FAGGOT.
HA HA HA!
WE CAN PUT SOAP ON THE FLOOR...
...TO MAKE A SLIDE!

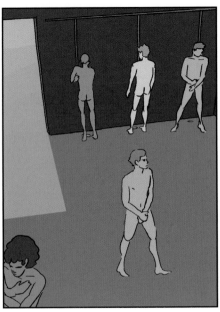

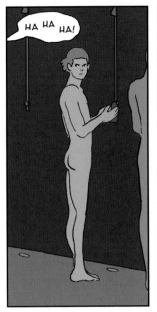

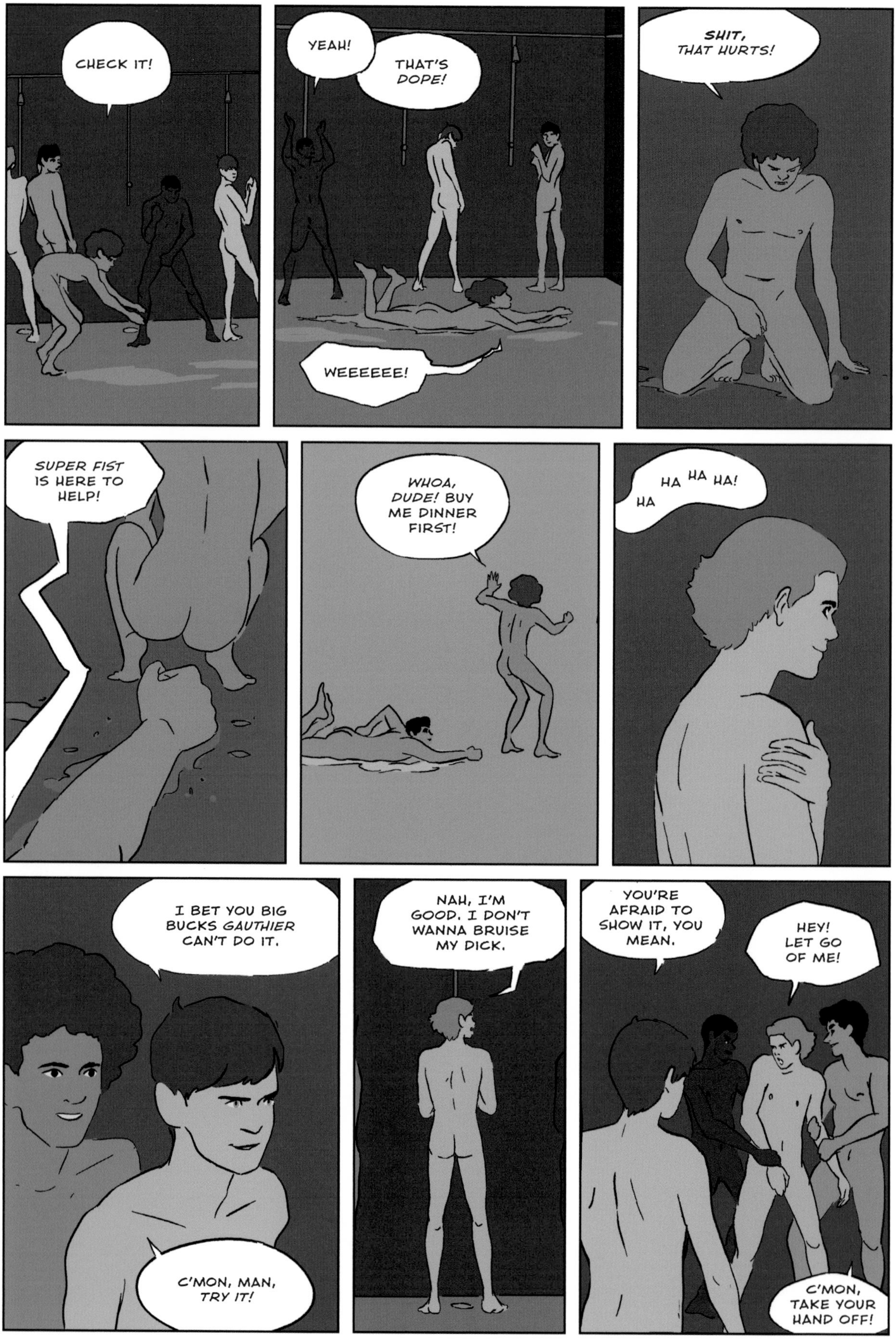
CHECK IT!
YEAH!
THAT'S DOPE!
WEEEEEE!
SHIT, THAT HURTS!
SUPER FIST IS HERE TO HELP!
WHOA, DUDE! BUY ME DINNER FIRST!
HA HA HA HA!
I BET YOU BIG BUCKS GAUTHIER CAN'T DO IT.
C'MON, MAN, TRY IT!
NAH, I'M GOOD. I DON'T WANNA BRUISE MY DICK.
YOU'RE AFRAID TO SHOW IT, YOU MEAN.
HEY! LET GO OF ME!
C'MON, TAKE YOUR HAND OFF!

WHY DON'T YOU GO PICK ON *CORENTIN* INSTEAD? THAT *FAT PIG* NEVER SHOWERS!

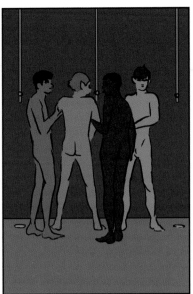

HE'S RIGHT! WHY ARE YOU STILL HERE IF YOU'RE NOT SHOWERING?

HE REEKS LIKE A DEAD DOG.

YOU THINK HE SHOULD WASH?

ABSOLUTELY.

NO! LET GO OF ME!

I'M NOT THE ONLY ONE WHO DOESN'T SHOWER!

MOVE, FATSO!

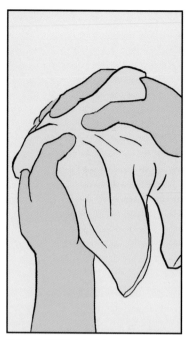

GRAB HIS LEGS.

LET GO OF ME!

CHECK OUT ALL THAT BLUBBER!

HA HA HA!

TIME FOR YOUR ANNUAL SHOWER!

MAKE SURE YOU WASH BETWEEN THE ROLLS!

HA HA HA!

GO AHEAD, TURN THE SHOWER ON.

AND THE NEXT ONE OVER, TOO!

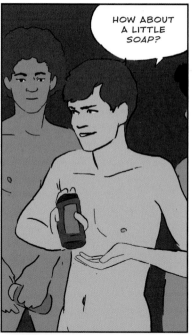

HOW ABOUT A LITTLE SOAP?

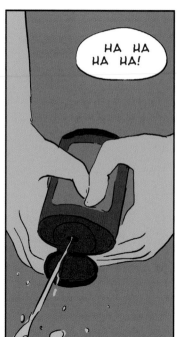

HA HA HA HA!

CIRCLE JERK!

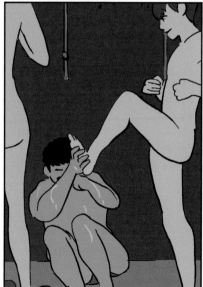

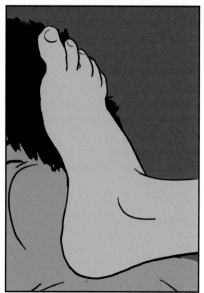

LISTEN TO THAT PIGGY SQUEAL!

HE WANTS MORE SOAP!

DON'T WORRY! YOU CAN SQUIRT IT IN HIS EYES, IT'S ORGANIC!

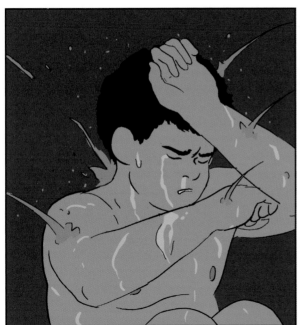

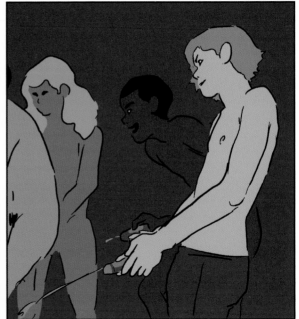

EMPTY.

PAM

YEAH, ME TOO.

HA HA HA!

ALL DONE.

I HOPE YOU REALIZE WE JUST SACRIFICED ALL OUR SHOWER GEL FOR YOUR HYGIENE...

HE SHOULD BUY US NEW ONES.

HA HA HA!

MINE HAD *EXFOLIATING* GRAINS.

ISN'T THAT ROUGH ON THE SKIN?

HA HA HA!

HA HA!

OKAY, EVERYBODY OUT?

I'M TURNING OFF THE LIGHTS.

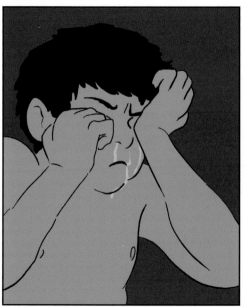

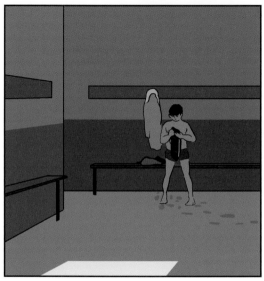

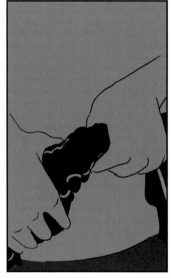

PLOC

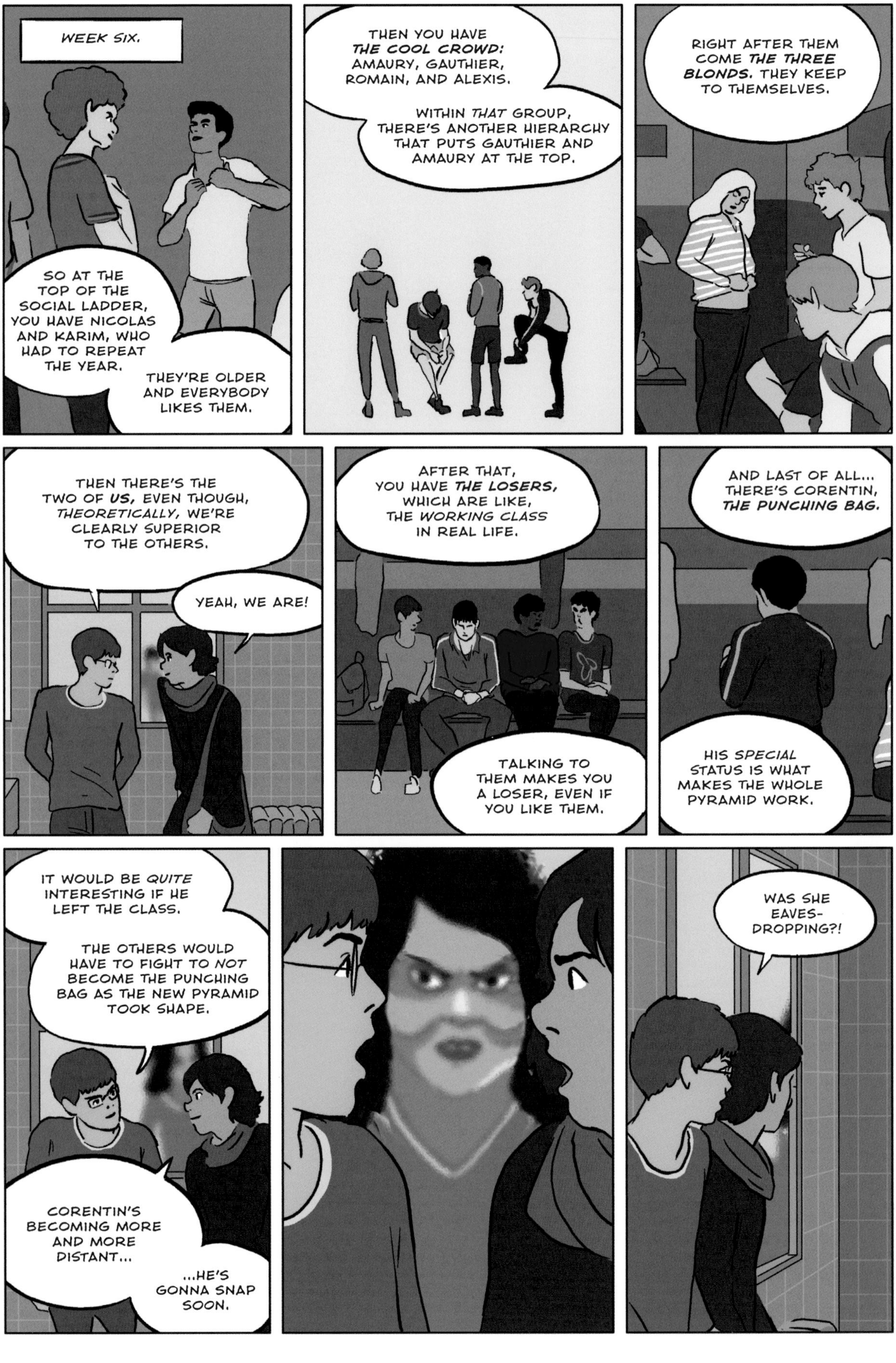
WEEK SIX.
SO AT THE TOP OF THE SOCIAL LADDER, YOU HAVE NICOLAS AND KARIM, WHO HAD TO REPEAT THE YEAR.
THEY'RE OLDER AND EVERYBODY LIKES THEM.
THEN YOU HAVE ***THE COOL CROWD:*** AMAURY, GAUTHIER, ROMAIN, AND ALEXIS.
WITHIN *THAT* GROUP, THERE'S ANOTHER HIERARCHY THAT PUTS GAUTHIER AND AMAURY AT THE TOP.
RIGHT AFTER THEM COME ***THE THREE BLONDS.*** THEY KEEP TO THEMSELVES.
THEN THERE'S THE TWO OF **US**, EVEN THOUGH, *THEORETICALLY*, WE'RE CLEARLY SUPERIOR TO THE OTHERS.
YEAH, WE ARE!
AFTER THAT, YOU HAVE ***THE LOSERS,*** WHICH ARE LIKE, THE *WORKING CLASS* IN REAL LIFE.
TALKING TO THEM MAKES YOU A LOSER, EVEN IF YOU LIKE THEM.
AND LAST OF ALL... THERE'S CORENTIN, ***THE PUNCHING BAG.***
HIS *SPECIAL* STATUS IS WHAT MAKES THE WHOLE PYRAMID WORK.
IT WOULD BE *QUITE* INTERESTING IF HE LEFT THE CLASS.
THE OTHERS WOULD HAVE TO FIGHT TO *NOT* BECOME THE PUNCHING BAG AS THE NEW PYRAMID TOOK SHAPE.
CORENTIN'S BECOMING MORE AND MORE DISTANT...
...HE'S GONNA SNAP SOON.
WAS SHE EAVES-DROPPING?!

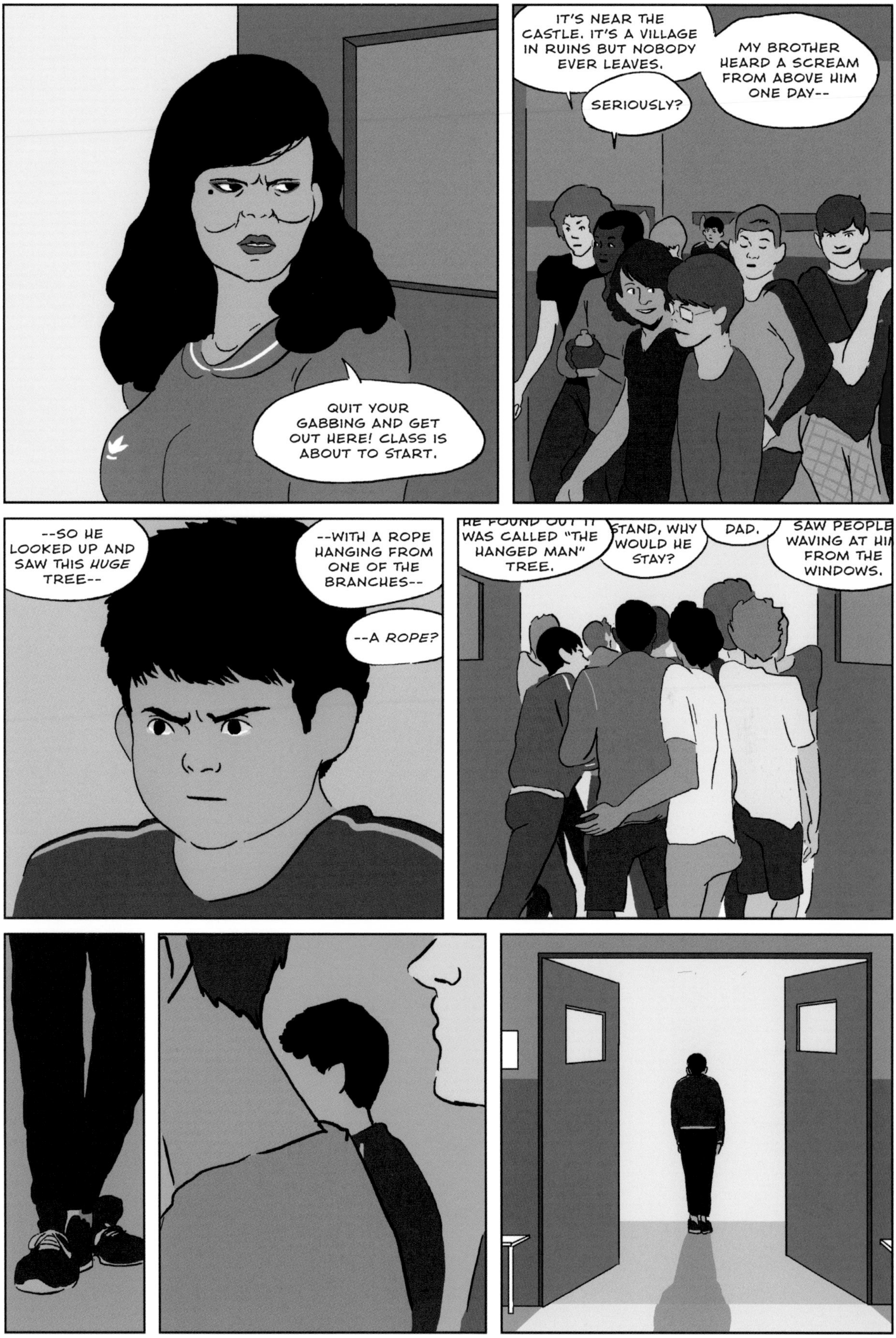
QUIT YOUR GABBING AND GET OUT HERE! CLASS IS ABOUT TO START.
IT'S NEAR THE CASTLE. IT'S A VILLAGE IN RUINS BUT NOBODY EVER LEAVES.
SERIOUSLY?
MY BROTHER HEARD A SCREAM FROM ABOVE HIM ONE DAY--
--SO HE LOOKED UP AND SAW THIS *HUGE* TREE--
--WITH A ROPE HANGING FROM ONE OF THE BRANCHES--
--A *ROPE?*
WAS CALLED "THE HANGED MAN" TREE.
STAND, WHY WOULD HE STAY?
DAD.
SAW PEOPLE WAVING AT HI FROM THE WINDOWS.

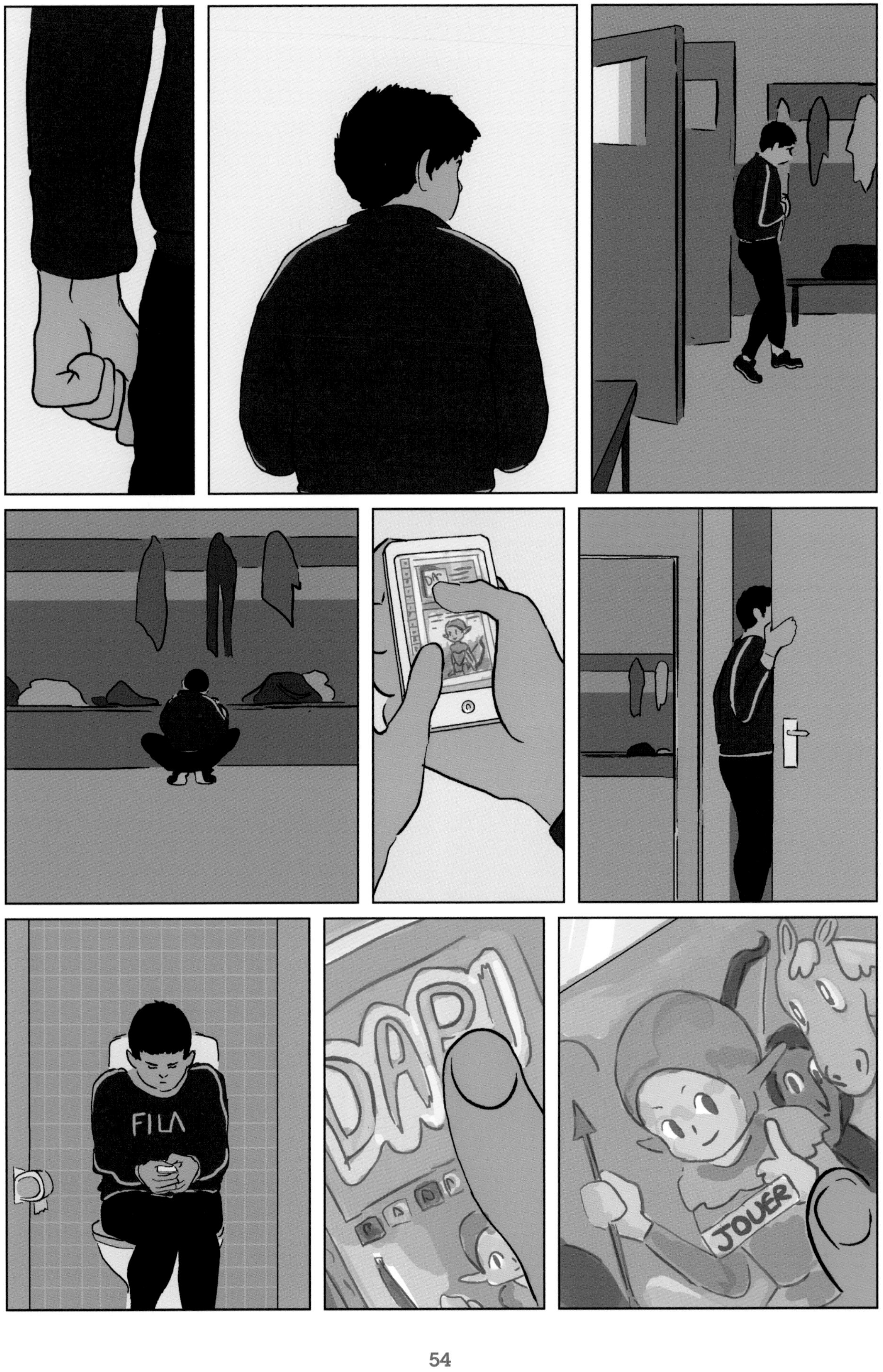
FILA
JOUER

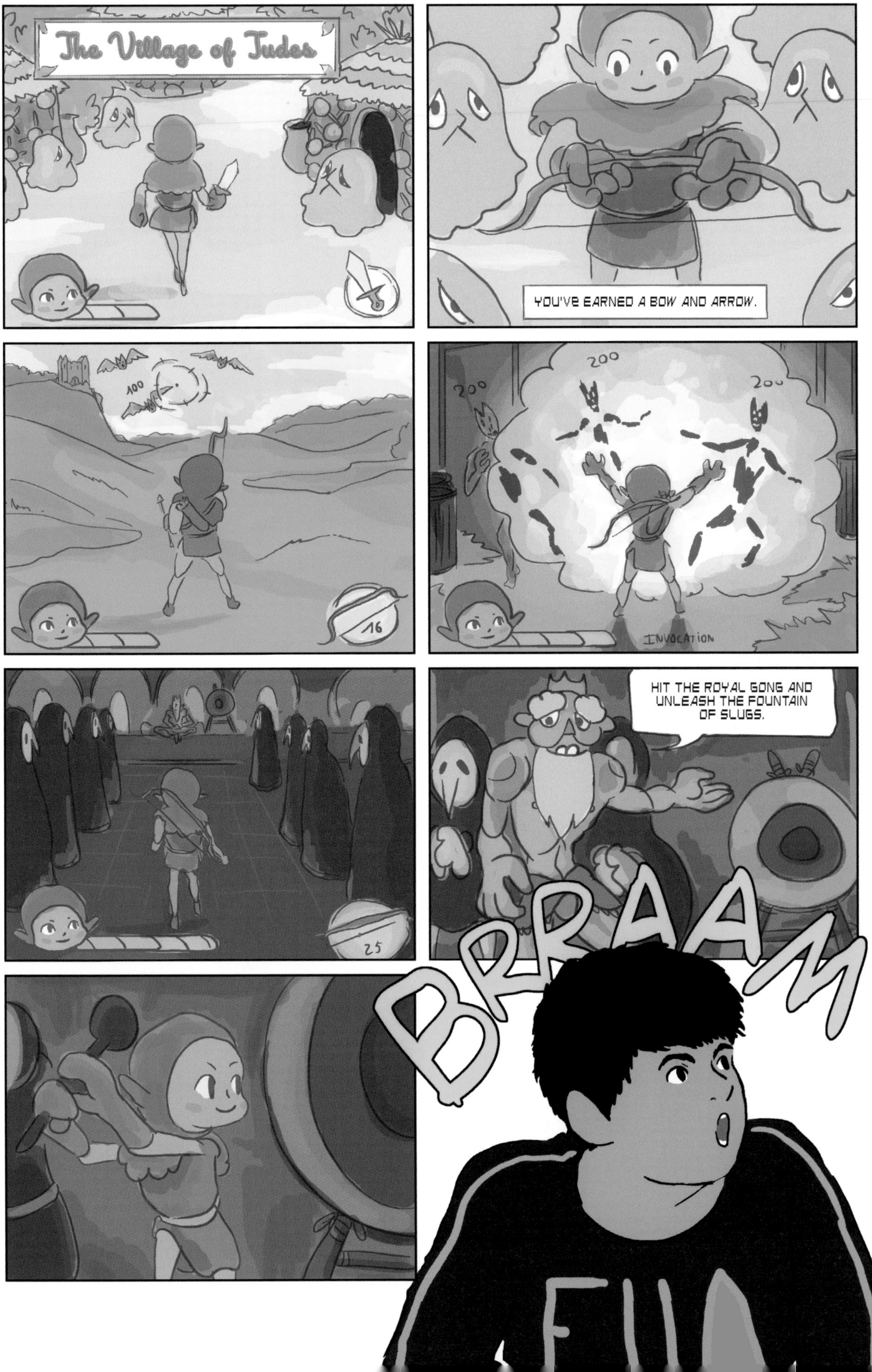

The Village of Judes
YOU'VE EARNED A BOW AND ARROW.
100
16
200
200
200
INVOCATION
25
HIT THE ROYAL GONG AND UNLEASH THE FOUNTAIN OF SLUGS.
BRRAAM

THAT CLASS SUCKED.

I CAN'T BELIEVE SHE MADE US RUN IN THE RAIN.

SHE'S A SADIST.

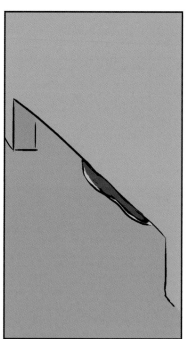

Click

56

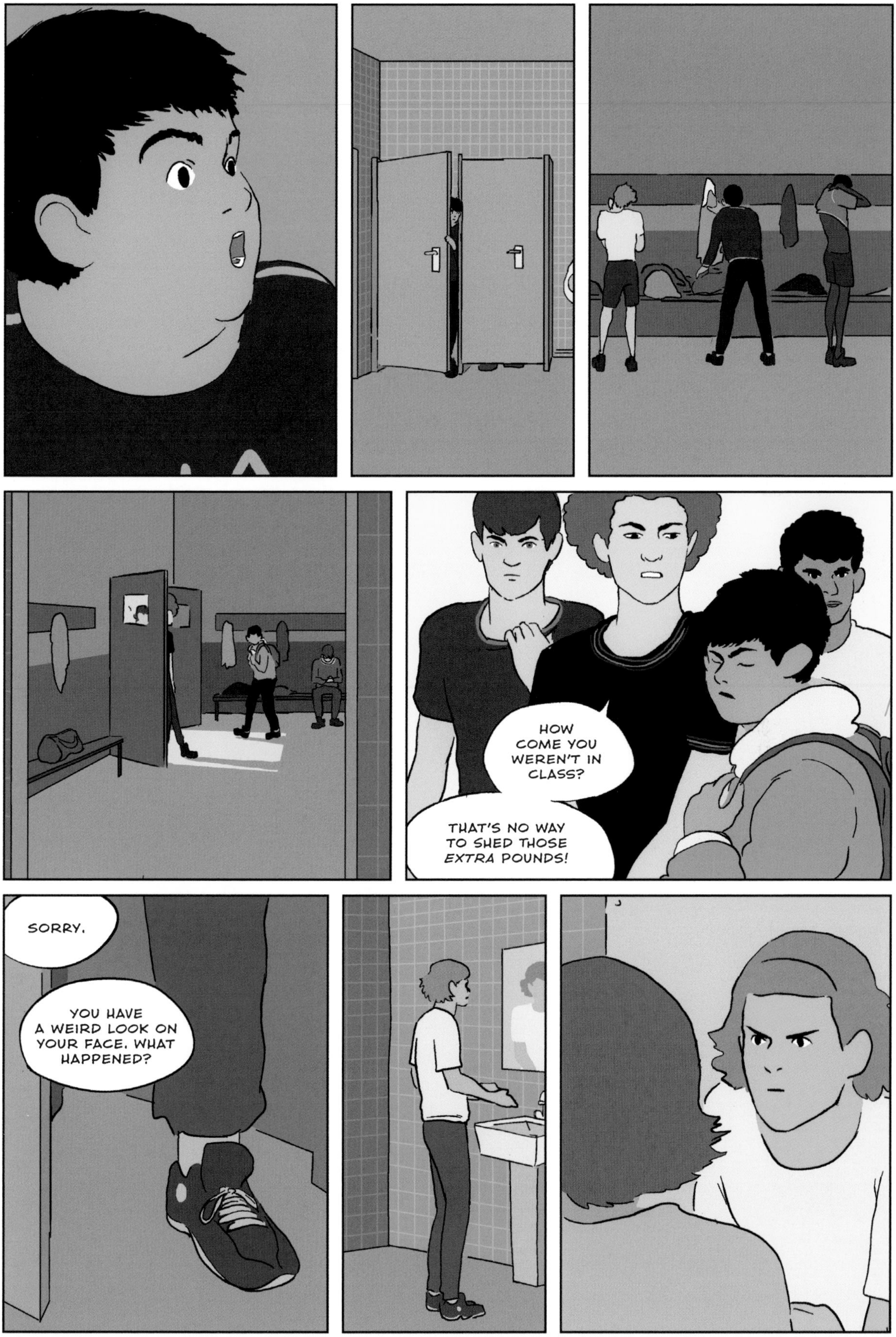
HOW COME YOU WEREN'T IN CLASS?
THAT'S NO WAY TO SHED THOSE *EXTRA* POUNDS!
SORRY.
YOU HAVE A WEIRD LOOK ON YOUR FACE. WHAT HAPPENED?

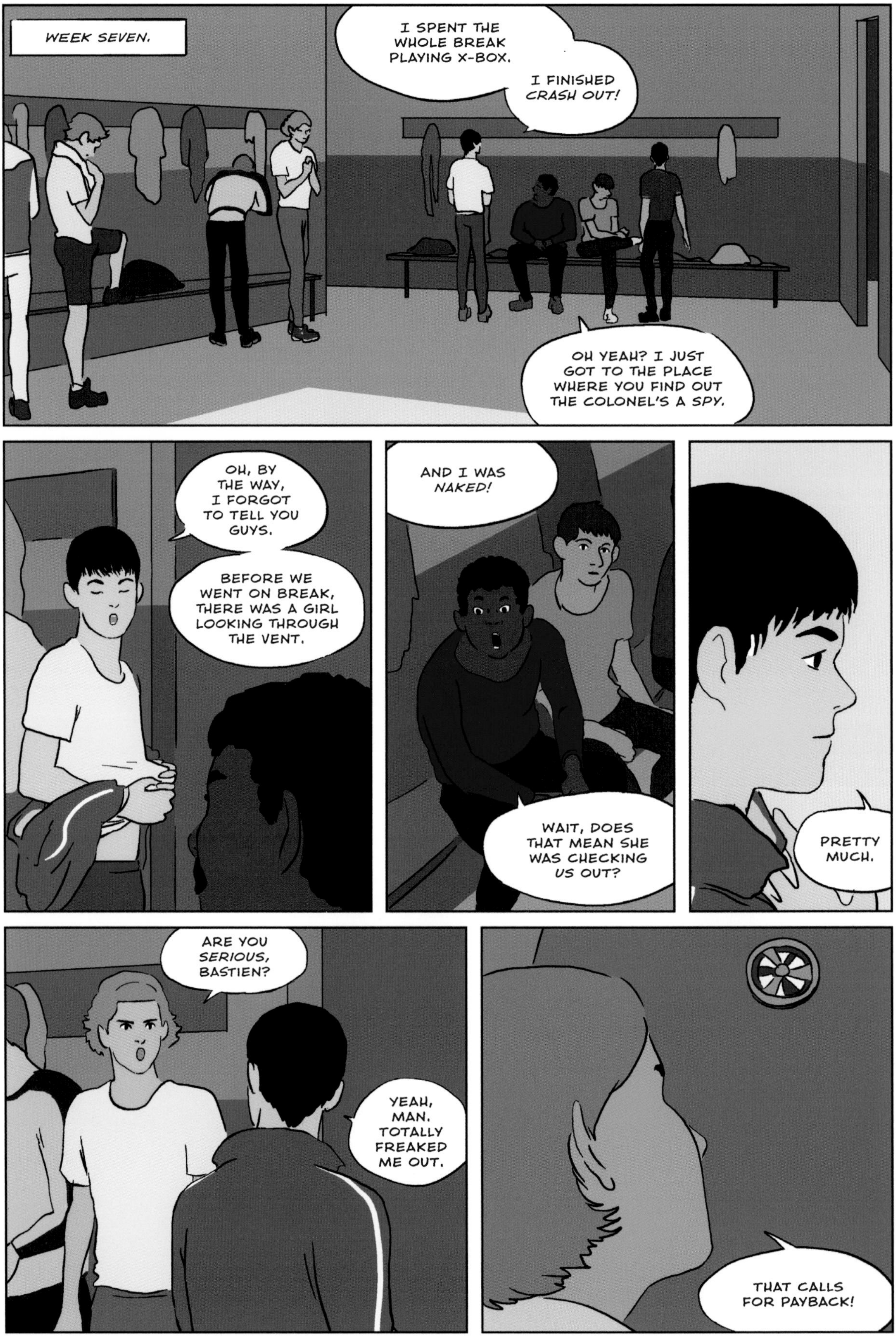
WEEK SEVEN.
I SPENT THE WHOLE BREAK PLAYING X-BOX.
I FINISHED *CRASH OUT!*
OH YEAH? I JUST GOT TO THE PLACE WHERE YOU FIND OUT THE COLONEL'S A SPY.
OH, BY THE WAY, I FORGOT TO TELL YOU GUYS.
BEFORE WE WENT ON BREAK, THERE WAS A GIRL LOOKING THROUGH THE VENT.
AND I WAS *NAKED!*
WAIT, DOES THAT MEAN SHE WAS CHECKING US OUT?
PRETTY MUCH.
ARE YOU *SERIOUS*, BASTIEN?
YEAH, MAN. TOTALLY FREAKED ME OUT.
THAT CALLS FOR PAYBACK!

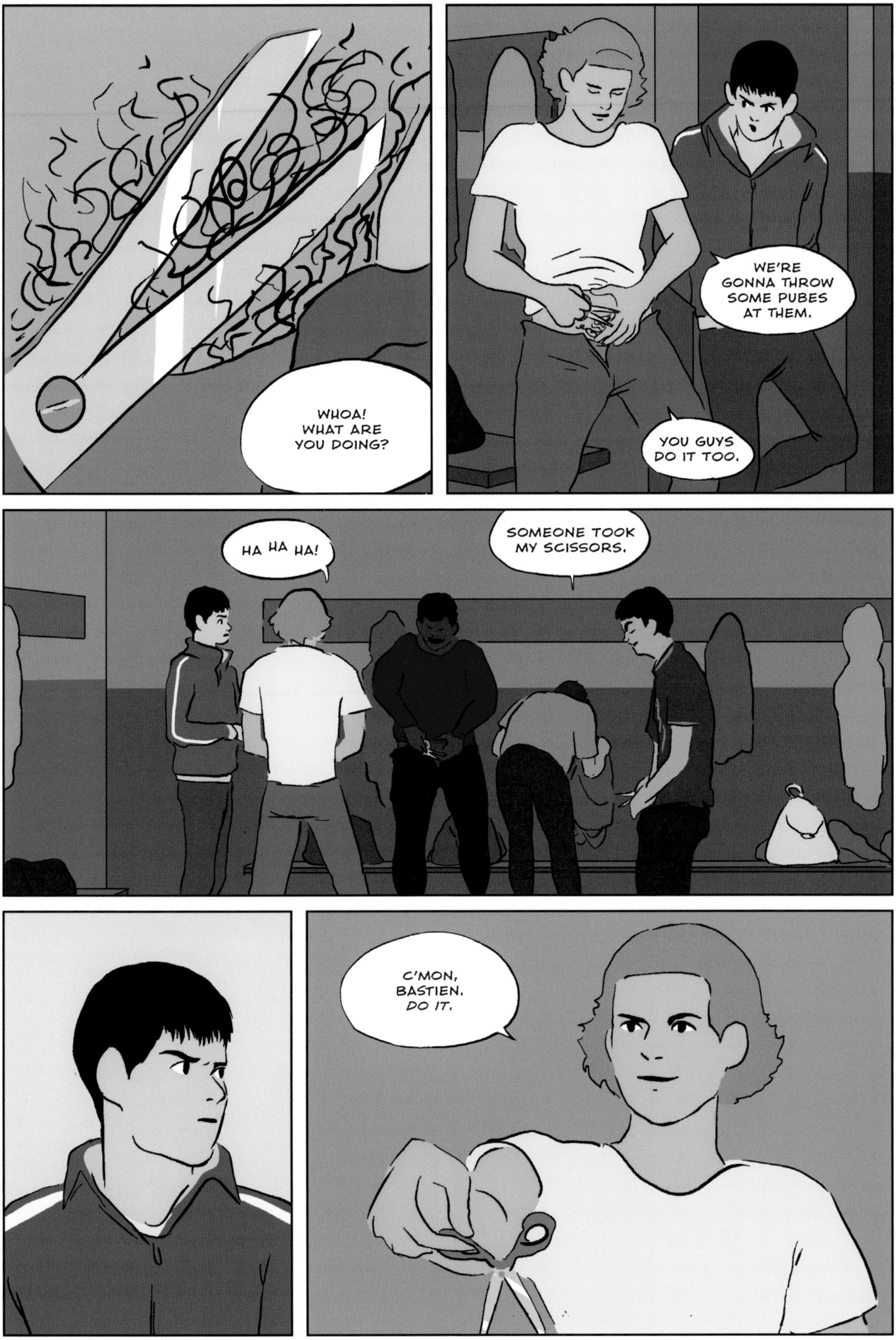
WHOA! WHAT ARE YOU DOING?
WE'RE GONNA THROW SOME PUBES AT THEM.
YOU GUYS DO IT TOO.
HA HA HA!
SOMEONE TOOK MY SCISSORS.
C'MON, BASTIEN. *DO IT.*

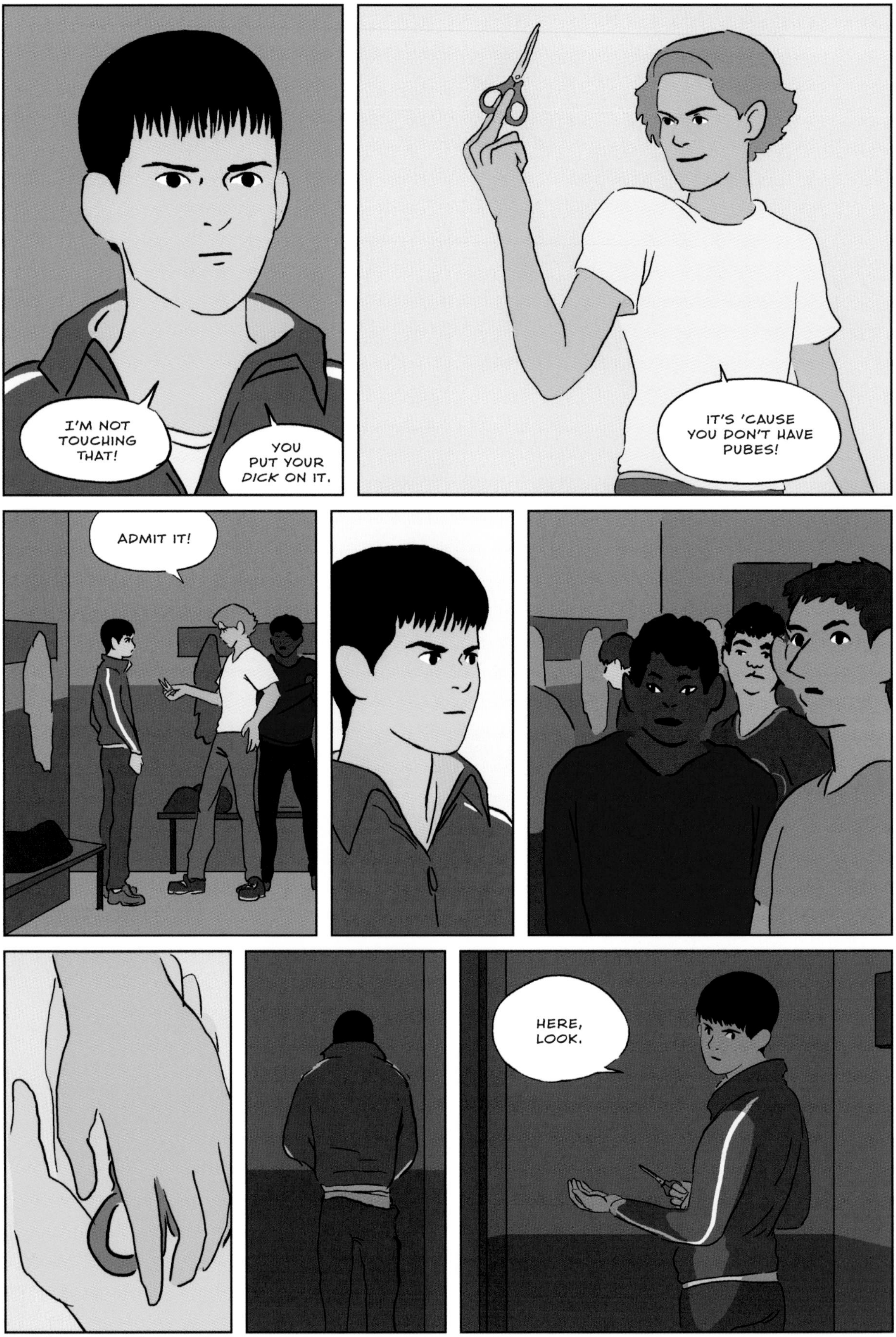

I'M NOT TOUCHING THAT!
YOU PUT YOUR *DICK* ON IT.
IT'S 'CAUSE YOU DON'T HAVE PUBES!
ADMIT IT!
HERE, LOOK.

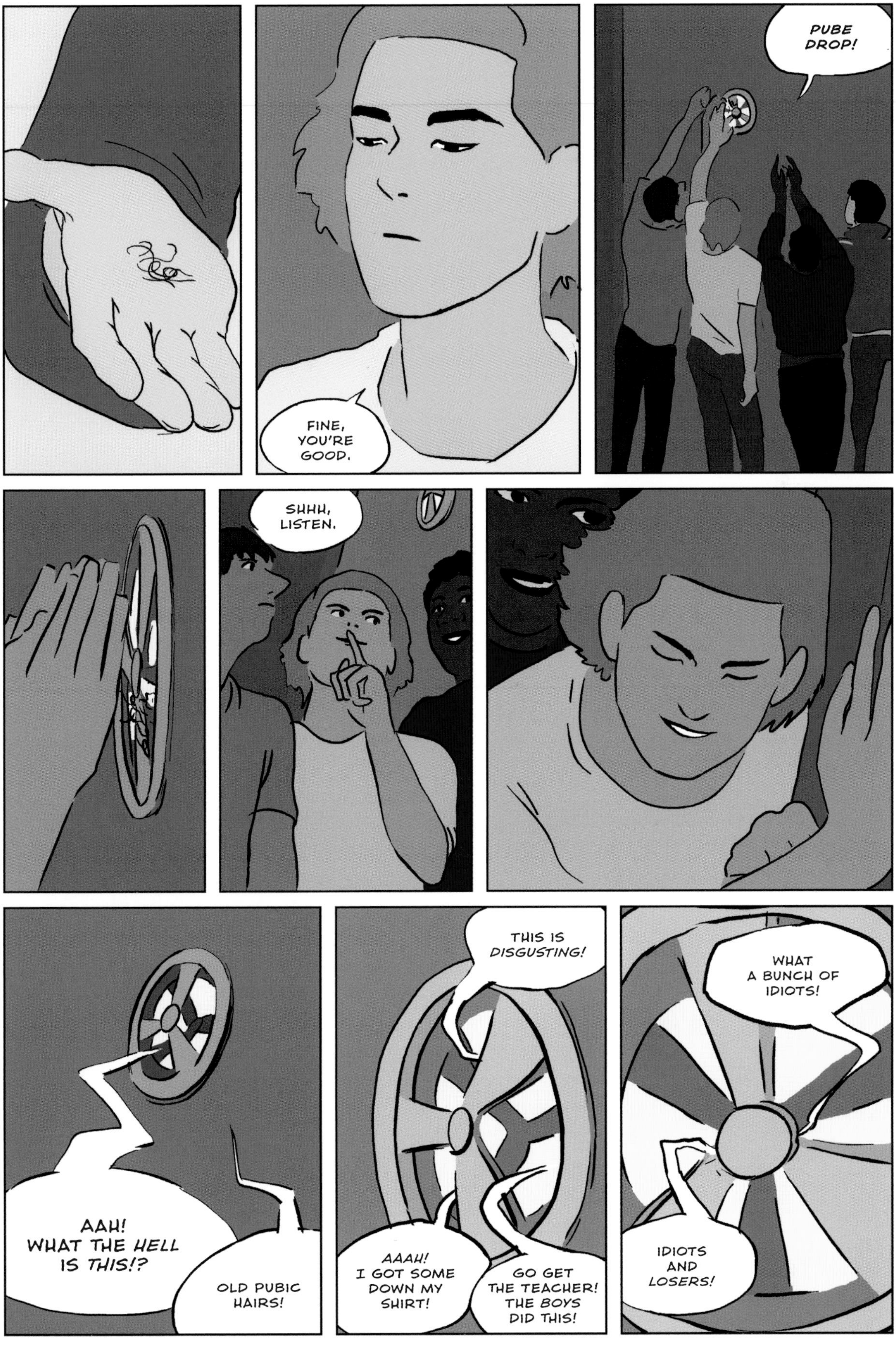
FINE, YOU'RE GOOD.
PUBE DROP!
SHHH, LISTEN.
AAH! WHAT THE *HELL* IS *THIS!?*
OLD PUBIC HAIRS!
THIS IS *DISGUSTING!*
AAAH! I GOT SOME DOWN MY SHIRT!
GO GET THE TEACHER! THE *BOYS* DID THIS!
WHAT A BUNCH OF IDIOTS!
IDIOTS AND *LOSERS!*

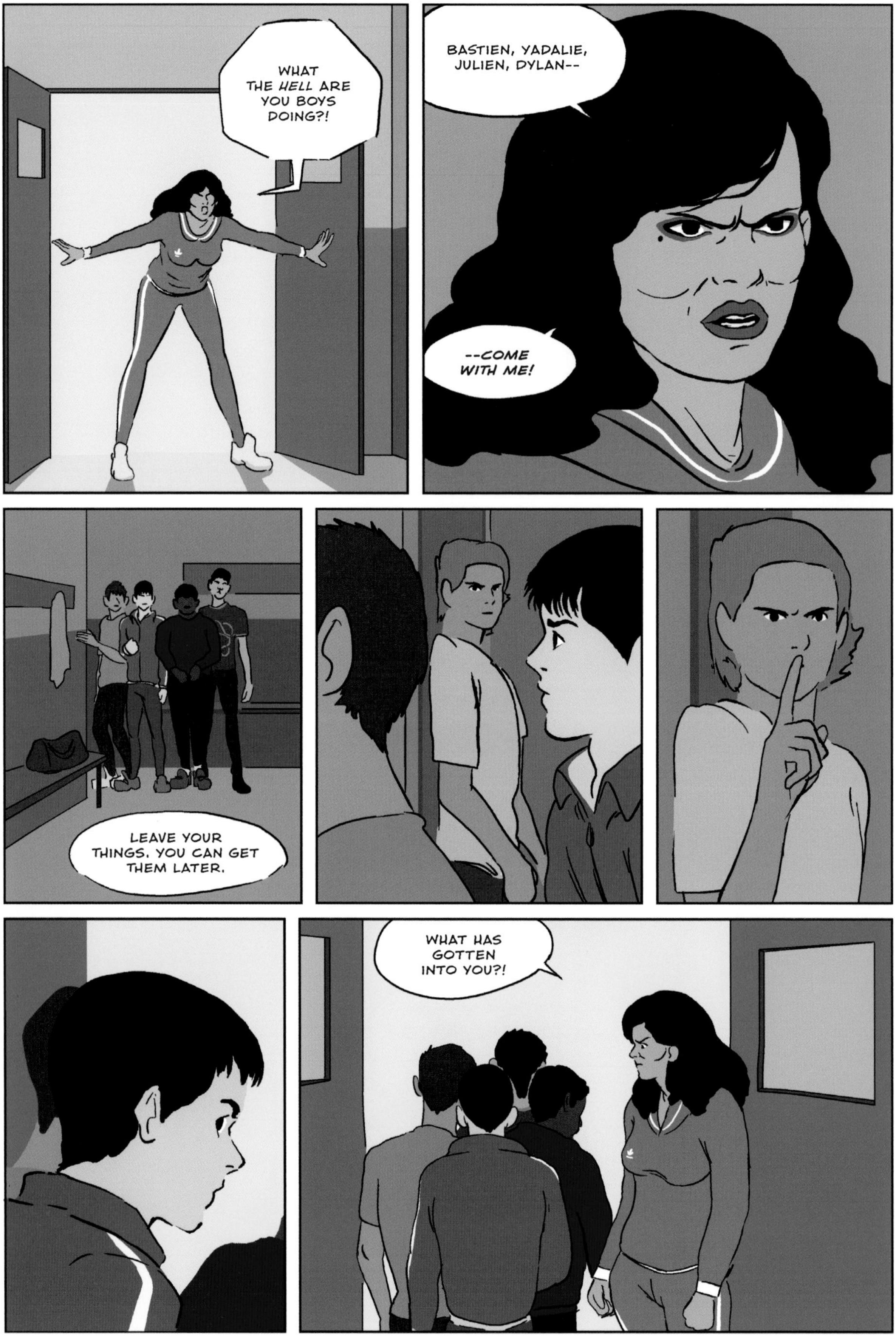
WHAT THE *HELL* ARE YOU BOYS DOING?!
BASTIEN, YADALIE, JULIEN, DYLAN--
--COME WITH ME!
LEAVE YOUR THINGS. YOU CAN GET THEM LATER.
WHAT HAS GOTTEN INTO YOU?!

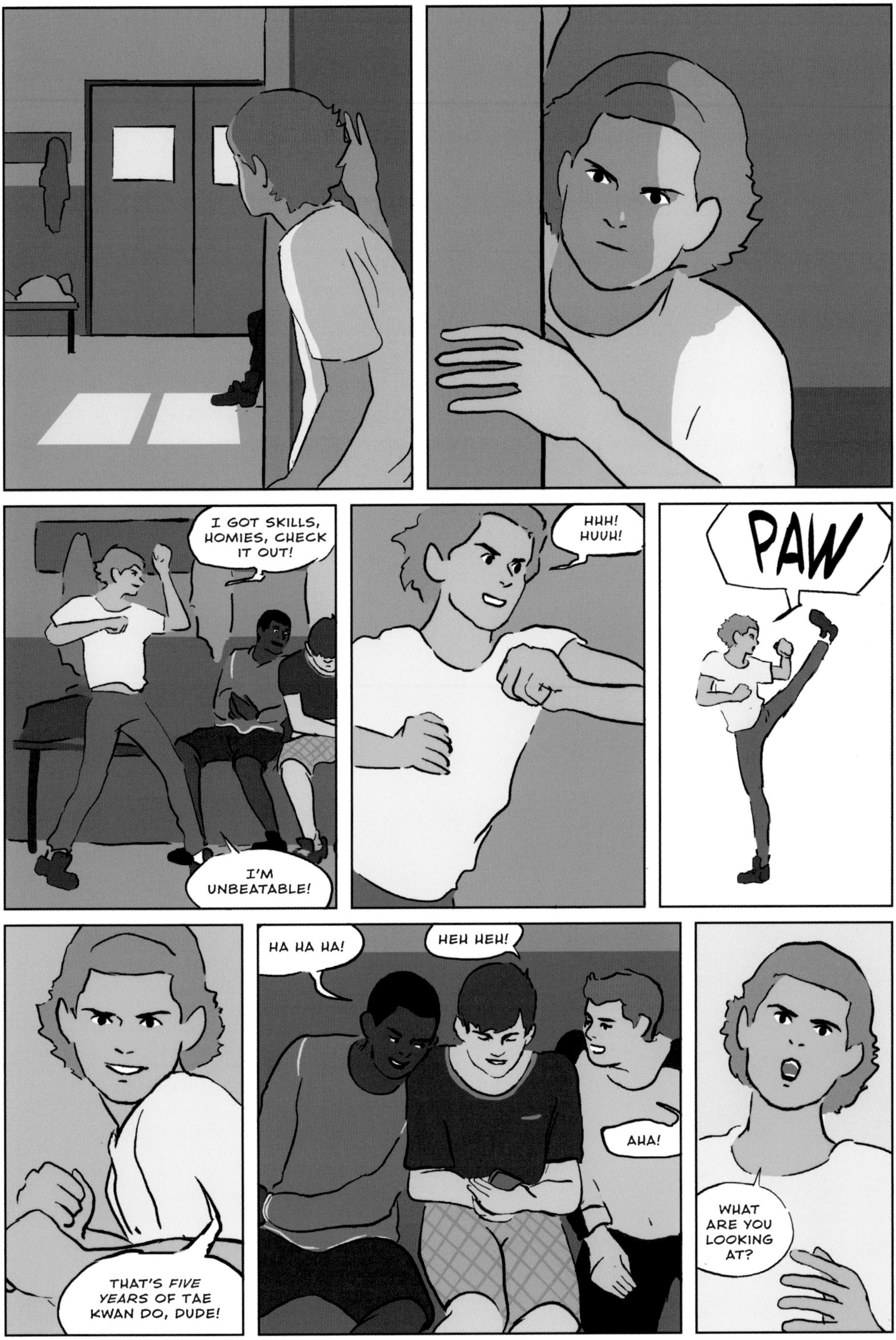
I GOT SKILLS, HOMIES, CHECK IT OUT!
I'M UNBEATABLE!
HHH! HUUH!
PAW
THAT'S *FIVE* YEARS OF TAE KWAN DO, DUDE!
HA HA HA!
HEH HEH!
AHA!
WHAT ARE YOU LOOKING AT?

BEAT IT, IT DOESN'T CONCERN YOU.

GIVEN YOUR REACTION...

...I'D SAY IT *DOES*.

LET GO OF IT!

GIVE ME BACK MY PHONE!

LET'S SEE WHAT YOU GUYS ARE *GIGGLING* ABOUT.

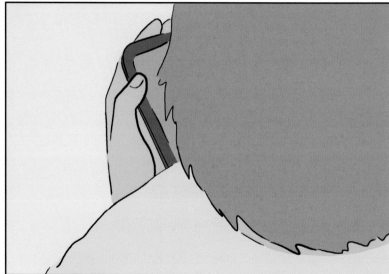

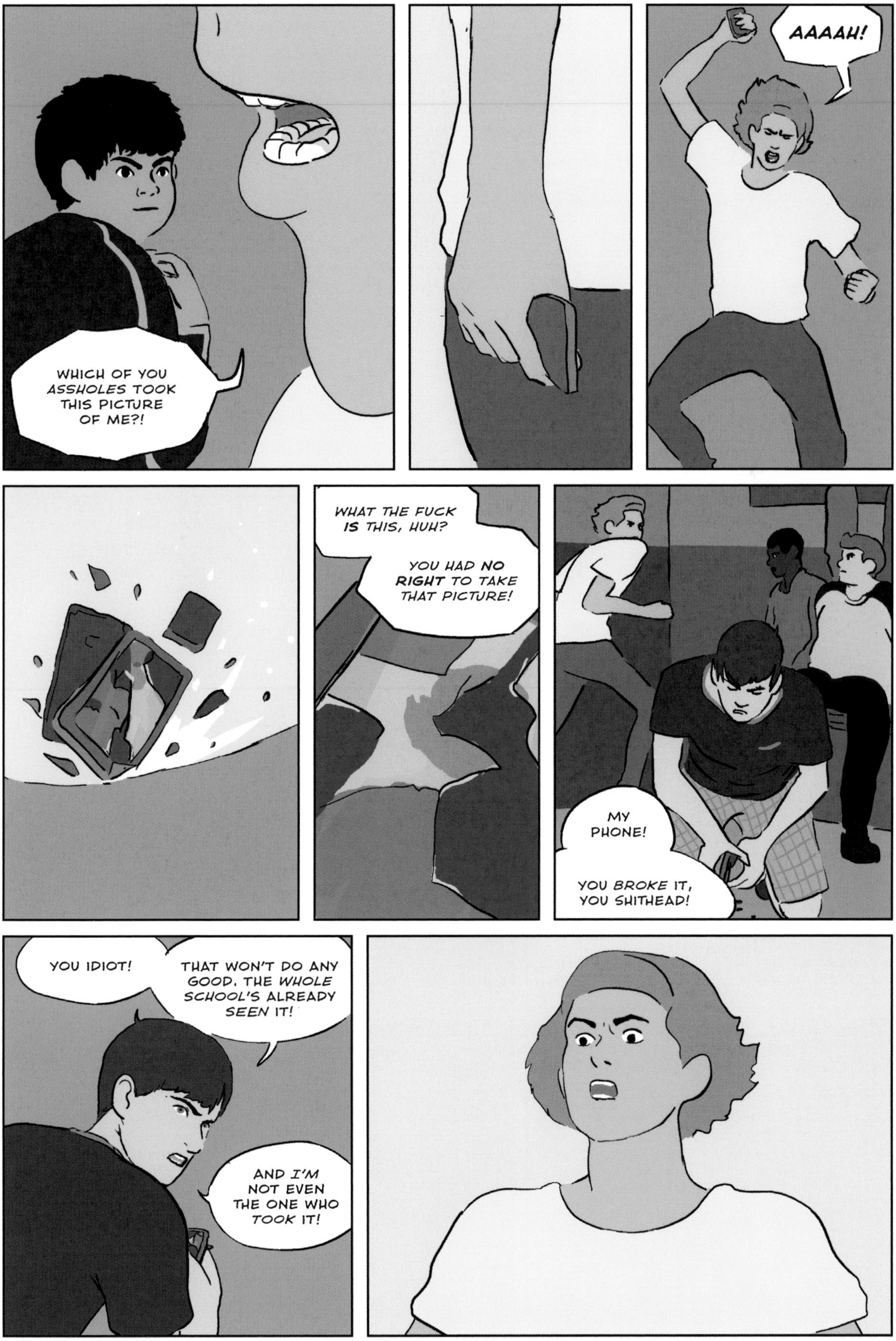
WHICH OF YOU ASSHOLES TOOK THIS PICTURE OF ME?!
AAAAH!
WHAT THE FUCK IS THIS, HUH?
YOU HAD NO RIGHT TO TAKE THAT PICTURE!
MY PHONE!
YOU BROKE IT, YOU SHITHEAD!
YOU IDIOT!
THAT WON'T DO ANY GOOD. THE WHOLE SCHOOL'S ALREADY SEEN IT!
AND I'M NOT EVEN THE ONE WHO TOOK IT!

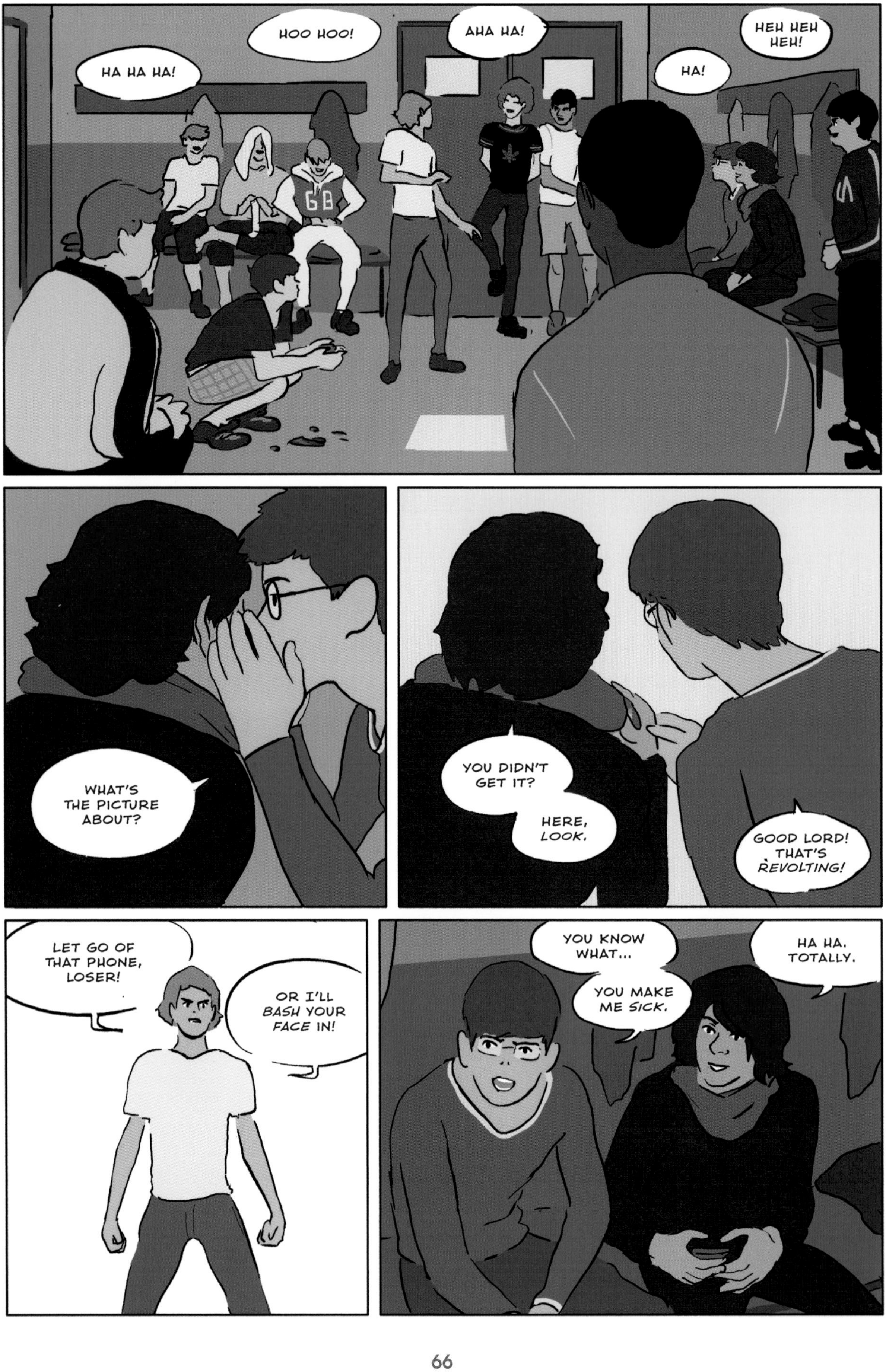
HA HA HA!
HOO HOO!
AHA HA!
HA!
HEH HEH HEH!
WHAT'S THE PICTURE ABOUT?
YOU DIDN'T GET IT?
HERE, LOOK.
GOOD LORD! THAT'S REVOLTING!
LET GO OF THAT PHONE, LOSER!
OR I'LL BASH YOUR FACE IN!
YOU KNOW WHAT...
YOU MAKE ME SICK.
HA HA. TOTALLY.

AHA HA!

HA HA HA!

HEH HEH HEH!

SHUUUUT UUUUP!

THAT PICTURE'S A FAKE!

SUUURE, WE BELIEVE YOU!

I KNEW IT FROM DAY ONE! YOU'RE A FREAK!

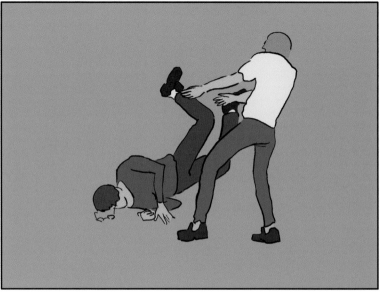

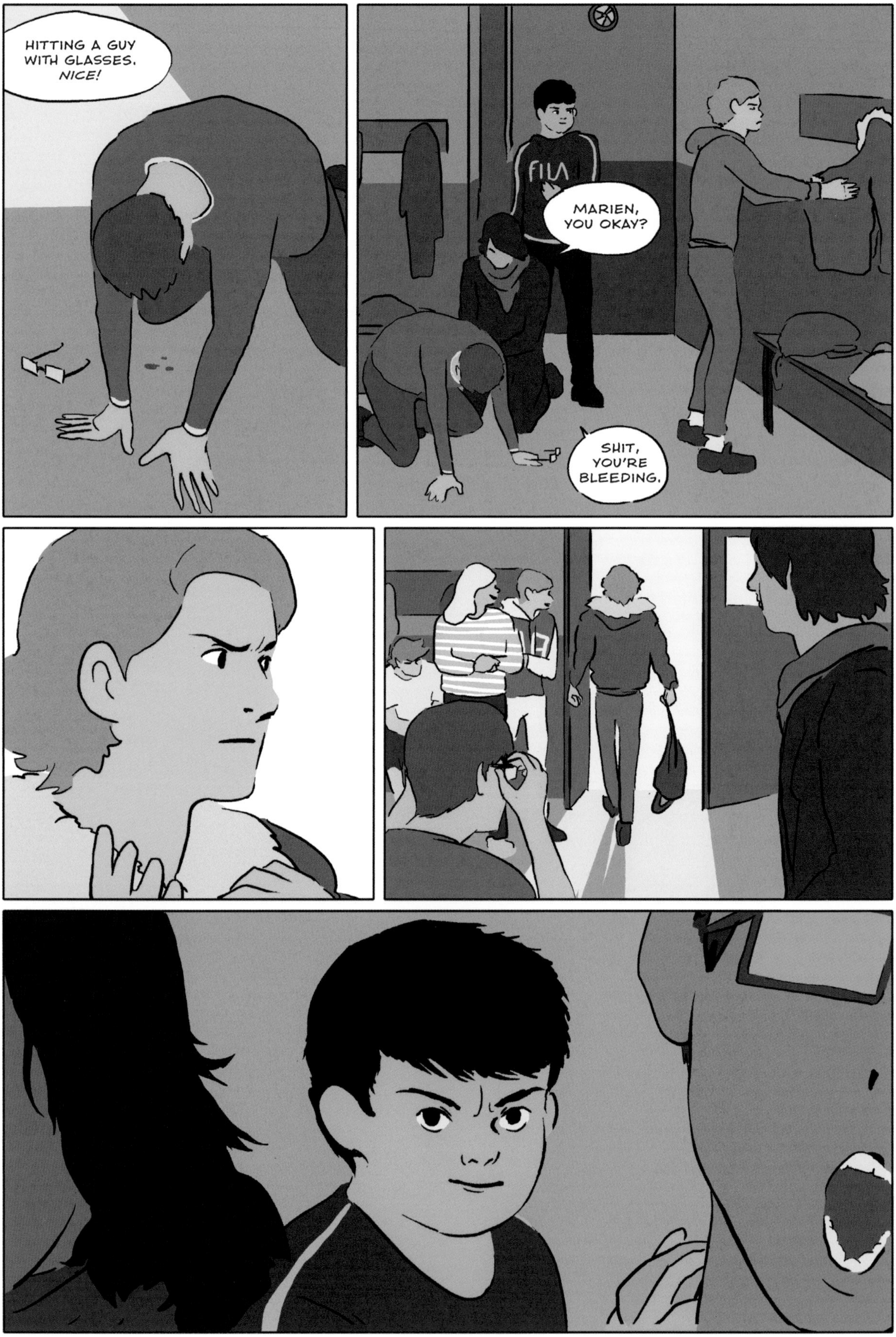
HITTING A GUY WITH GLASSES. NICE!
MARIEN, YOU OKAY?
SHIT, YOU'RE BLEEDING.

WEEK EIGHT.

DIRTY BOXERS FOR DIRTY BOYS!

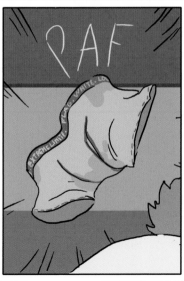

HEY! WHAT THE HELL, MAN!

OLÉ!

ASSHOLE.

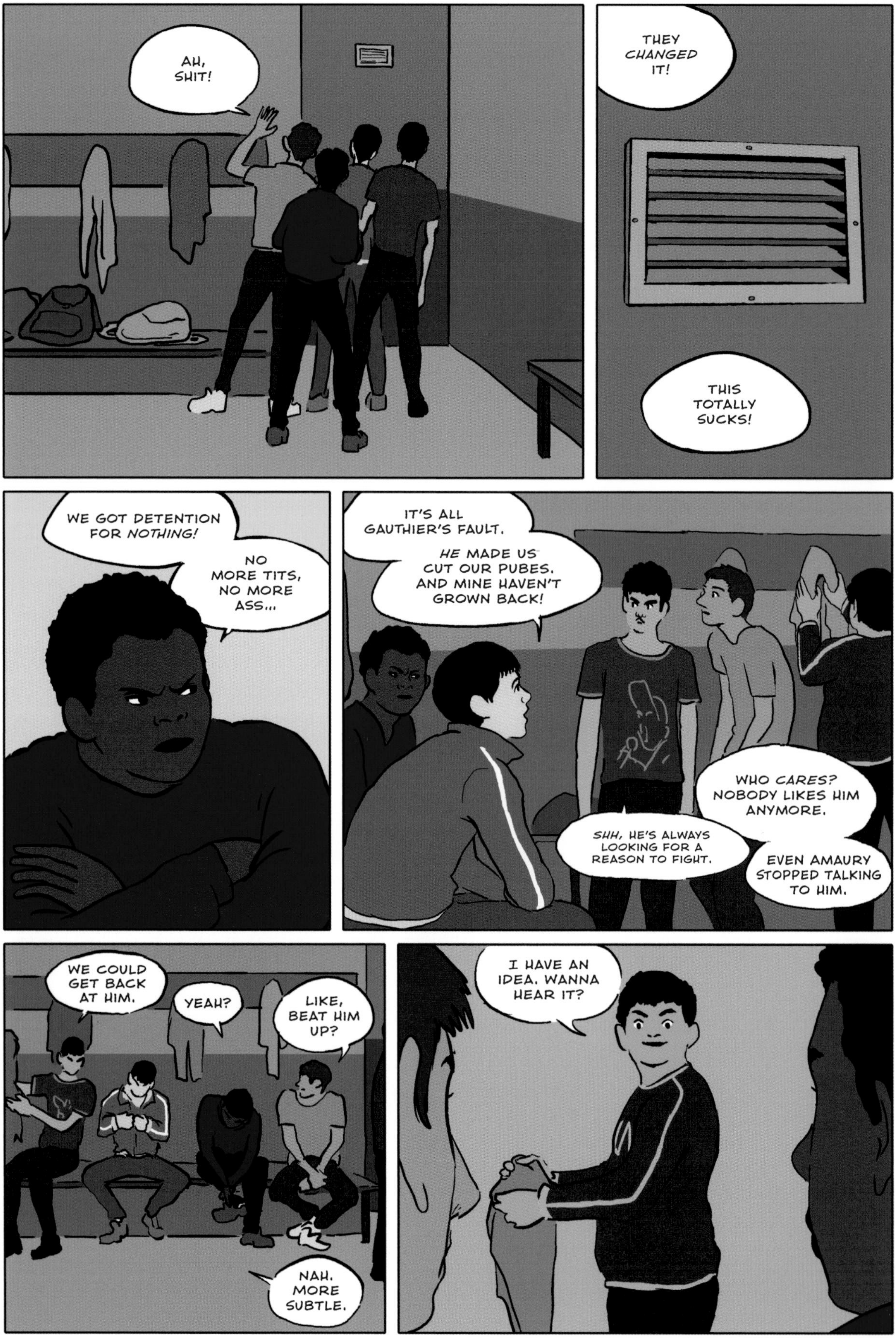
AH, SHIT!
THEY CHANGED IT!
THIS TOTALLY SUCKS!
WE GOT DETENTION FOR *NOTHING!*
NO MORE TITS, NO MORE ASS...
IT'S ALL GAUTHIER'S FAULT.
HE MADE US CUT OUR PUBES. AND MINE HAVEN'T GROWN BACK!
WHO *CARES?* NOBODY LIKES HIM ANYMORE.
SHH, HE'S ALWAYS LOOKING FOR A REASON TO FIGHT.
EVEN AMAURY STOPPED TALKING TO HIM.
WE COULD GET BACK AT HIM.
YEAH?
LIKE, BEAT HIM UP?
NAH. MORE SUBTLE.
I HAVE AN IDEA. WANNA HEAR IT?

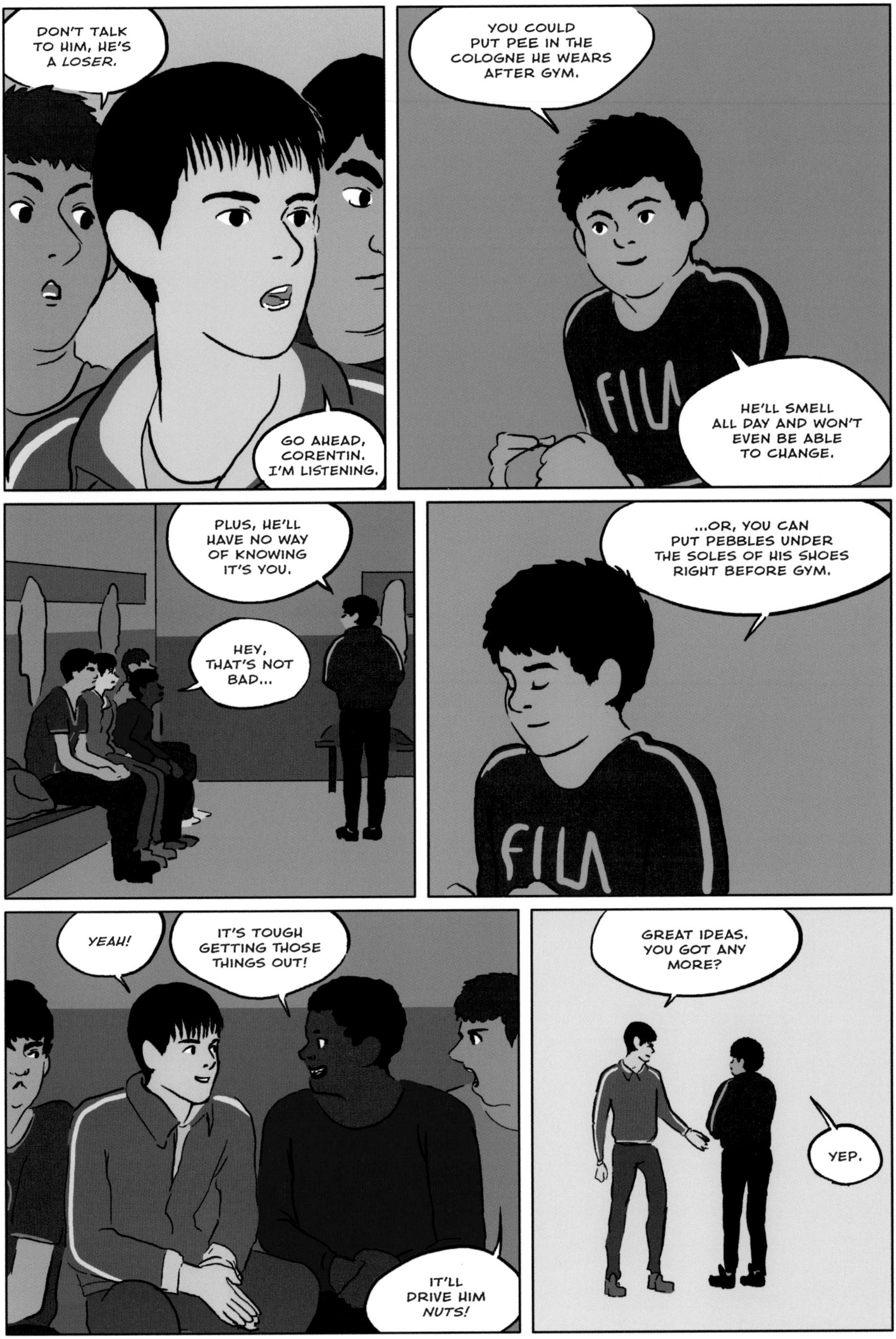
DON'T TALK TO HIM, HE'S A *LOSER.*
GO AHEAD, CORENTIN. I'M LISTENING.
YOU COULD PUT PEE IN THE COLOGNE HE WEARS AFTER GYM.
FILA
HE'LL SMELL ALL DAY AND WON'T EVEN BE ABLE TO CHANGE.
PLUS, HE'LL HAVE NO WAY OF KNOWING IT'S YOU.
HEY, THAT'S NOT BAD...
...OR, YOU CAN PUT PEBBLES UNDER THE SOLES OF HIS SHOES RIGHT BEFORE GYM.
FILA
YEAH!
IT'S TOUGH GETTING THOSE THINGS OUT!
IT'LL DRIVE HIM *NUTS!*
GREAT IDEAS. YOU GOT ANY MORE?
YEP.

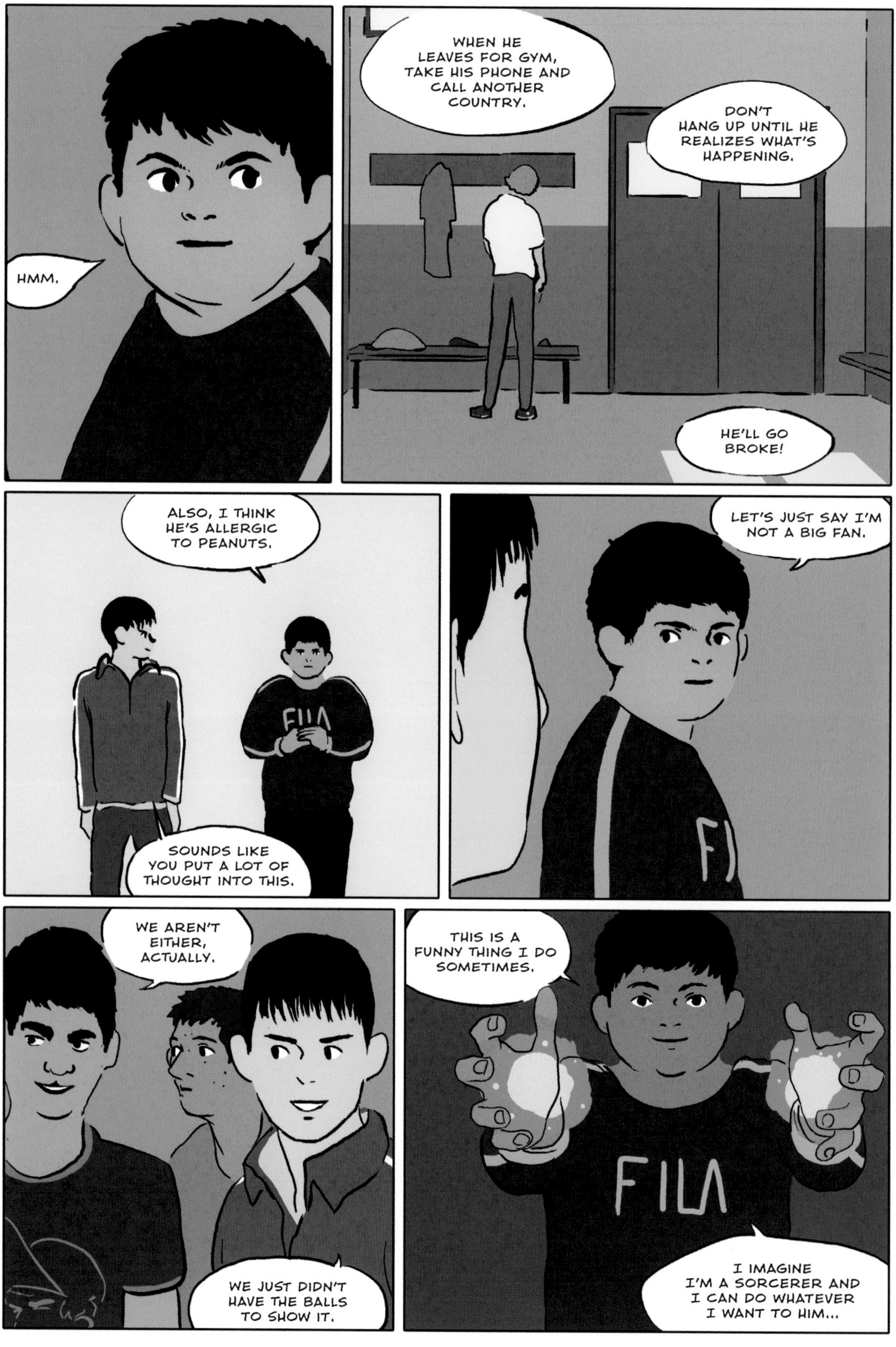
HMM.
WHEN HE LEAVES FOR GYM, TAKE HIS PHONE AND CALL ANOTHER COUNTRY.
DON'T HANG UP UNTIL HE REALIZES WHAT'S HAPPENING.
HE'LL GO BROKE!
ALSO, I THINK HE'S ALLERGIC TO PEANUTS.
FILA
SOUNDS LIKE YOU PUT A LOT OF THOUGHT INTO THIS.
LET'S JUST SAY I'M NOT A BIG FAN.
WE AREN'T EITHER, ACTUALLY.
WE JUST DIDN'T HAVE THE BALLS TO SHOW IT.
THIS IS A FUNNY THING I DO SOMETIMES.
FILA
I IMAGINE I'M A SORCERER AND I CAN DO WHATEVER I WANT TO HIM...

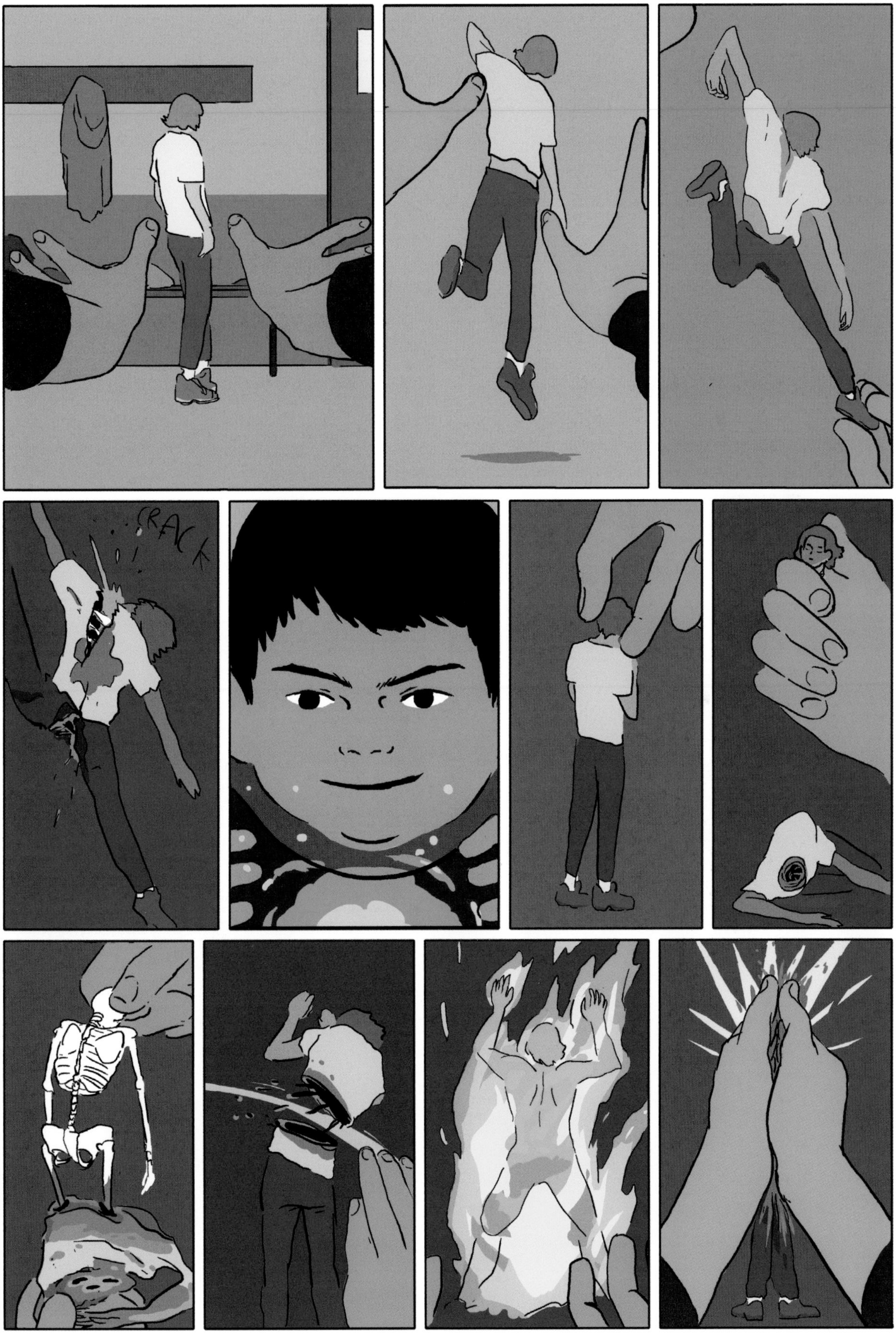
CRACK

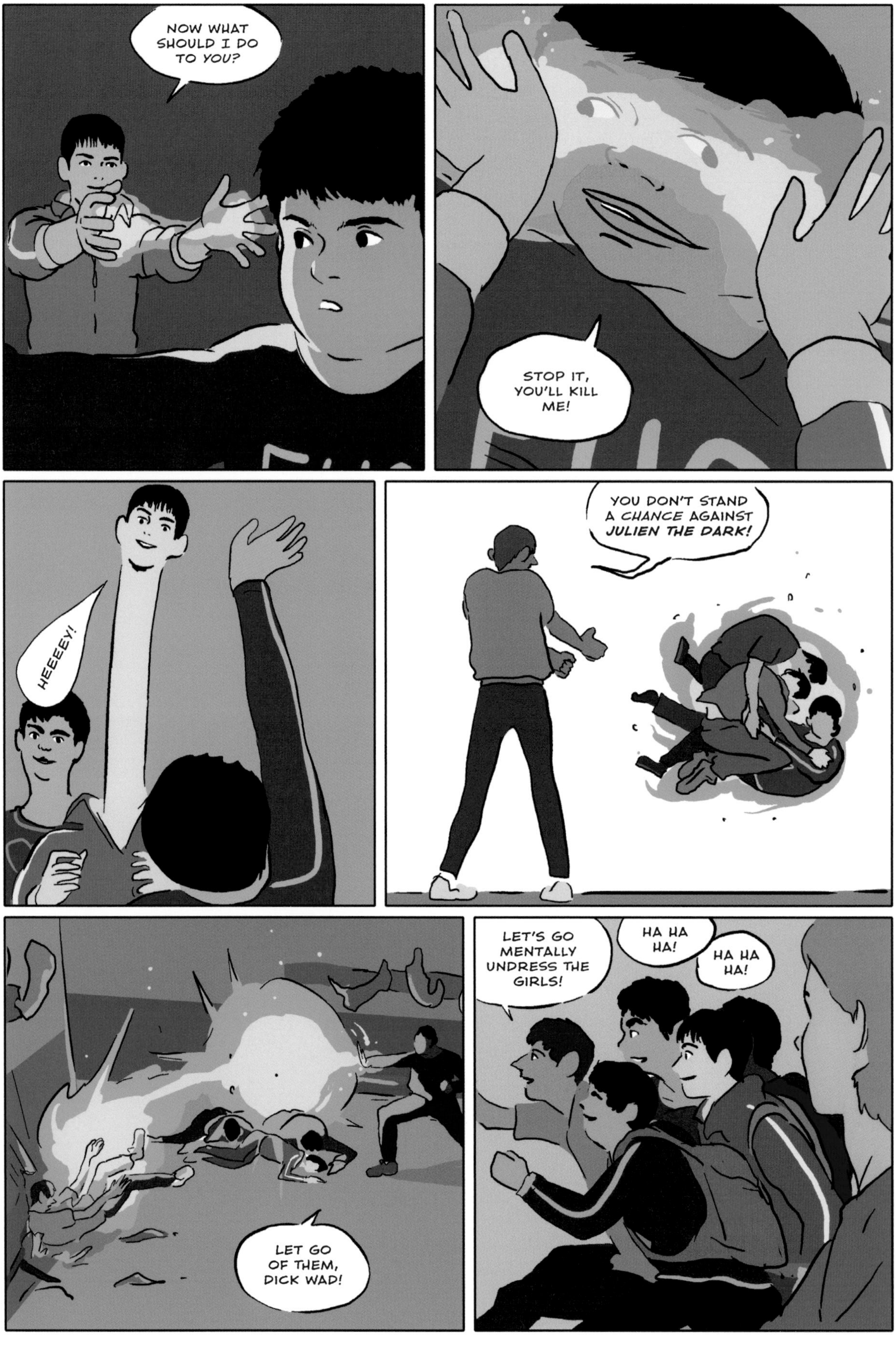
NOW WHAT SHOULD I DO TO YOU?
STOP IT, YOU'LL KILL ME!
HEEEEY!
YOU DON'T STAND A CHANCE AGAINST JULIEN THE DARK!
LET GO OF THEM, DICK WAD!
LET'S GO MENTALLY UNDRESS THE GIRLS!
HA HA HA!
HA HA HA!

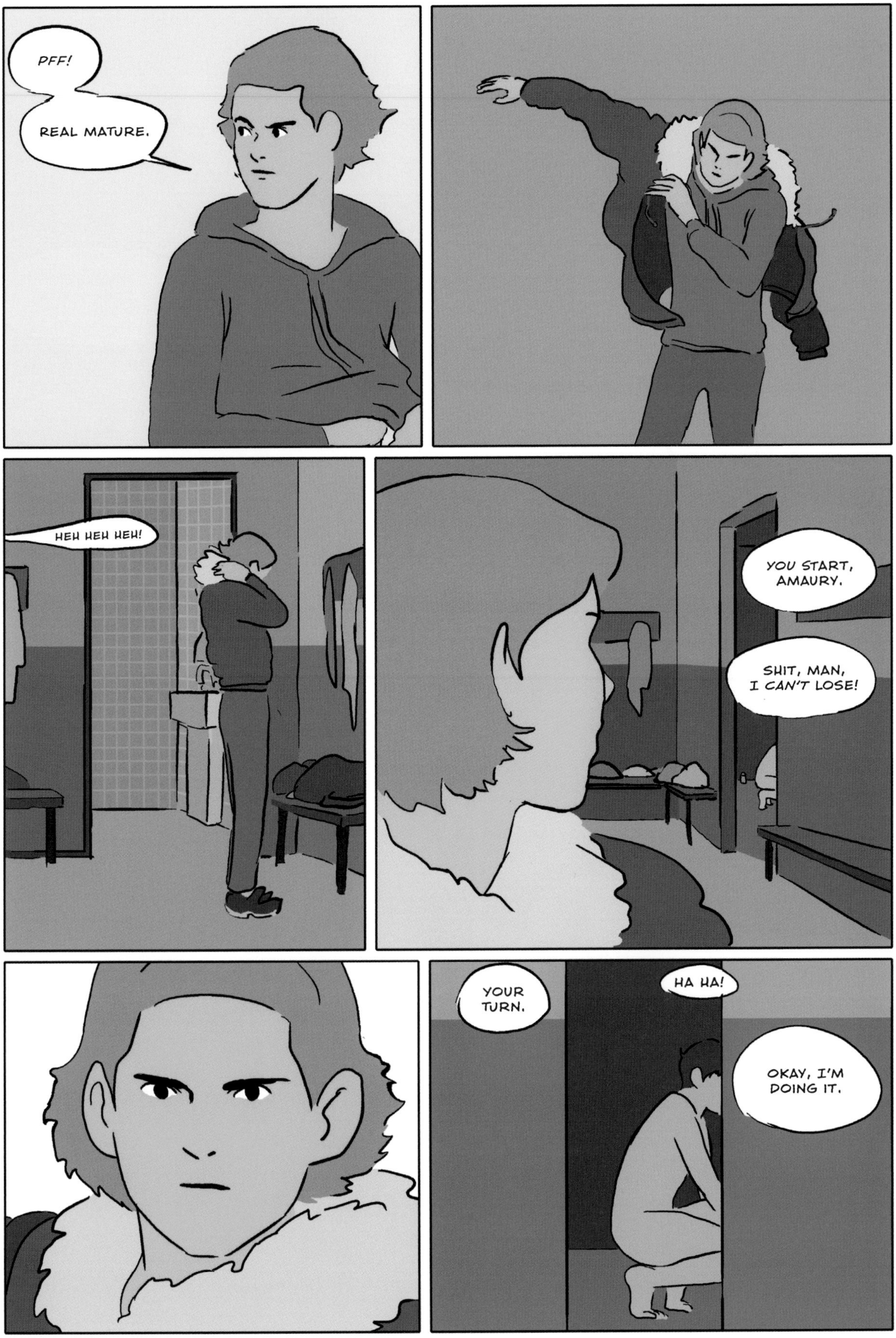
PFF!
REAL MATURE.
HEH HEH HEH!
YOU START, AMAURY.
SHIT, MAN, I CAN'T LOSE!
YOUR TURN.
HA HA!
OKAY, I'M DOING IT.

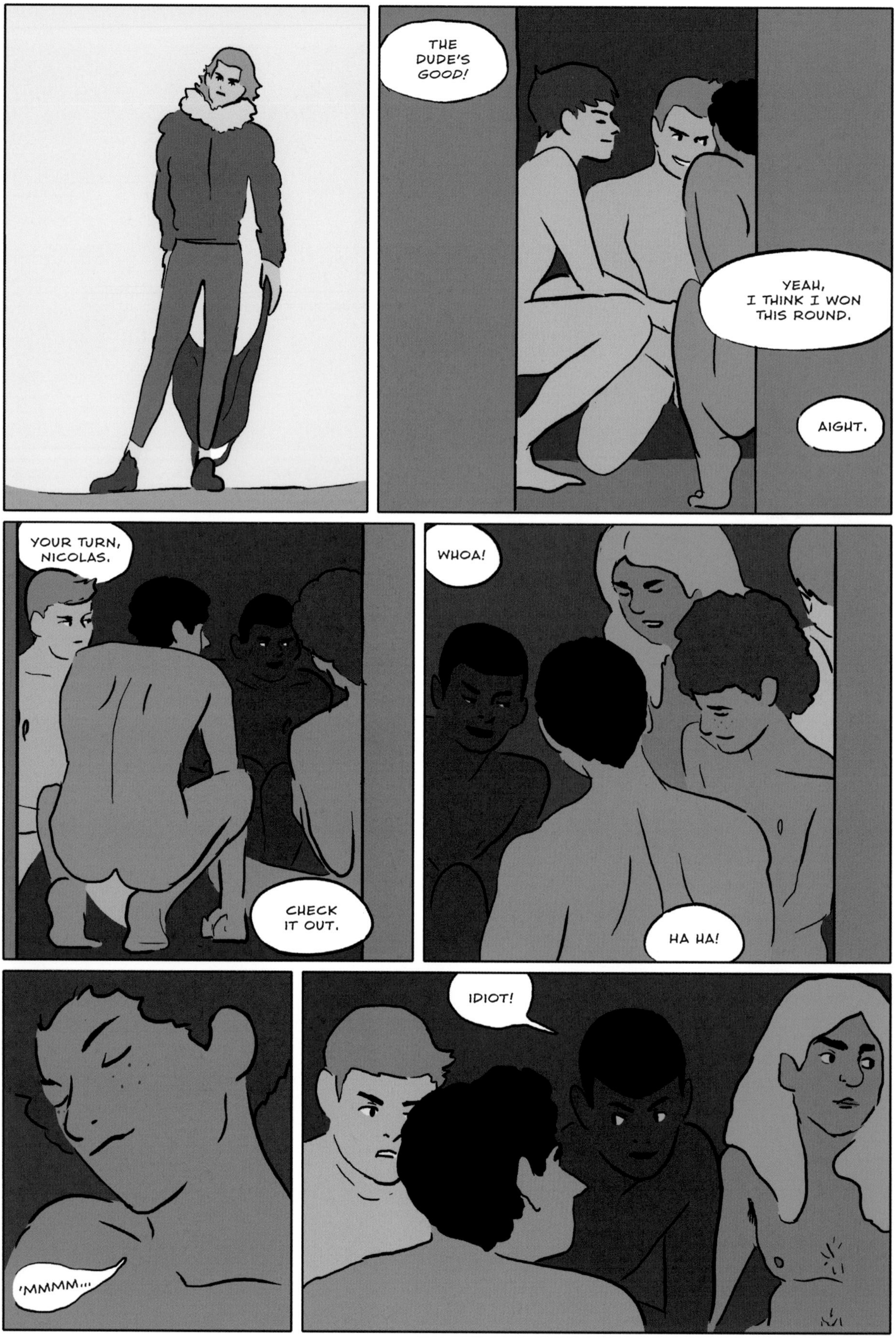
THE DUDE'S GOOD!
YEAH, I THINK I WON THIS ROUND.
AIGHT.
YOUR TURN, NICOLAS.
CHECK IT OUT.
WHOA!
HA HA!
'MMMM...
IDIOT!

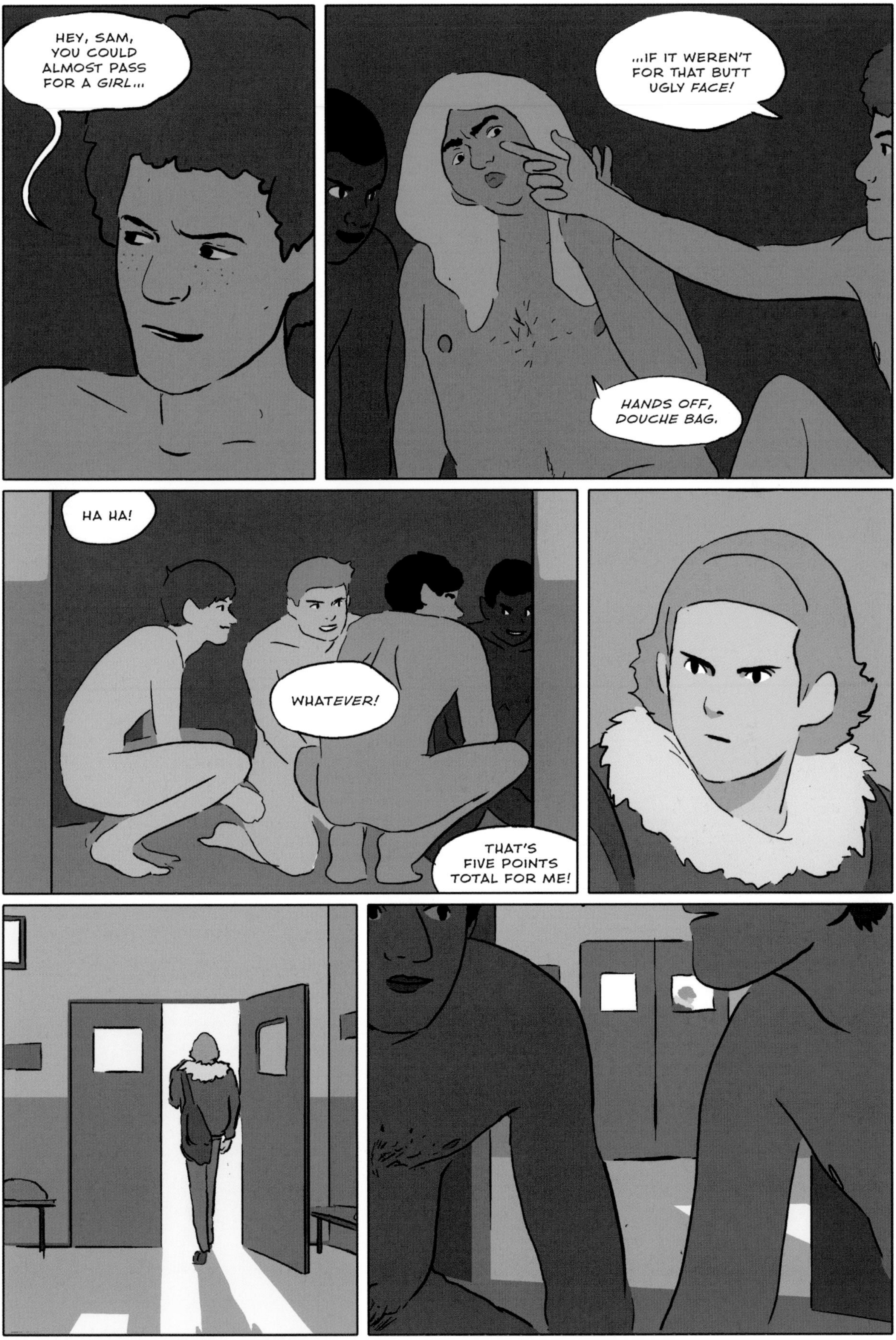
HEY, SAM, YOU COULD ALMOST PASS FOR A *GIRL*...
...IF IT WEREN'T FOR THAT BUTT UGLY *FACE!*
HANDS OFF, DOUCHE BAG.
HA HA!
WHATEVER!
THAT'S FIVE POINTS TOTAL FOR ME!

WEEK NINE.

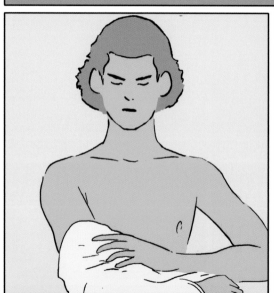

LISTEN, GAUTHIER, I KNOW WE DON'T TALK MUCH THESE DAYS...

...BUT I'M REALLY SORRY ABOUT YOUR DAD.

78

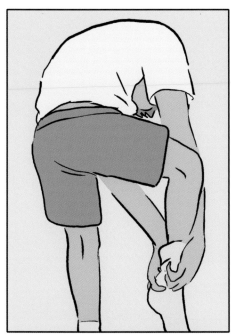

YOU DON'T SEEM VERY SAD.

WHAT DO YOU WANT ME TO SAY?

THE ONLY THING HE'S EVER DONE FOR ME IN THE LAST FEW YEARS IS GIVE ME THIS STUPID NECKLACE.

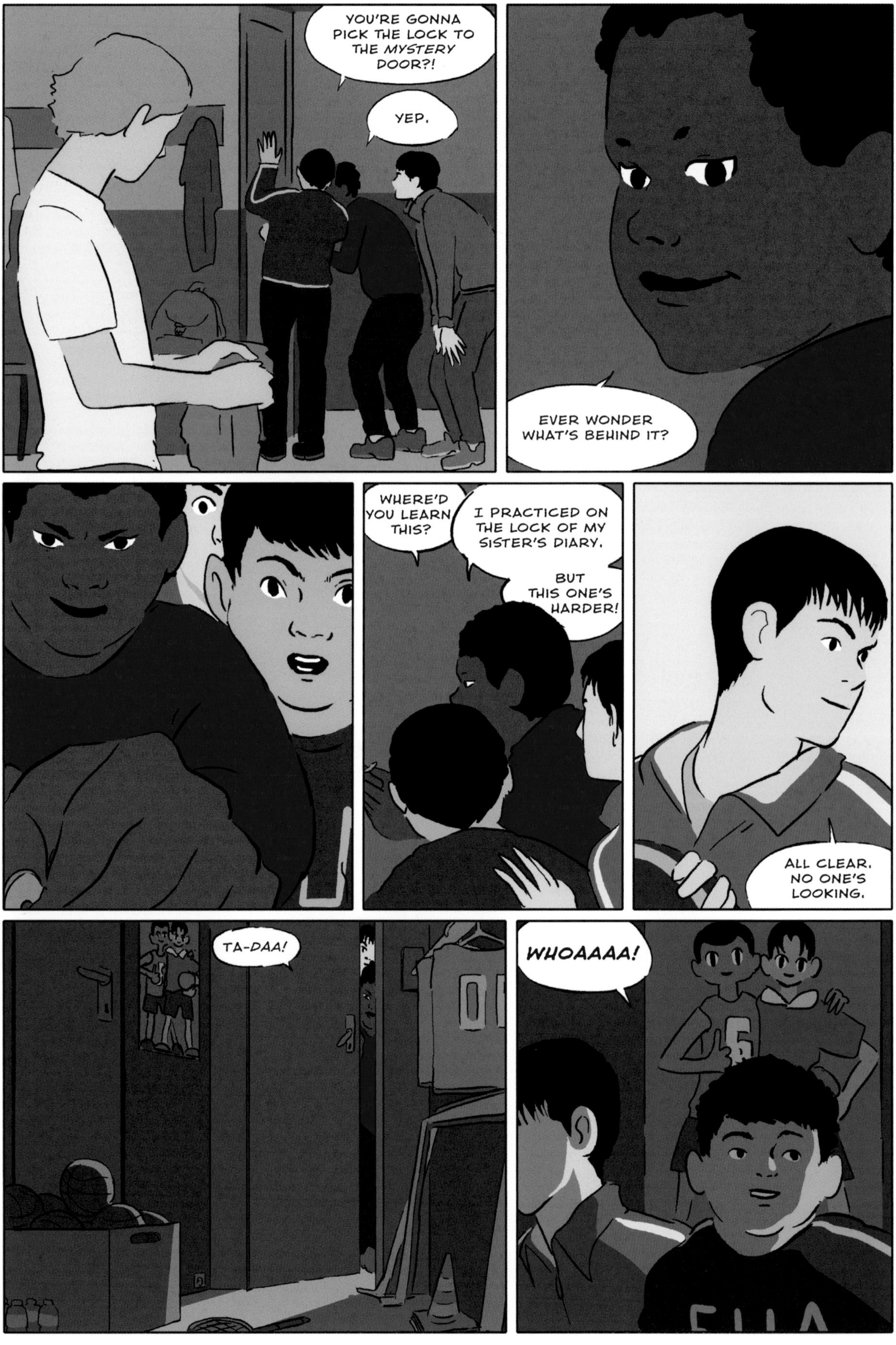
YOU'RE GONNA PICK THE LOCK TO THE *MYSTERY* DOOR?!
YEP.
EVER WONDER WHAT'S BEHIND IT?
WHERE'D YOU LEARN THIS?
I PRACTICED ON THE LOCK OF MY SISTER'S DIARY.
BUT THIS ONE'S HARDER!
ALL CLEAR. NO ONE'S LOOKING.
TA-DAA!
WHOAAAA!

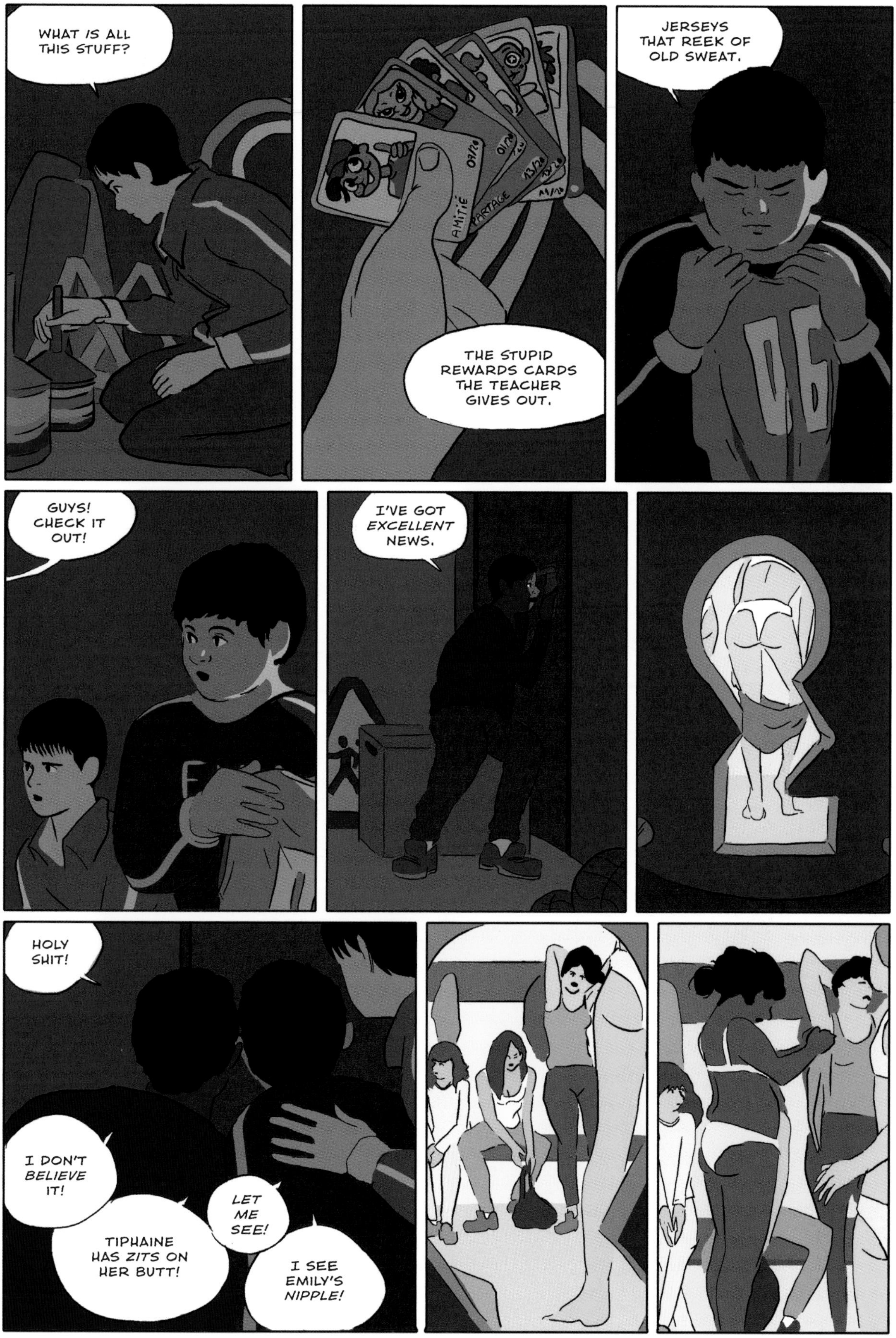
WHAT IS ALL THIS STUFF?
AMITIÉ
PARTAGE
THE STUPID REWARDS CARDS THE TEACHER GIVES OUT.
JERSEYS THAT REEK OF OLD SWEAT.
06
GUYS! CHECK IT OUT!
I'VE GOT *EXCELLENT* NEWS.
HOLY SHIT!
I DON'T *BELIEVE* IT!
TIPHAINE HAS *ZITS* ON HER BUTT!
LET ME SEE!
I SEE EMILY'S *NIPPLE!*

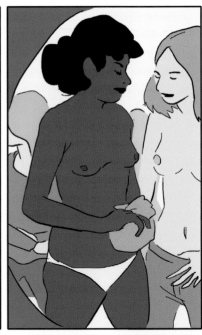

LET'S MAKE THIS OUR SECRET BASE FROM NOW ON!

THE H.Q. FOR SPYING ON THE GIRLS!

HA HA!

JUST MAKE SURE YOU DON'T TELL JULIEN!

HE'S THE ONE WHO TOLD THE BLONDS ABOUT THE AIR VENT.

DEAL!

THIS IS OUR SECRET.

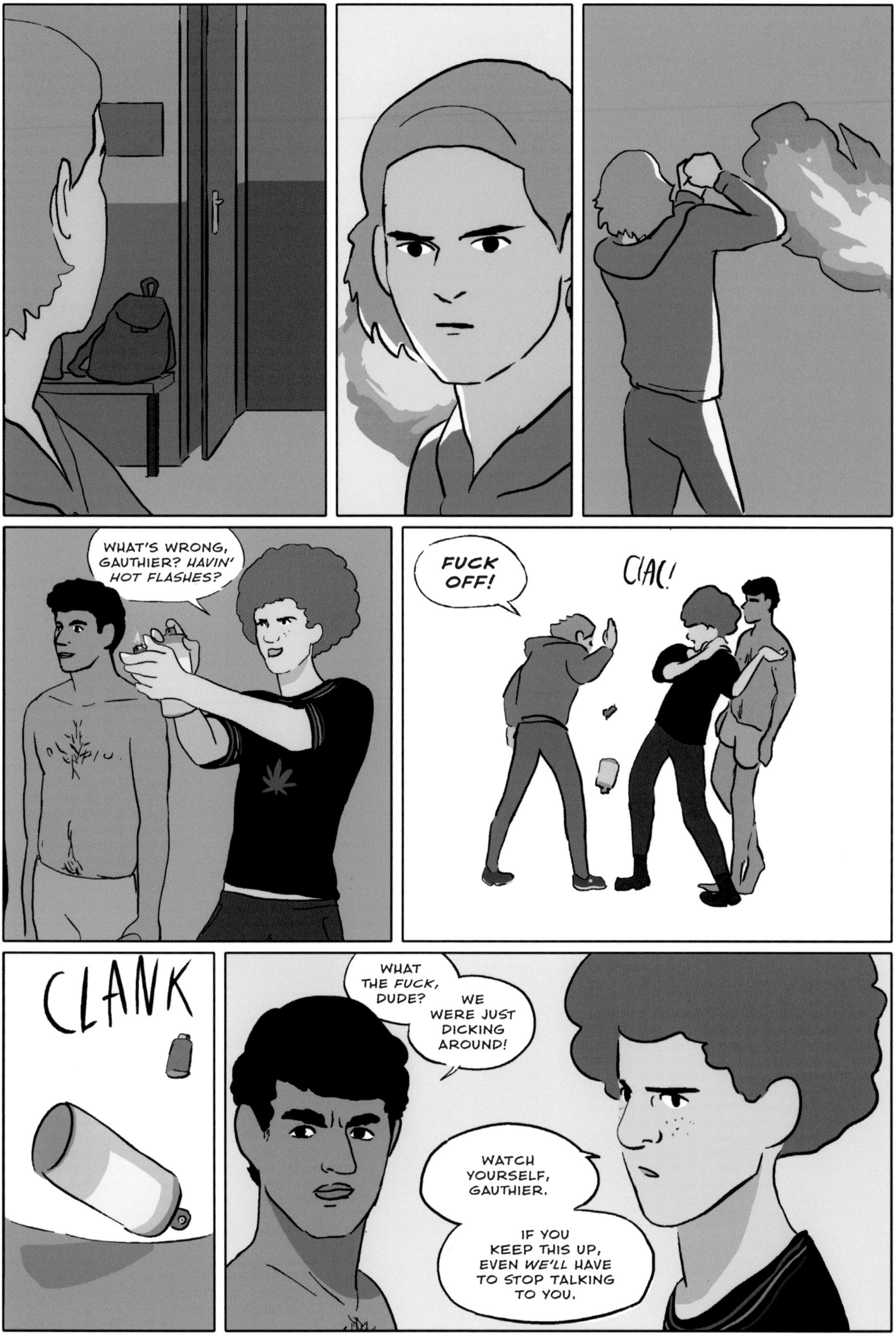
WHAT'S WRONG, GAUTHIER? *HAVIN' HOT FLASHES?*
FUCK OFF!
CIAC!
CLANK
WHAT THE *FUCK*, DUDE?
WE WERE JUST DICKING AROUND!
WATCH YOURSELF, GAUTHIER.
IF YOU KEEP THIS UP, EVEN *WE'LL* HAVE TO STOP TALKING TO YOU.

SORRY, GUYS.

YOU SHOULD BE CAREFUL.

MY COUSIN TOLD ME A GUY IN HIS CLASS GOT HIS HAND BLOWN OFF.

BLOOD EVERYWHERE.

FORREAL?

YOU CAN'T LET THE FLAME GO UP.

OTHERWISE, YOU'LL HAVE A STUMP FOR A HAND.

I DARE YOU!

CHECK IT OUT. I'M GONNA SHOW YOU SOMETHING ELSE...

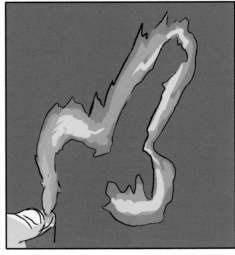

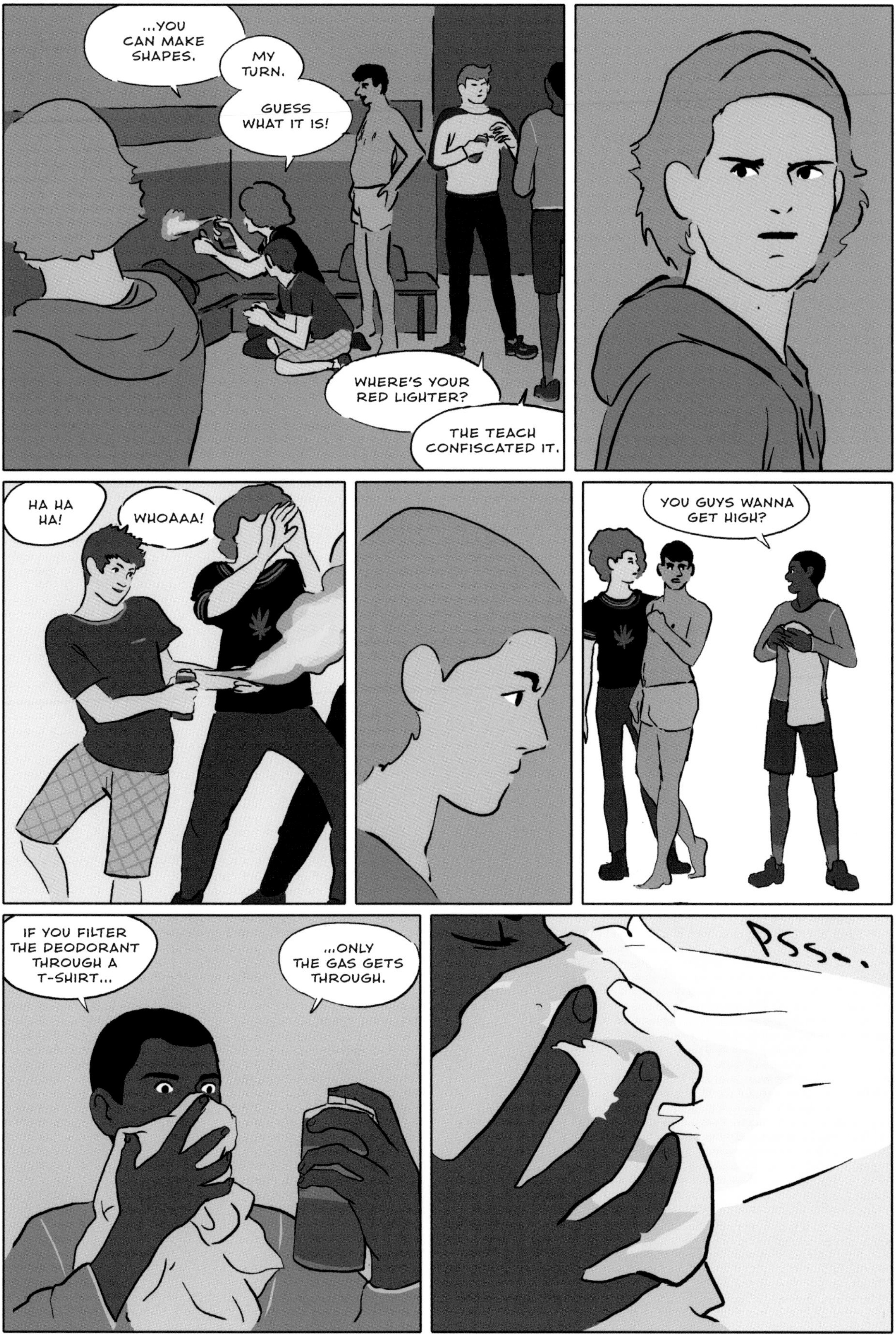
...YOU CAN MAKE SHAPES.
MY TURN.
GUESS WHAT IT IS!
WHERE'S YOUR RED LIGHTER?
THE TEACH CONFISCATED IT.
HA HA HA!
WHOAAA!
YOU GUYS WANNA GET HIGH?
IF YOU FILTER THE DEODORANT THROUGH A T-SHIRT...
...ONLY THE GAS GETS THROUGH.
PSS..

AAAAAH...

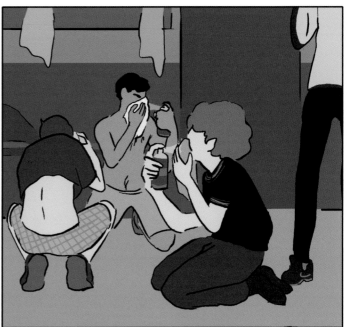

I'M FLYING, MAN.

HA HA HA!

WHOA...

PAM

GAUTHIER'S A TOTAL *BUZZ KILL,* ISN'T HE?

HE JUST STANDS THERE AND STARES AT US AND DOESN'T SAY A WORD.

THE DUDE JUST *LOST HIS DAD,* AMAURY.

CAN YOU IMAGINE WHAT THAT MUST FEEL LIKE?

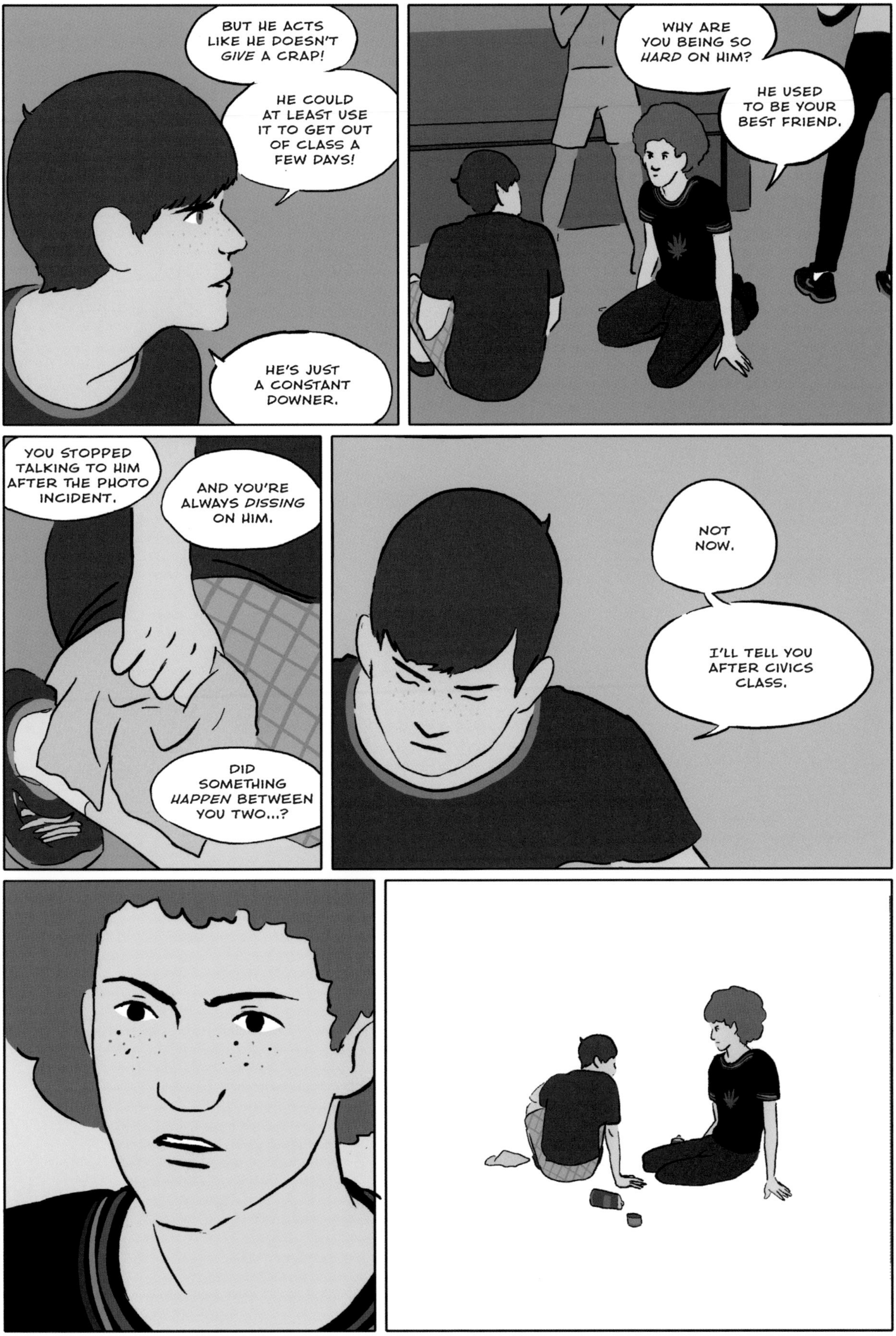
BUT HE ACTS LIKE HE DOESN'T *GIVE* A CRAP!
HE COULD AT LEAST USE IT TO GET OUT OF CLASS A FEW DAYS!
HE'S JUST A CONSTANT DOWNER.
WHY ARE YOU BEING SO *HARD* ON HIM?
HE USED TO BE YOUR BEST FRIEND.
YOU STOPPED TALKING TO HIM AFTER THE PHOTO INCIDENT.
AND YOU'RE ALWAYS *DISSING* ON HIM.
DID SOMETHING *HAPPEN* BETWEEN YOU TWO...?
NOT NOW.
I'LL TELL YOU AFTER CIVICS CLASS.

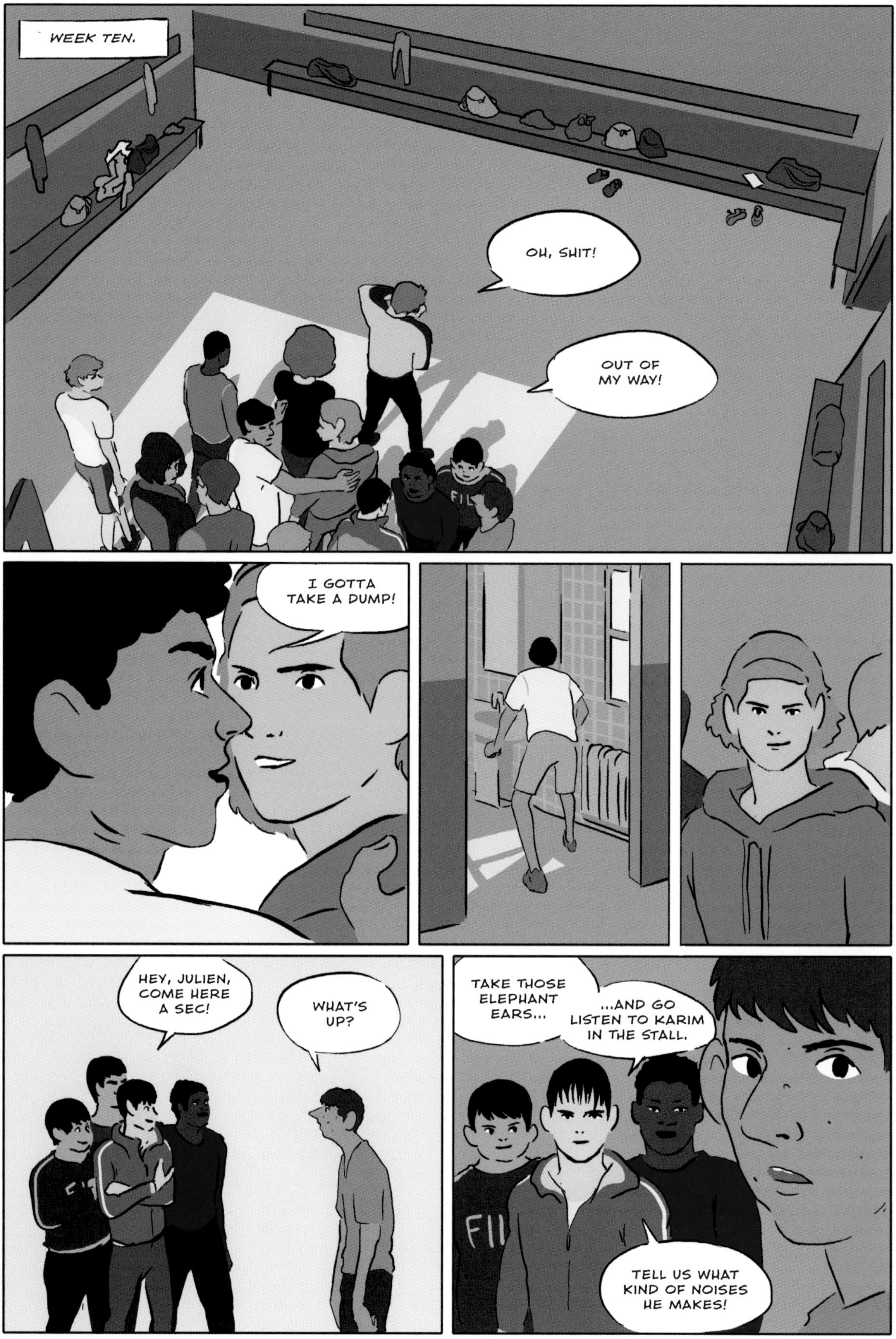
WEEK TEN.
OH, SHIT!
OUT OF MY WAY!
I GOTTA TAKE A DUMP!
HEY, JULIEN, COME HERE A SEC!
WHAT'S UP?
TAKE THOSE ELEPHANT EARS...
...AND GO LISTEN TO KARIM IN THE STALL.
TELL US WHAT KIND OF NOISES HE MAKES!

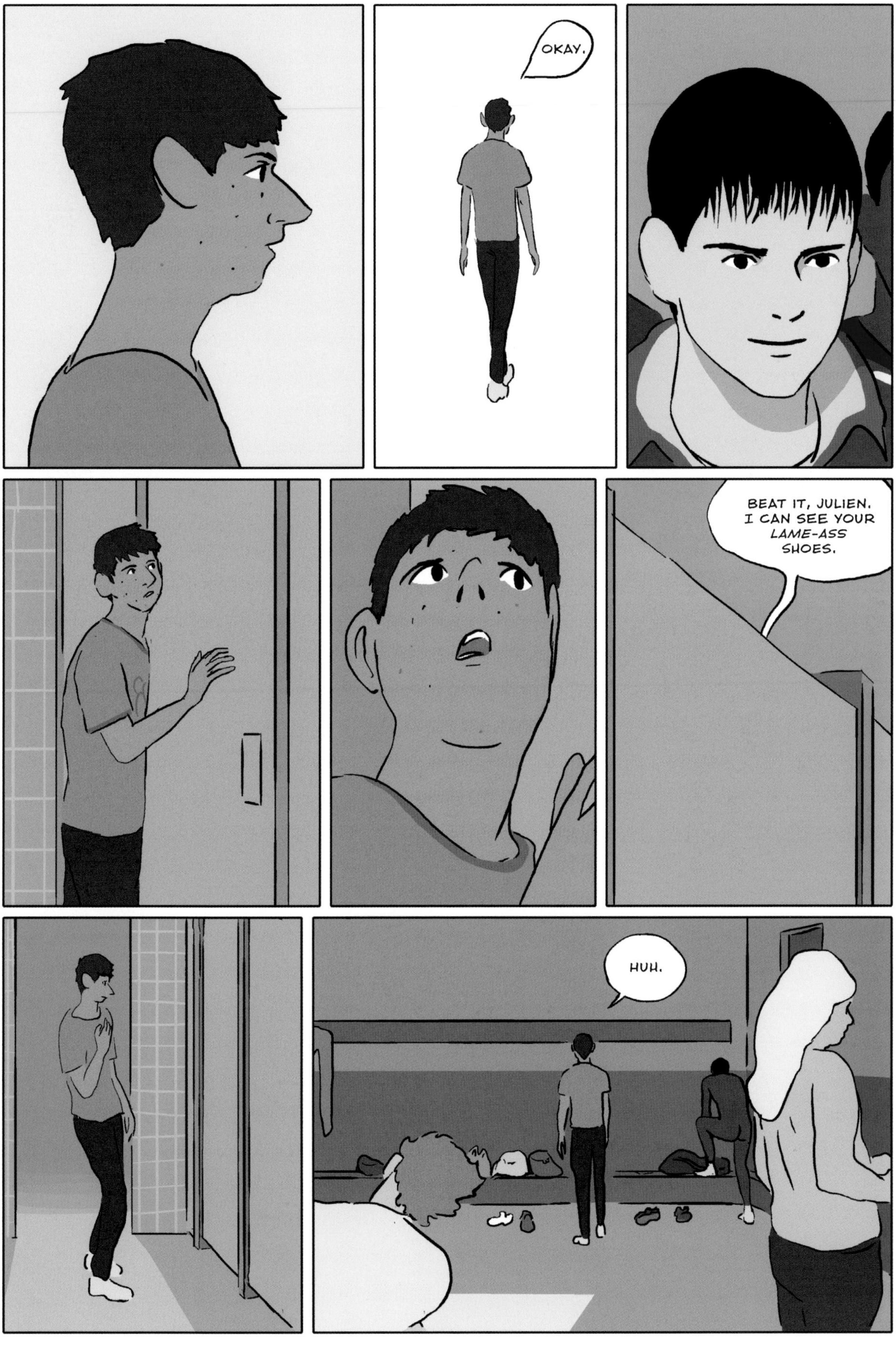
OKAY.
BEAT IT, JULIEN. I CAN SEE YOUR *LAME-ASS* SHOES.
HUH.

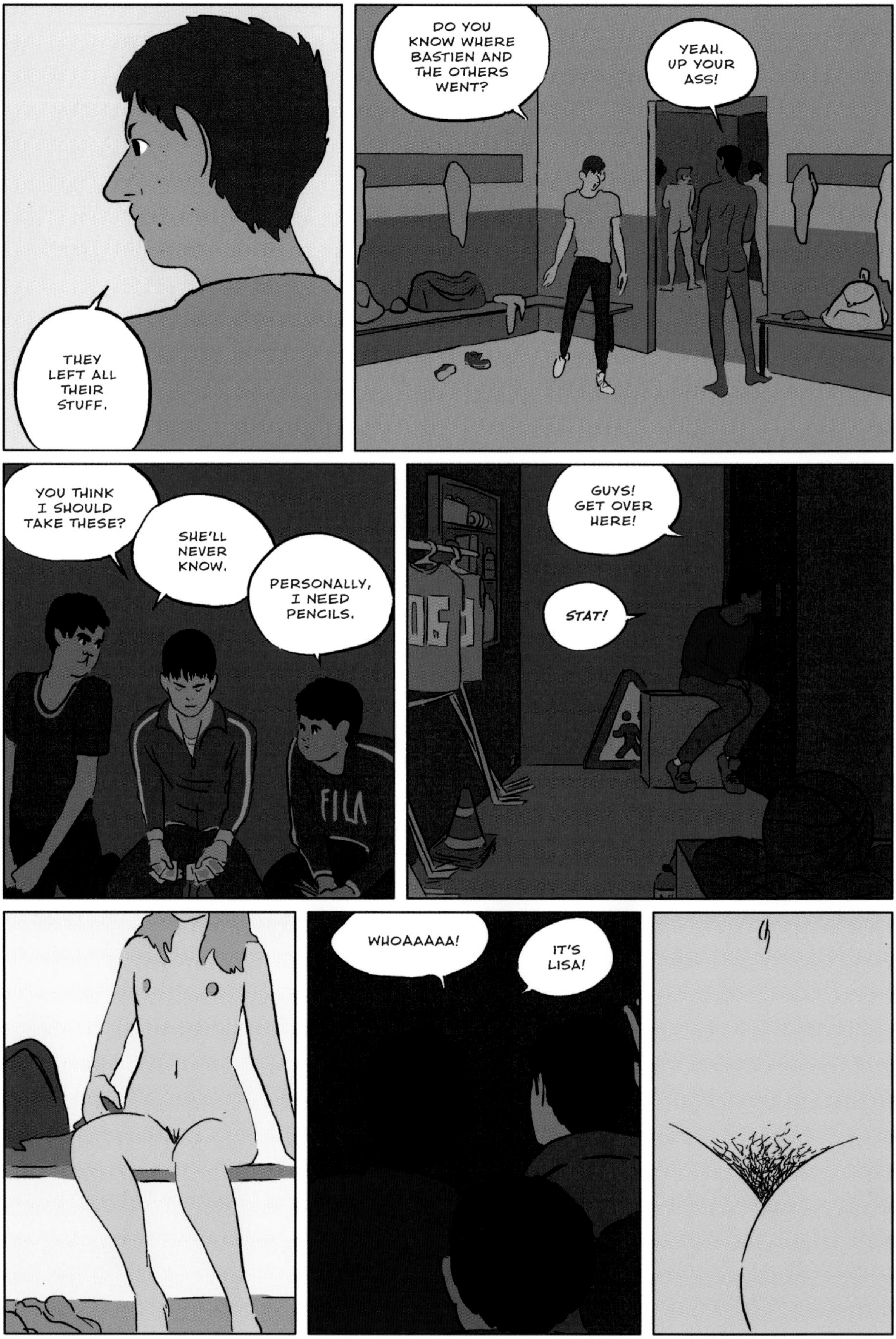
THEY LEFT ALL THEIR STUFF.
DO YOU KNOW WHERE BASTIEN AND THE OTHERS WENT?
YEAH. UP YOUR ASS!
YOU THINK I SHOULD TAKE THESE?
SHE'LL NEVER KNOW.
PERSONALLY, I NEED PENCILS.
FILA
GUYS! GET OVER HERE!
STAT!
WHOAAAAA!
IT'S LISA!

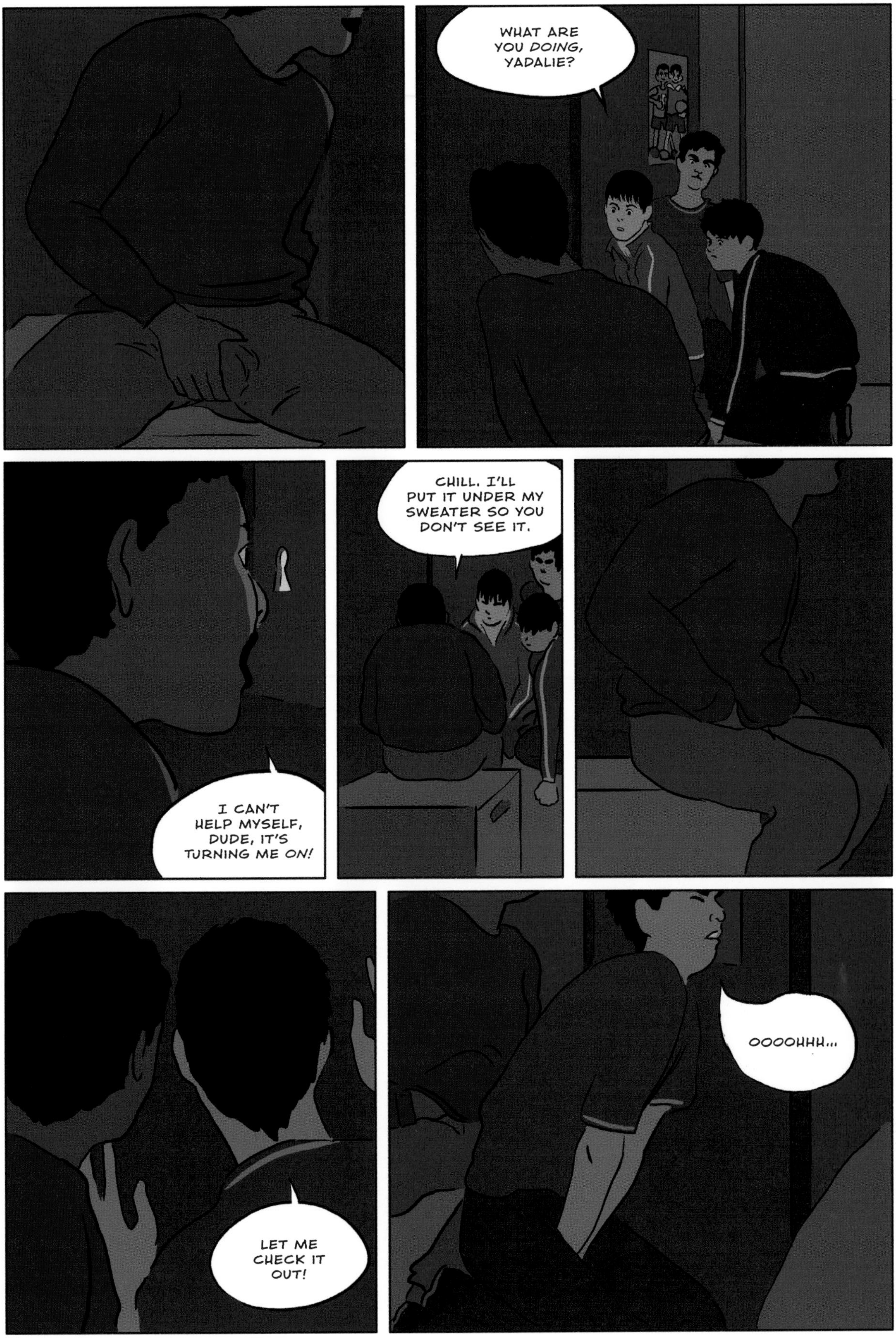
WHAT ARE YOU DOING, YADALIE?
I CAN'T HELP MYSELF, DUDE, IT'S TURNING ME ON!
CHILL. I'LL PUT IT UNDER MY SWEATER SO YOU DON'T SEE IT.
LET ME CHECK IT OUT!
OOOOHHH...

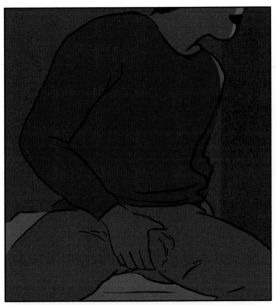

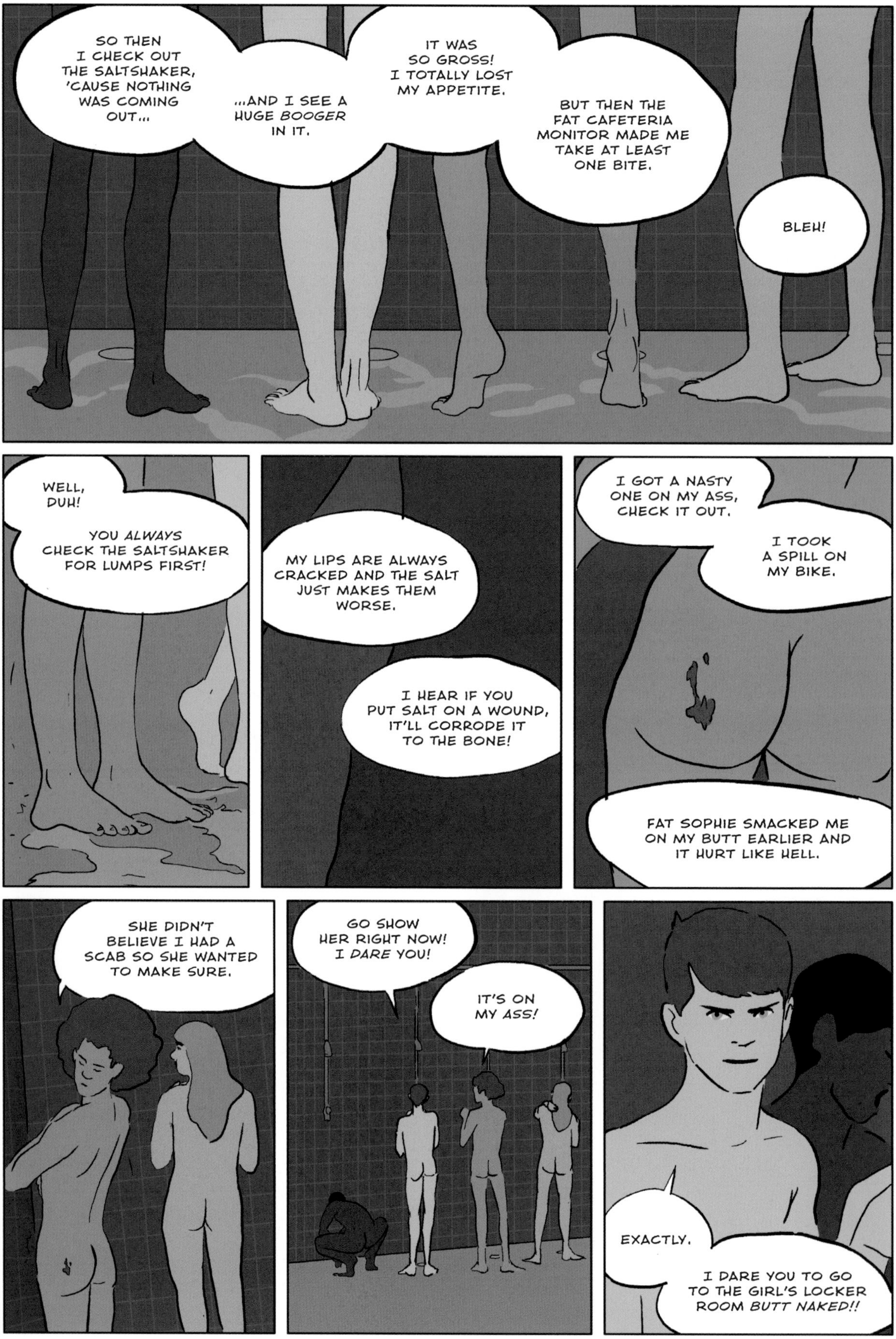
SO THEN I CHECK OUT THE SALTSHAKER, 'CAUSE NOTHING WAS COMING OUT...
...AND I SEE A HUGE *BOOGER* IN IT.
IT WAS SO GROSS! I TOTALLY LOST MY APPETITE.
BUT THEN THE FAT CAFETERIA MONITOR MADE ME TAKE AT LEAST ONE BITE.
BLEH!
WELL, DUH!
YOU *ALWAYS* CHECK THE SALTSHAKER FOR LUMPS FIRST!
MY LIPS ARE ALWAYS CRACKED AND THE SALT JUST MAKES THEM WORSE.
I HEAR IF YOU PUT SALT ON A WOUND, IT'LL CORRODE IT TO THE BONE!
I GOT A NASTY ONE ON MY ASS, CHECK IT OUT.
I TOOK A SPILL ON MY BIKE.
FAT SOPHIE SMACKED ME ON MY BUTT EARLIER AND IT HURT LIKE HELL.
SHE DIDN'T BELIEVE I HAD A SCAB SO SHE WANTED TO MAKE SURE.
GO SHOW HER RIGHT NOW! I *DARE* YOU!
IT'S ON MY *ASS!*
EXACTLY.
I DARE YOU TO GO TO THE GIRL'S LOCKER ROOM *BUTT NAKED!!*

FINE.
I'LL DO IT.

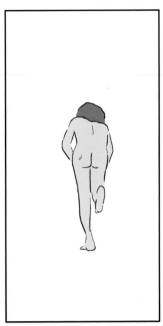

FLOP

FLOP

FLOP

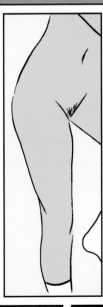

UNGH,
I'M
GONNA
COME!

HELLO,
LADIES!

AAAAAHHH!

AAAAAAAAH!

MOVE,
DAMMIT!

AAH!

OOOH,
YOU ASSHOLE!

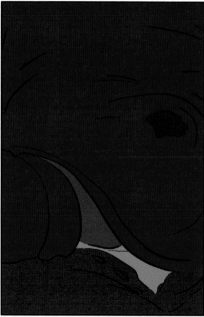

AH, SHIT.

ALL DONE.

PUT THEM AWAY, THE GIRLS ARE ALL DRESSED.

DID YOU HEAR THEM SCREAM?

OH, SWEET JESUS! A NAKED BOY!

YOU ARE A GOD!

HEY, IS KARIM STILL ON THE CRAPPER?

TAKE IT TO THE FACE, BEEYATCH!

WHAT THE HELL IS THIS?

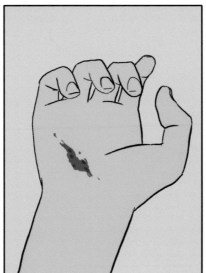

IS THIS YOUR *SHIT?*

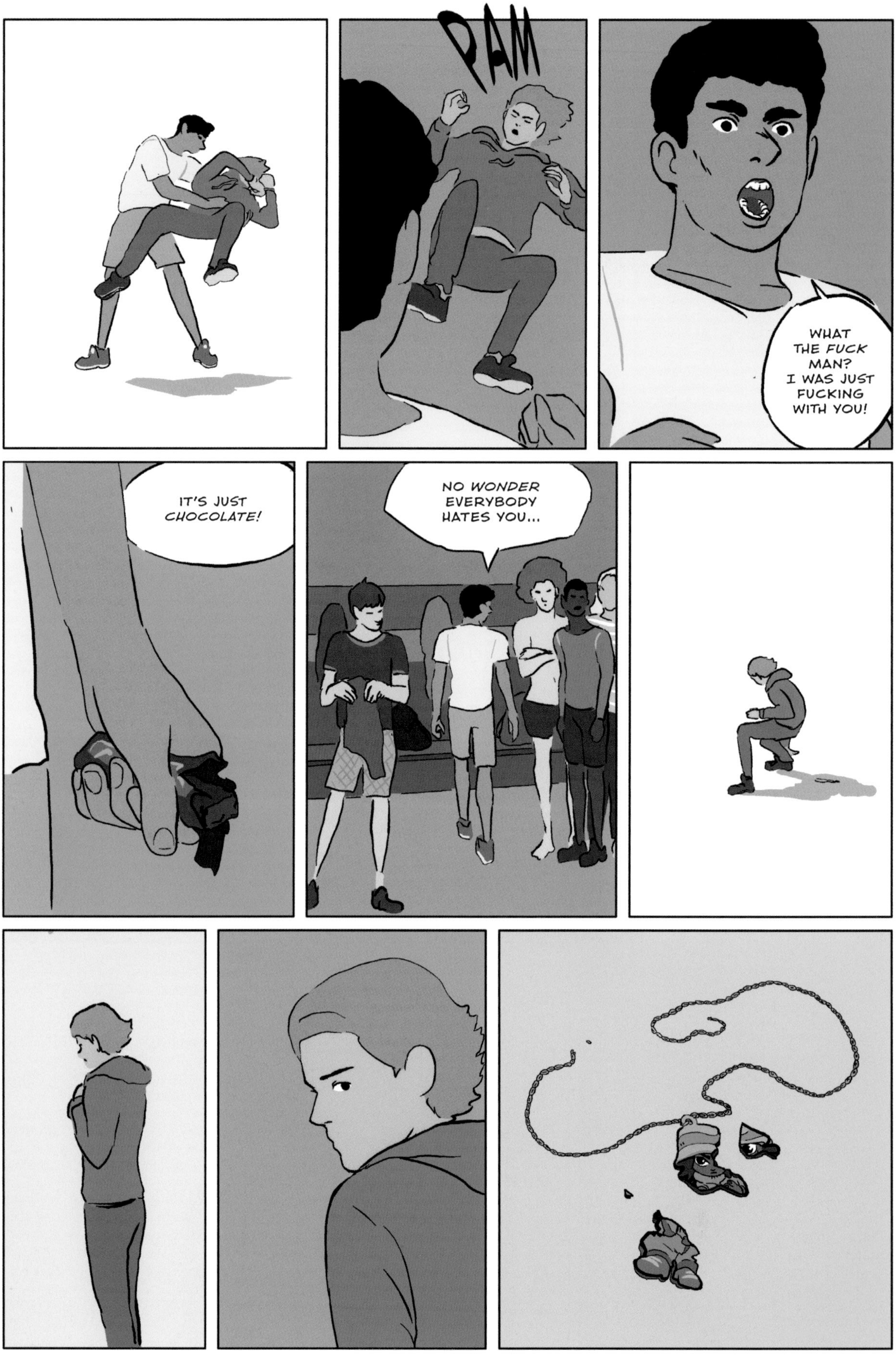
PAM
WHAT THE FUCK MAN? I WAS JUST FUCKING WITH YOU!
IT'S JUST CHOCOLATE!
NO WONDER EVERYBODY HATES YOU...

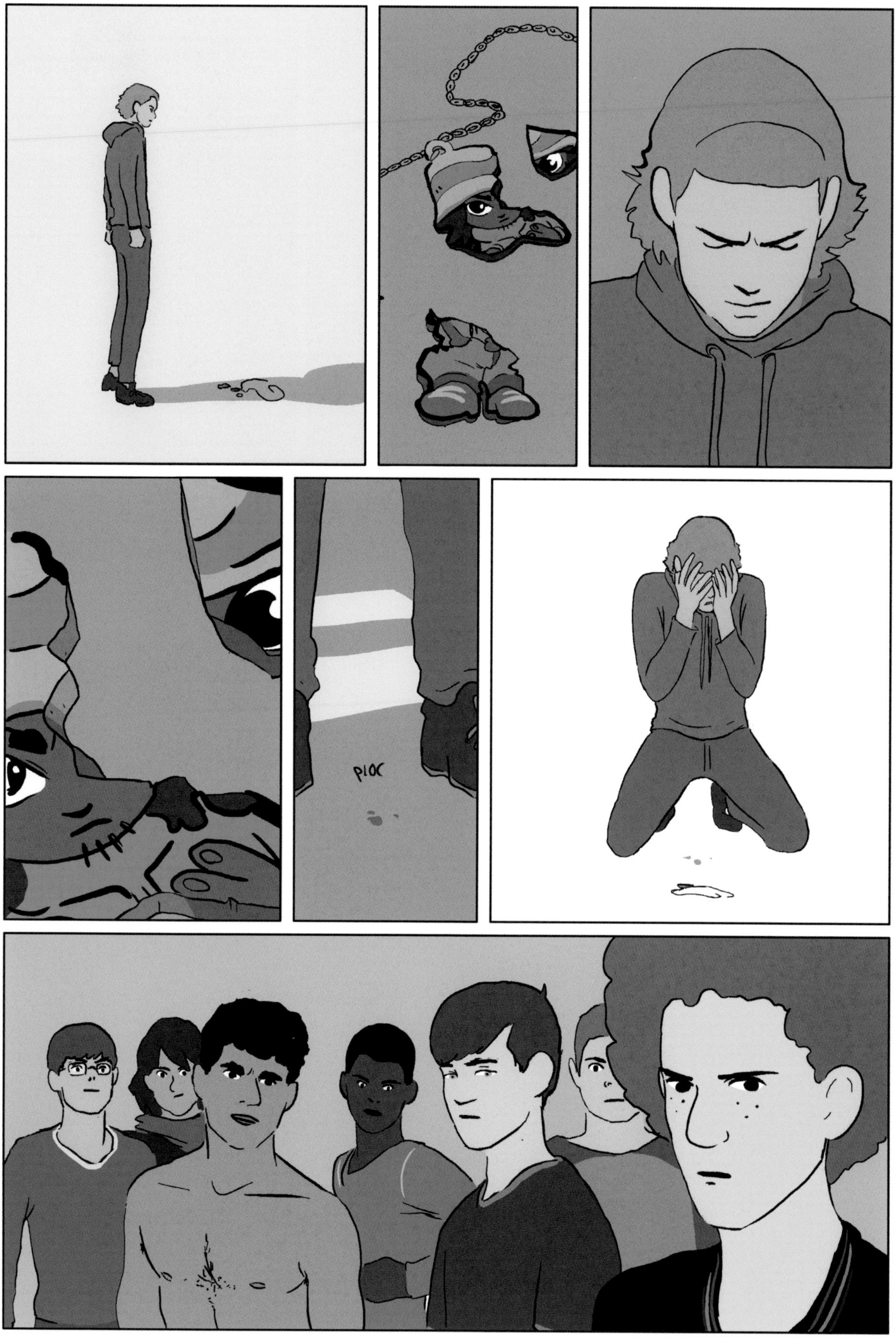
PLOC

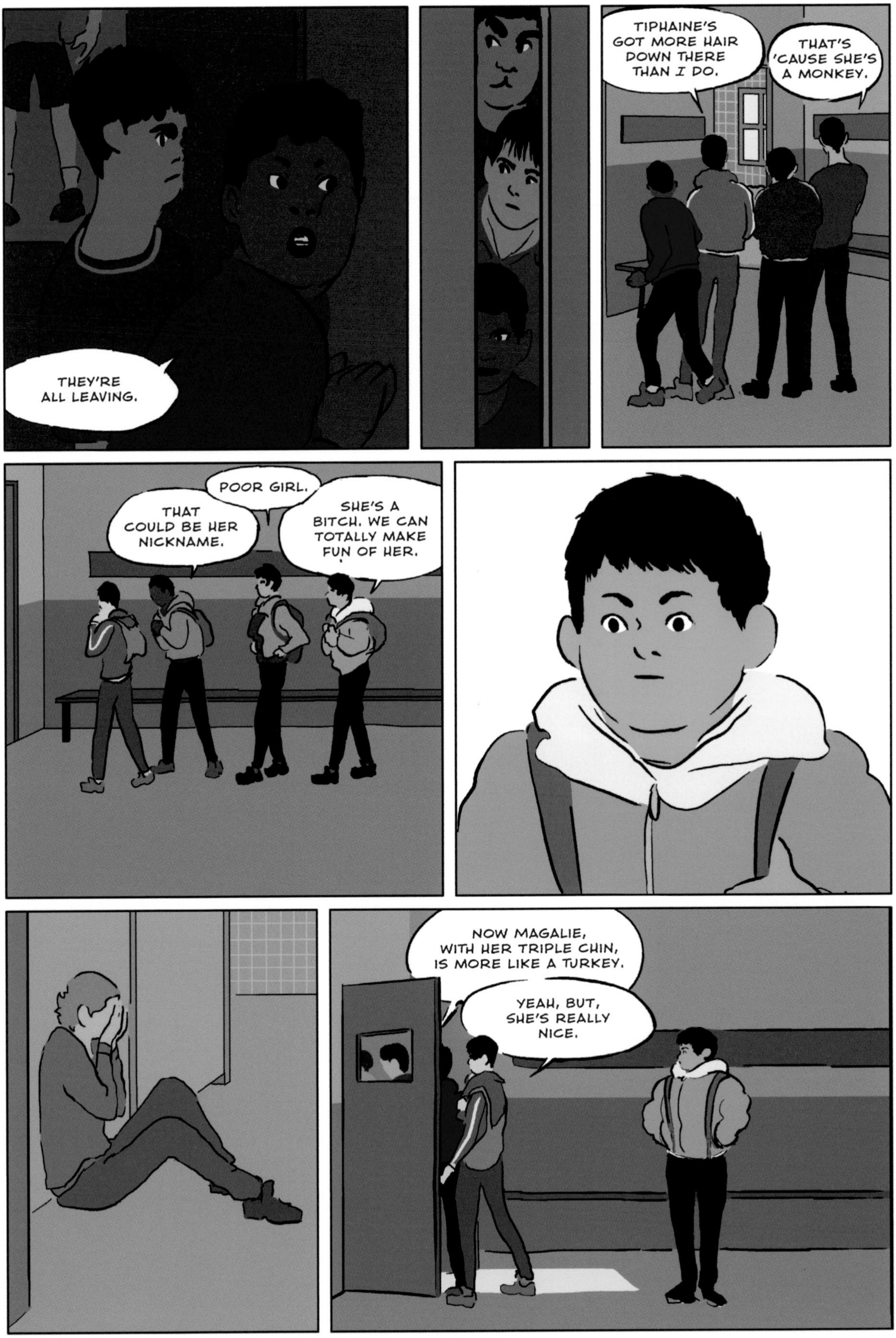
THEY'RE ALL LEAVING.
TIPHAINE'S GOT MORE HAIR DOWN THERE THAN I DO.
THAT'S 'CAUSE SHE'S A MONKEY.
THAT COULD BE HER NICKNAME.
POOR GIRL.
SHE'S A BITCH. WE CAN TOTALLY MAKE FUN OF HER.
NOW MAGALIE, WITH HER TRIPLE CHIN, IS MORE LIKE A TURKEY.
YEAH, BUT, SHE'S REALLY NICE.

HEY, WAIT FOR ME!

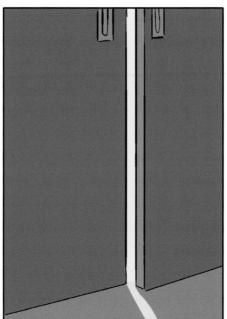

WHAT DO YOU WANT?

I BET YOU GET A KICK OUTTA SEEING ME LIKE THIS, DON'T YOU?

YEAH.

BUT I CAN'T HELP FEELING SORRY FOR YOU...

...I'VE BEEN THERE.

WELL, IT'S NOT *RIGHT* FOR IT TO HAPPEN TO *ME*. I'M NOT THE TYPE TO GET PICKED ON.

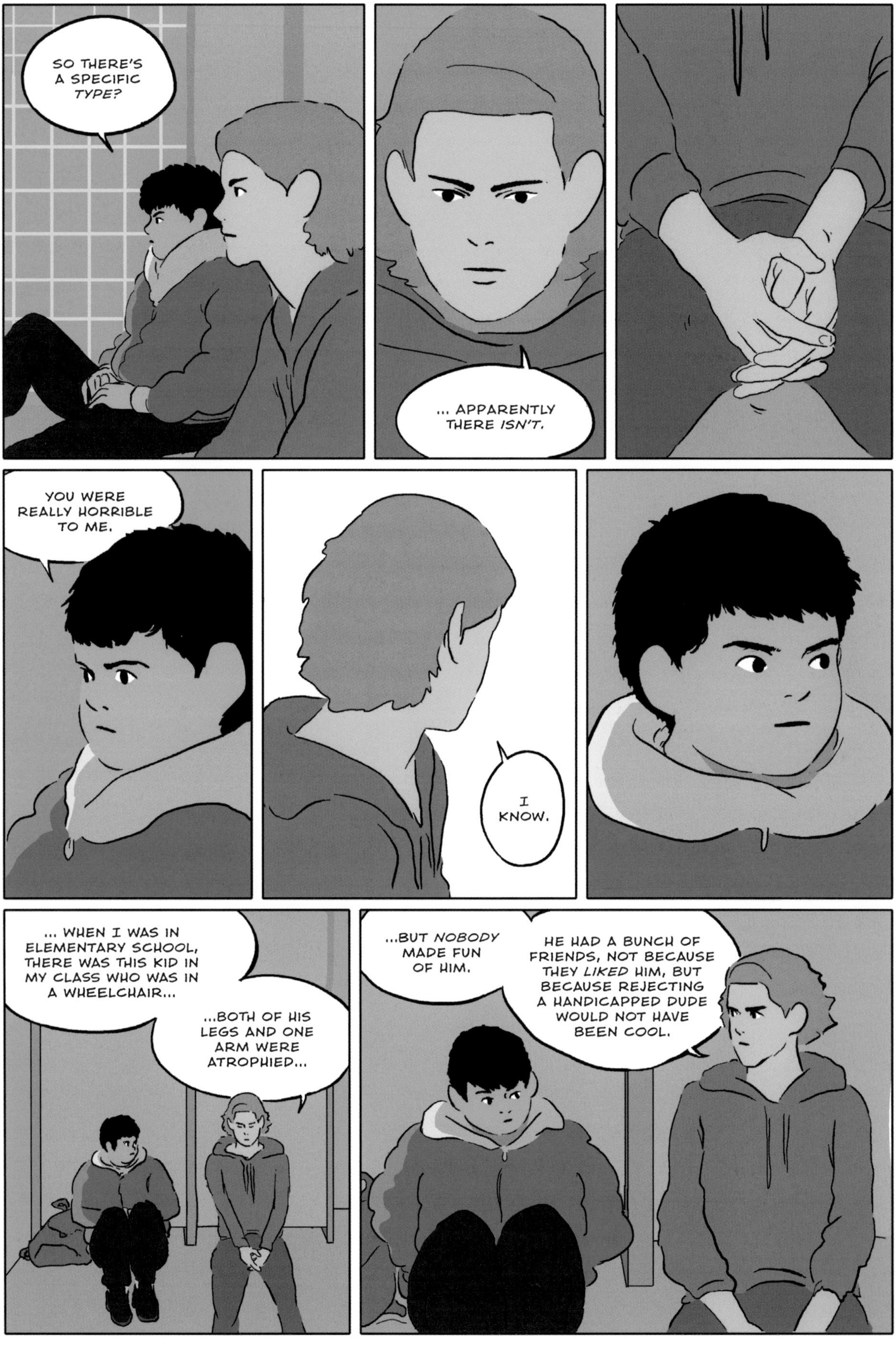
SO THERE'S A SPECIFIC *TYPE*?
... APPARENTLY THERE *ISN'T*.
YOU WERE REALLY HORRIBLE TO ME.
I KNOW.
... WHEN I WAS IN ELEMENTARY SCHOOL, THERE WAS THIS KID IN MY CLASS WHO WAS IN A WHEELCHAIR...
...BOTH OF HIS LEGS AND ONE ARM WERE ATROPHIED...
...BUT *NOBODY* MADE FUN OF HIM.
HE HAD A BUNCH OF FRIENDS, NOT BECAUSE THEY *LIKED* HIM, BUT BECAUSE REJECTING A HANDICAPPED DUDE WOULD NOT HAVE BEEN COOL.

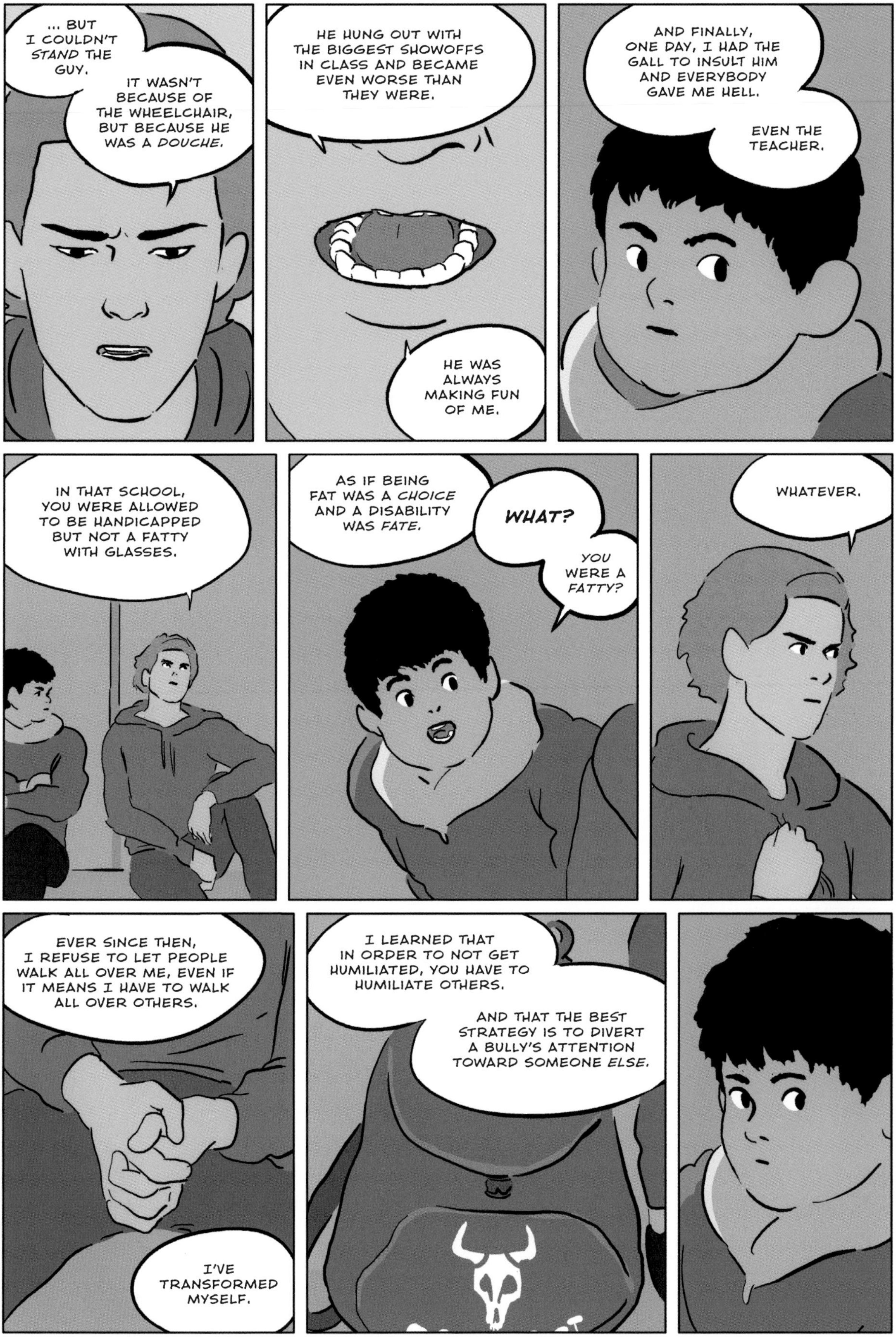
... BUT I COULDN'T *STAND* THE GUY.
IT WASN'T BECAUSE OF THE WHEELCHAIR, BUT BECAUSE HE WAS A *DOUCHE*.
HE HUNG OUT WITH THE BIGGEST SHOWOFFS IN CLASS AND BECAME EVEN WORSE THAN THEY WERE.
HE WAS ALWAYS MAKING FUN OF ME.
AND FINALLY, ONE DAY, I HAD THE GALL TO INSULT HIM AND EVERYBODY GAVE ME HELL.
EVEN THE TEACHER.
IN THAT SCHOOL, YOU WERE ALLOWED TO BE HANDICAPPED BUT NOT A FATTY WITH GLASSES.
AS IF BEING FAT WAS A *CHOICE* AND A DISABILITY WAS *FATE*.
WHAT?
YOU WERE A *FATTY?*
WHATEVER.
EVER SINCE THEN, I REFUSE TO LET PEOPLE WALK ALL OVER ME, EVEN IF IT MEANS I HAVE TO WALK ALL OVER OTHERS.
I'VE TRANSFORMED MYSELF.
I LEARNED THAT IN ORDER TO NOT GET HUMILIATED, YOU HAVE TO HUMILIATE OTHERS.
AND THAT THE BEST STRATEGY IS TO DIVERT A BULLY'S ATTENTION TOWARD SOMEONE *ELSE*.

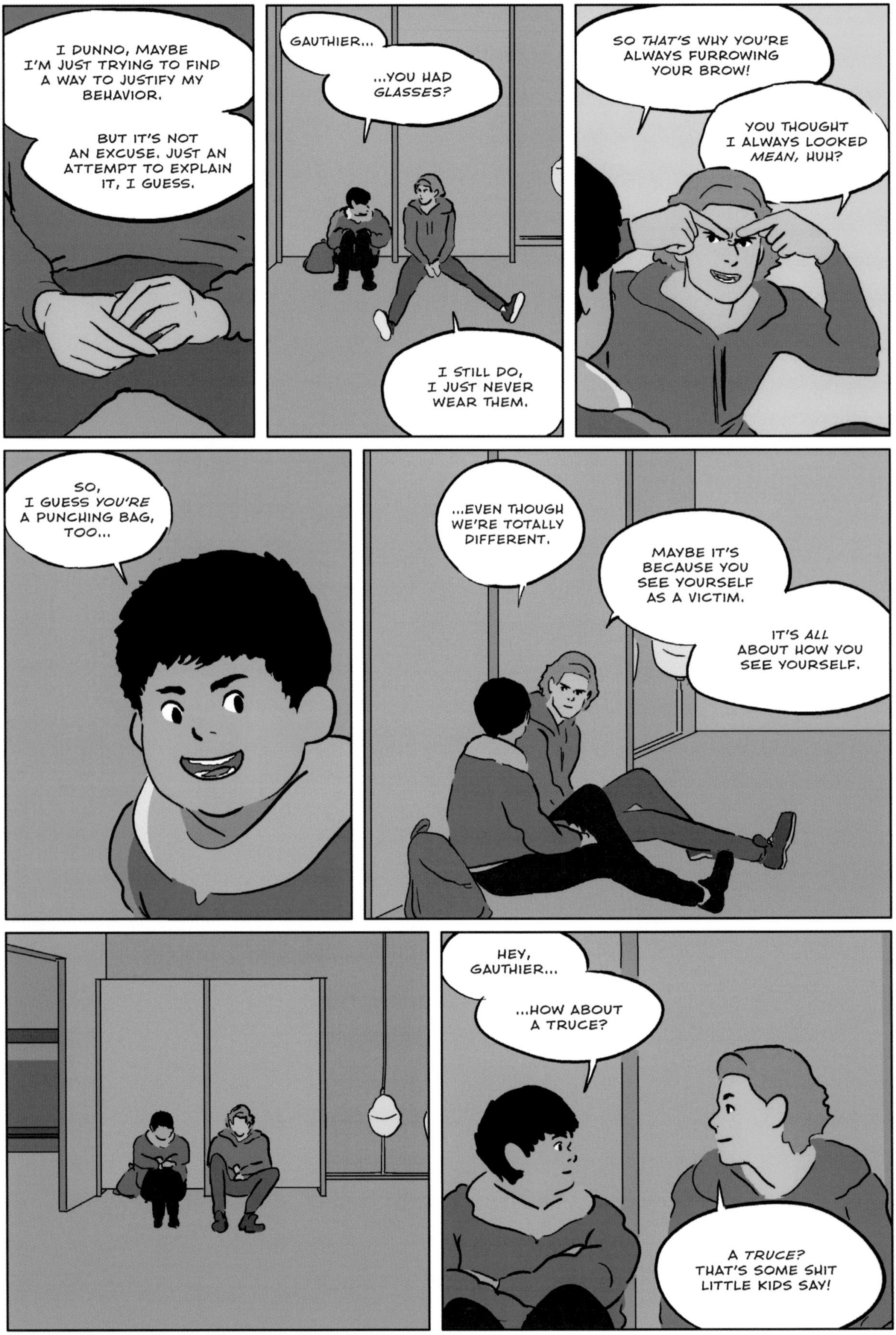
I DUNNO, MAYBE I'M JUST TRYING TO FIND A WAY TO JUSTIFY MY BEHAVIOR.
BUT IT'S NOT AN EXCUSE. JUST AN ATTEMPT TO EXPLAIN IT, I GUESS.
GAUTHIER...
...YOU HAD *GLASSES?*
I STILL DO, I JUST NEVER WEAR THEM.
SO *THAT'S* WHY YOU'RE ALWAYS FURROWING YOUR BROW!
YOU THOUGHT I ALWAYS LOOKED *MEAN*, HUH?
SO, I GUESS *YOU'RE* A PUNCHING BAG, TOO...
...EVEN THOUGH WE'RE TOTALLY DIFFERENT.
MAYBE IT'S BECAUSE YOU SEE YOURSELF AS A VICTIM.
IT'S *ALL* ABOUT HOW YOU SEE YOURSELF.
HEY, GAUTHIER...
...HOW ABOUT A TRUCE?
A *TRUCE?* THAT'S SOME SHIT LITTLE KIDS SAY!

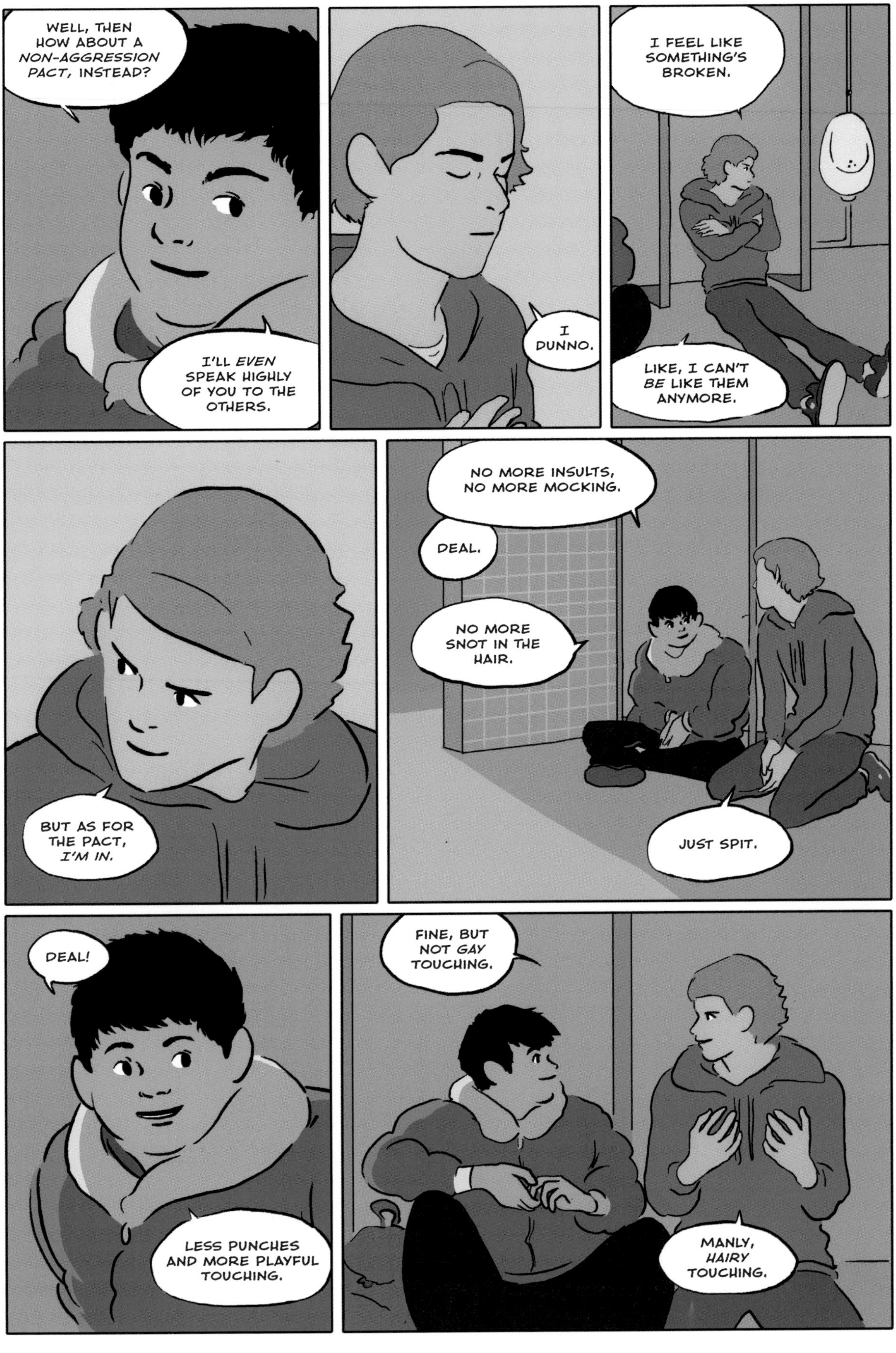
WELL, THEN HOW ABOUT A *NON-AGGRESSION PACT*, INSTEAD?
I'LL *EVEN* SPEAK HIGHLY OF YOU TO THE OTHERS.
I DUNNO.
I FEEL LIKE SOMETHING'S BROKEN.
LIKE, I CAN'T *BE* LIKE THEM ANYMORE.
BUT AS FOR THE PACT, *I'M IN.*
NO MORE INSULTS, NO MORE MOCKING.
DEAL.
NO MORE SNOT IN THE HAIR.
JUST SPIT.
DEAL!
LESS PUNCHES AND MORE PLAYFUL TOUCHING.
FINE, BUT *NOT GAY* TOUCHING.
MANLY, *HAIRY* TOUCHING.

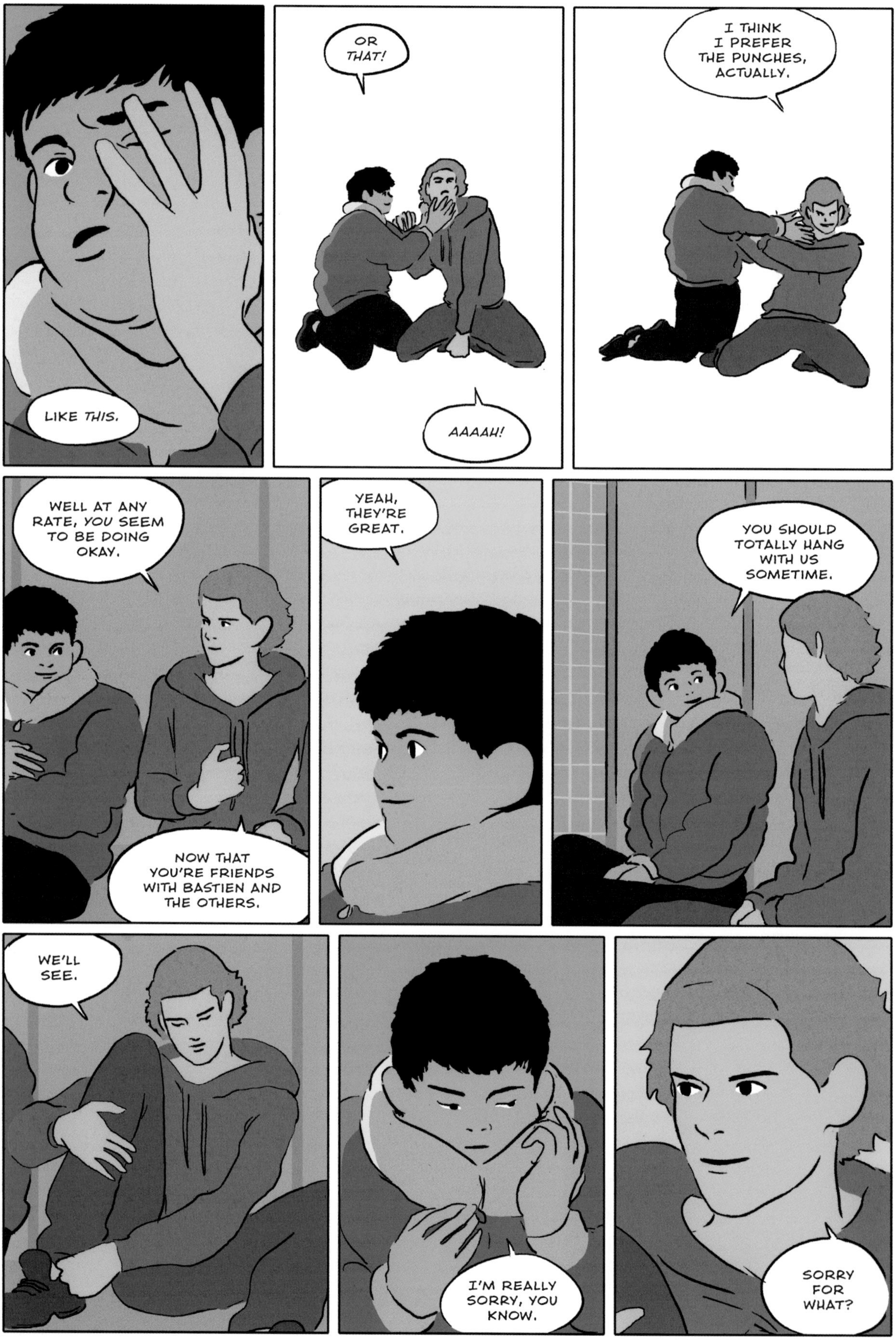
LIKE *THIS*.
OR *THAT!*
AAAAH!
I THINK I PREFER THE PUNCHES, ACTUALLY.
WELL AT ANY RATE, *YOU* SEEM TO BE DOING OKAY.
NOW THAT YOU'RE FRIENDS WITH BASTIEN AND THE OTHERS.
YEAH, THEY'RE GREAT.
YOU SHOULD TOTALLY HANG WITH US SOMETIME.
WE'LL SEE.
I'M REALLY SORRY, YOU KNOW.
SORRY FOR WHAT?

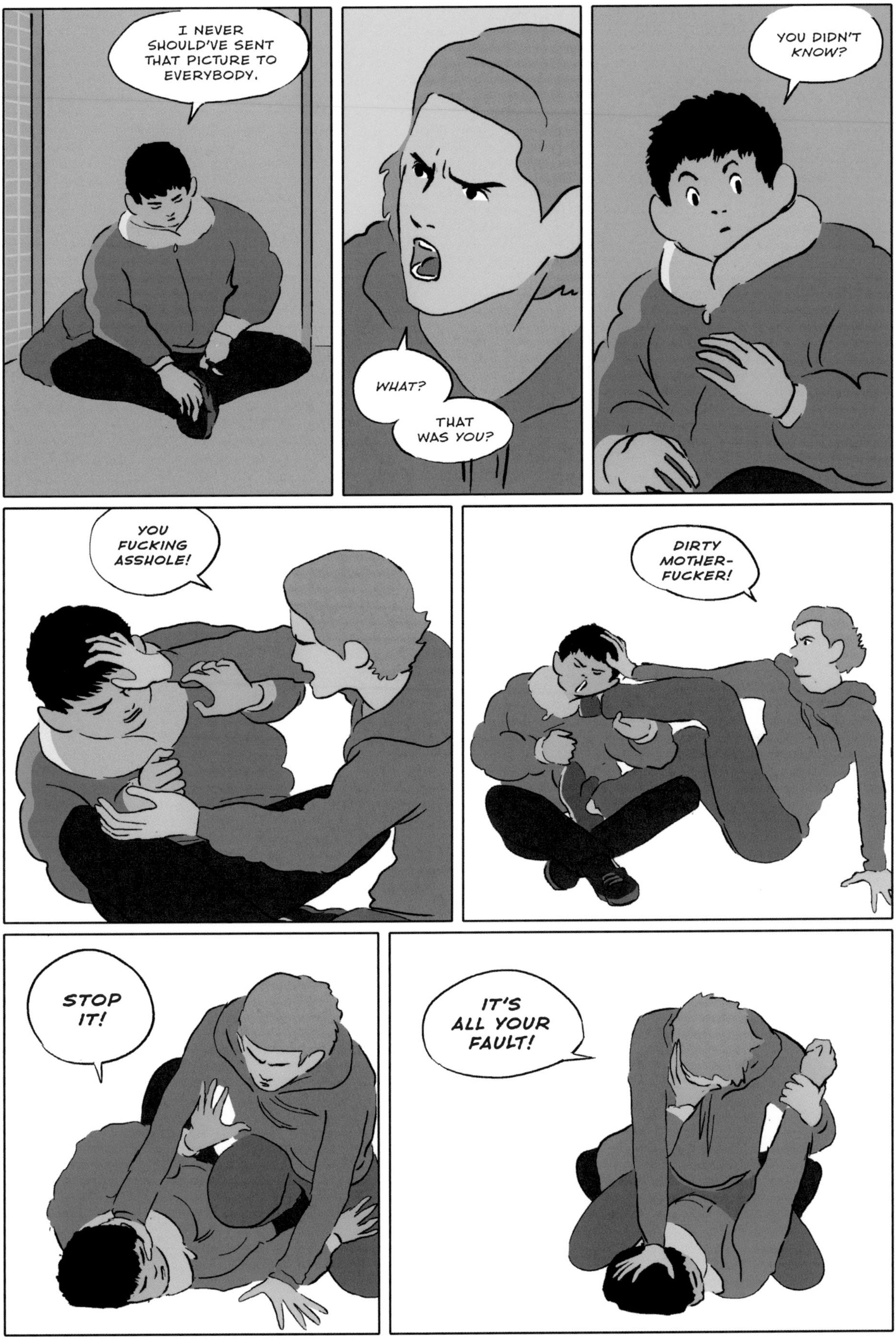
I NEVER SHOULD'VE SENT THAT PICTURE TO EVERYBODY.
WHAT?
THAT WAS YOU?
YOU DIDN'T KNOW?
YOU FUCKING ASSHOLE!
DIRTY MOTHER-FUCKER!
STOP IT!
IT'S ALL YOUR FAULT!

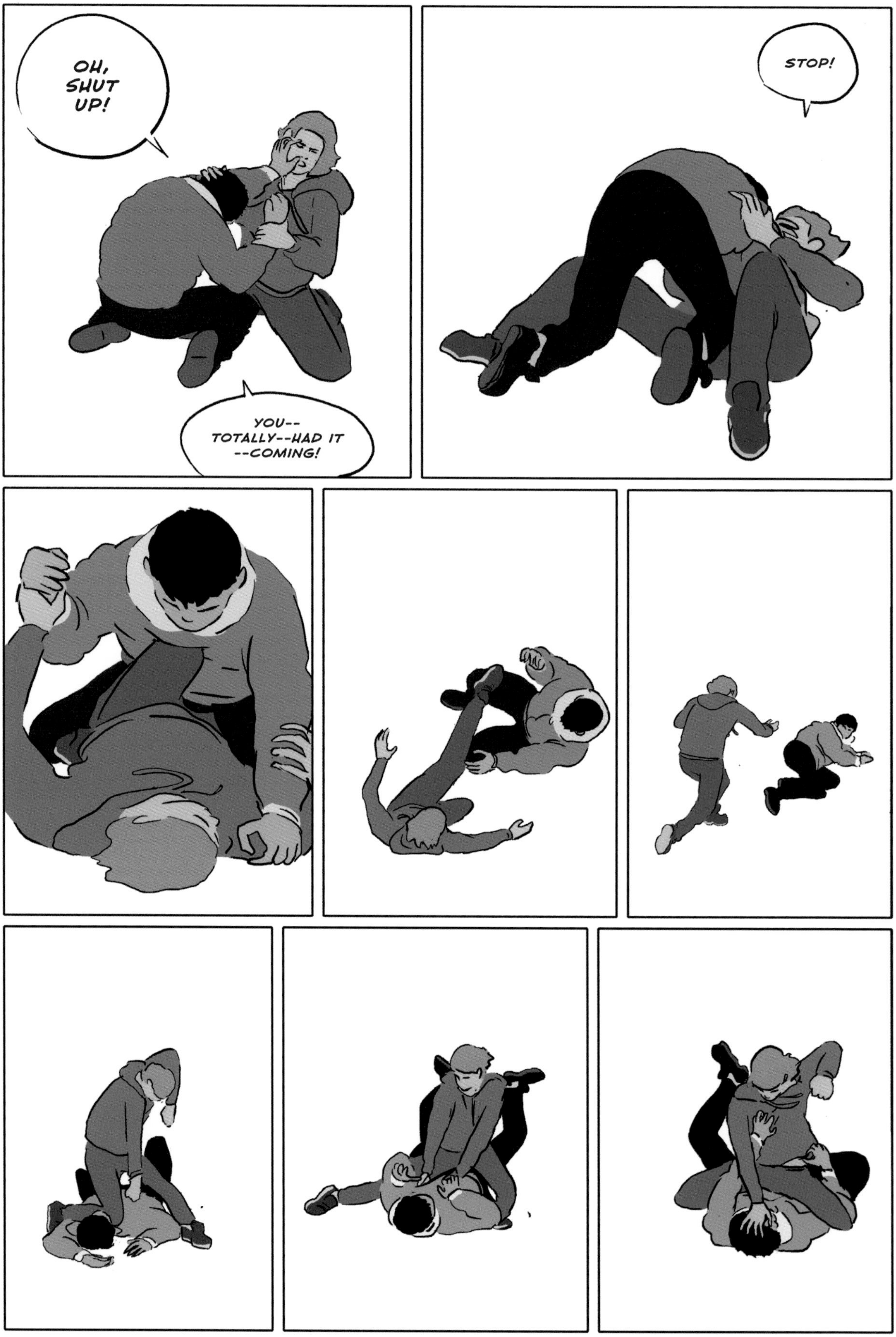
OH, SHUT UP!
YOU-- TOTALLY--HAD IT --COMING!
STOP!

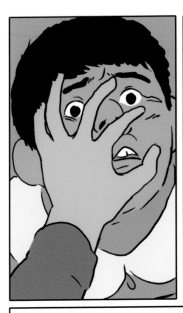

I'M SORRY.

I'M SORRY!

I'M SORRY!

PAM

WHAT ARE YOU BOYS DOING?!

GAUTHIER!

YOU'RE COMING WITH ME TO THE PRINCIPAL'S OFFICE.

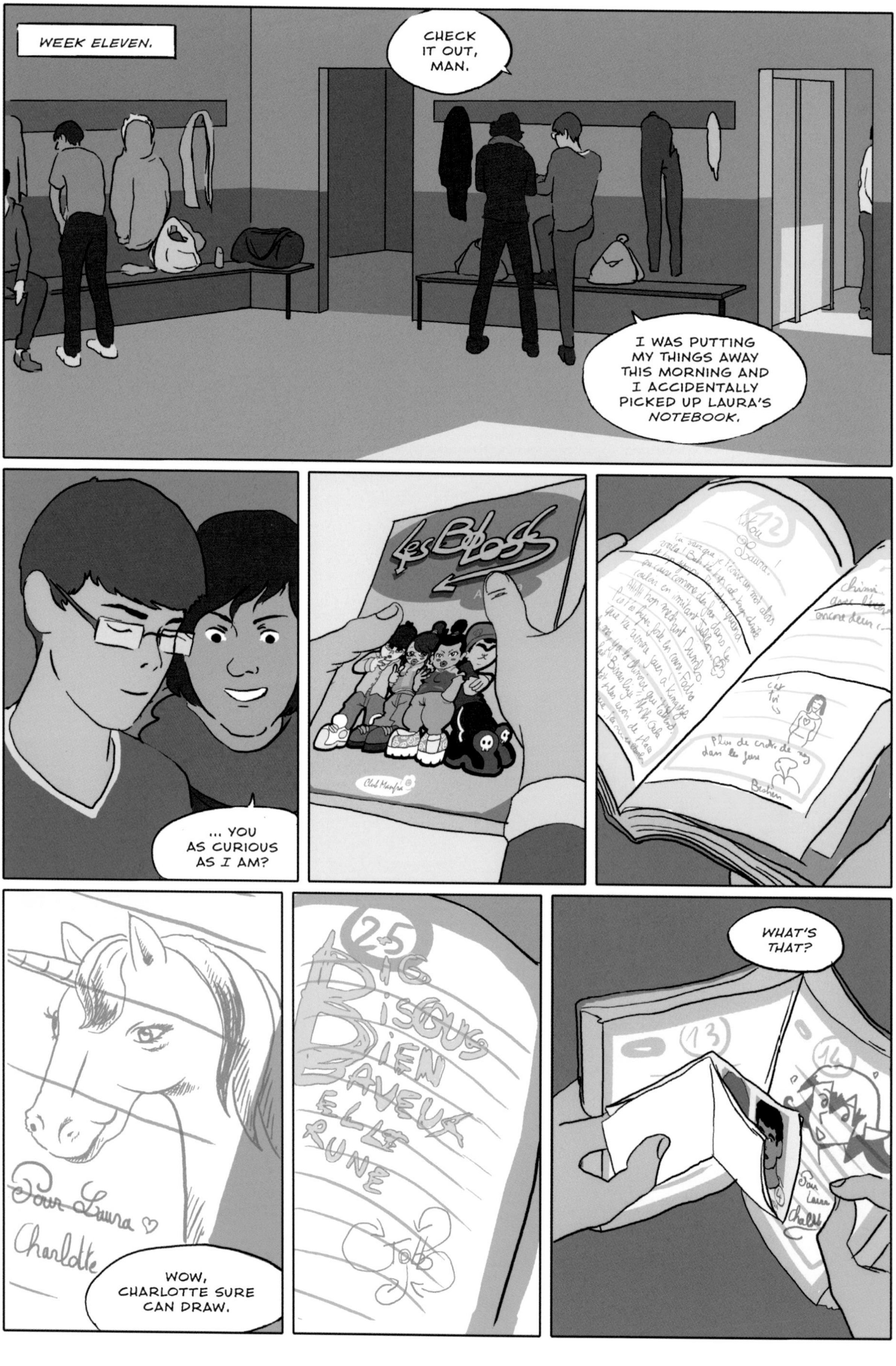
WEEK ELEVEN.
CHECK IT OUT, MAN.
I WAS PUTTING MY THINGS AWAY THIS MORNING AND I ACCIDENTALLY PICKED UP LAURA'S *NOTEBOOK*.
... YOU AS CURIOUS AS *I* AM?
Pour Laura ♡
Charlotte
WOW, CHARLOTTE SURE CAN DRAW.
WHAT'S THAT?

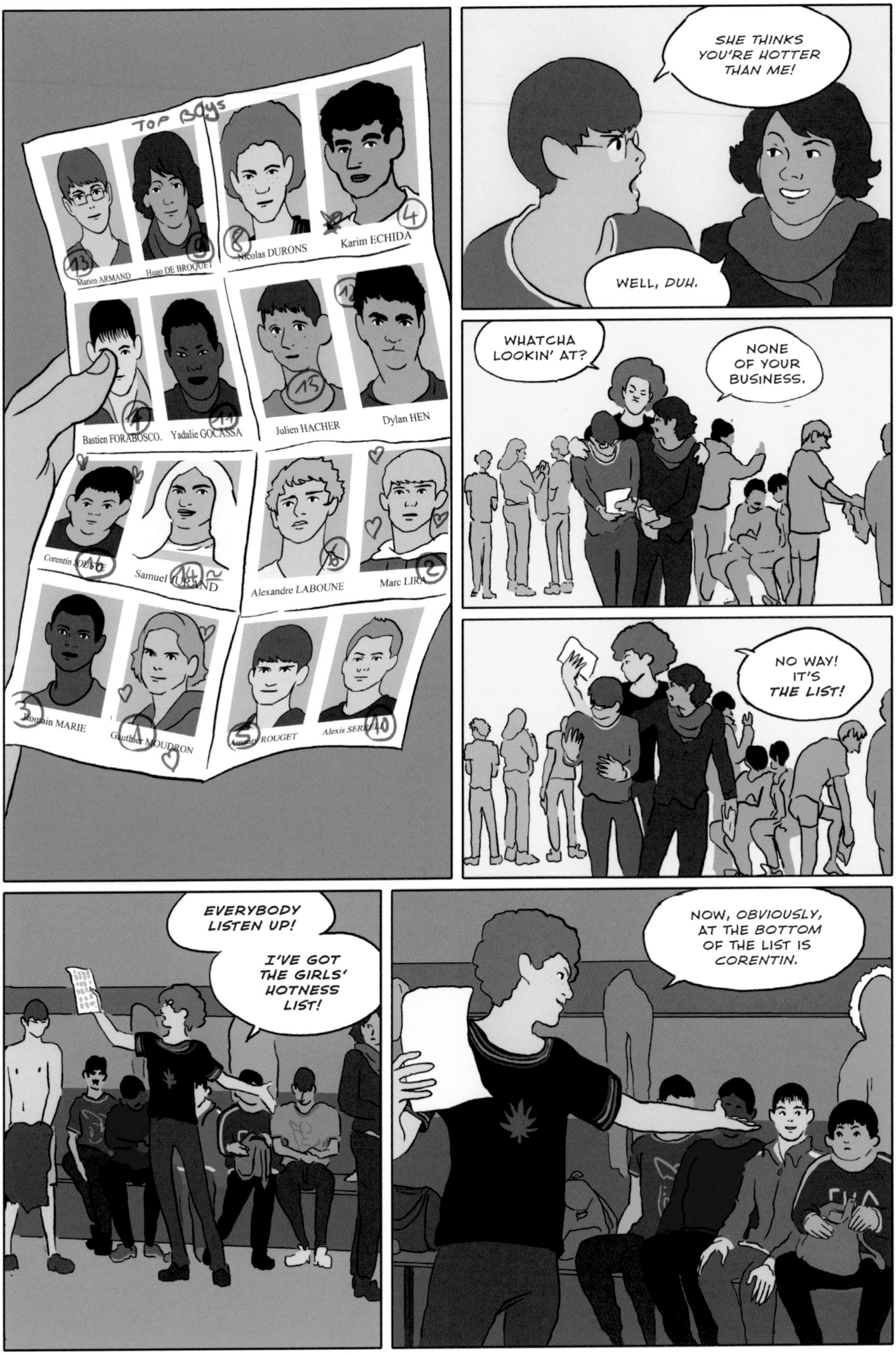
TOP BOYS
Marien ARMAND
Hugo DE BROQUET
Nicolas DURONS
Karim ECHIDA
Bastien FORABOSCO.
Yadalie GOCASSA
Julien HACHER
Dylan HEN
Corentin
Samuel
Alexandre LABOUNE
Romain MARIE
Gauthier MOUDRON
ROUGET
Alexis
SHE THINKS YOU'RE HOTTER THAN ME!
WELL, DUH.
WHATCHA LOOKIN' AT?
NONE OF YOUR BUSINESS.
NO WAY! IT'S THE LIST!
EVERYBODY LISTEN UP!
I'VE GOT THE GIRLS' HOTNESS LIST!
NOW, OBVIOUSLY, AT THE BOTTOM OF THE LIST IS CORENTIN.

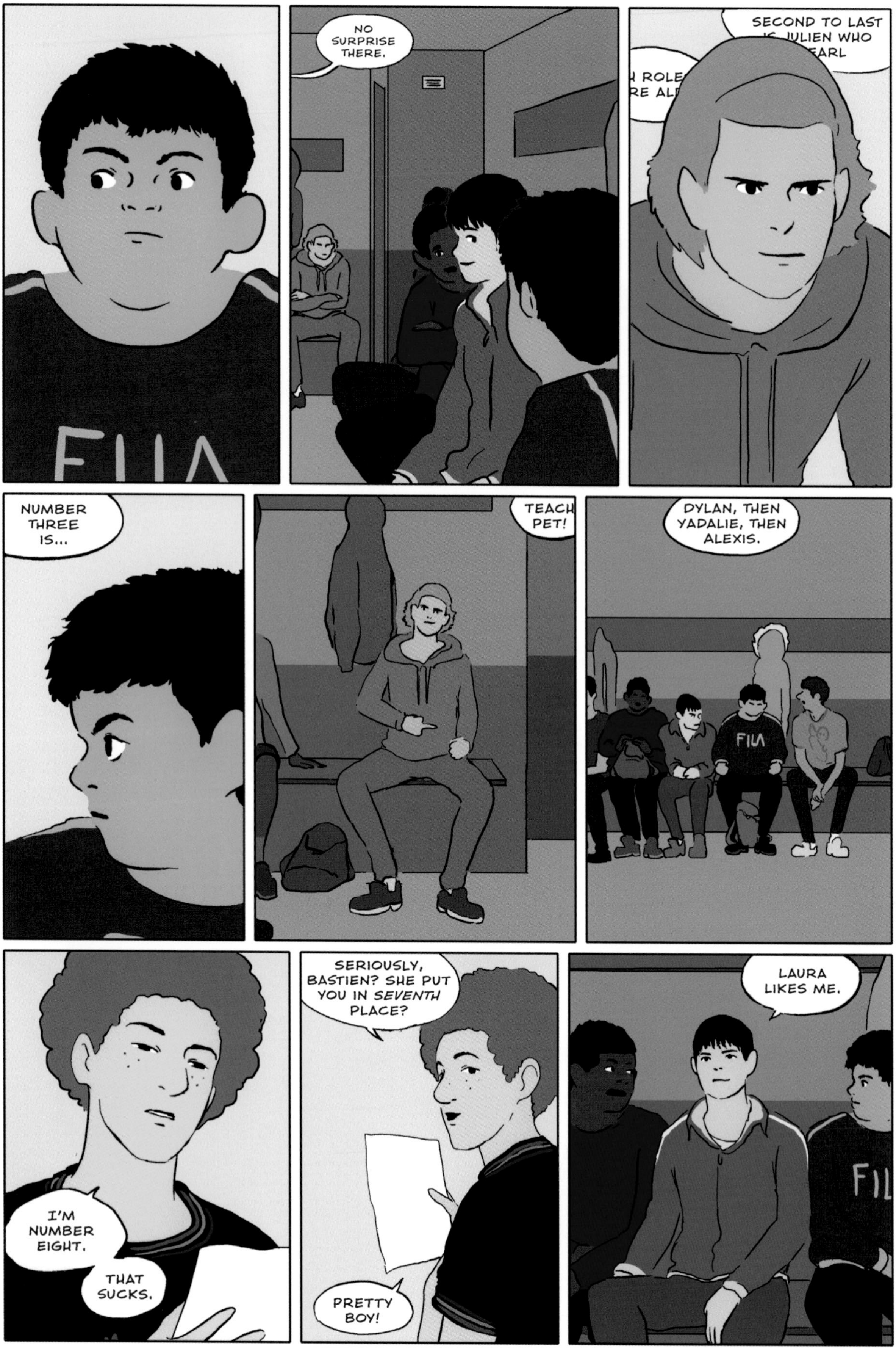
NO SURPRISE THERE.
SECOND TO LAST
JULIEN WHO
NUMBER THREE IS...
TEACH PET!
DYLAN, THEN YADALIE, THEN ALEXIS.
I'M NUMBER EIGHT.
THAT SUCKS.
SERIOUSLY, BASTIEN? SHE PUT YOU IN *SEVENTH* PLACE?
PRETTY BOY!
LAURA LIKES ME.

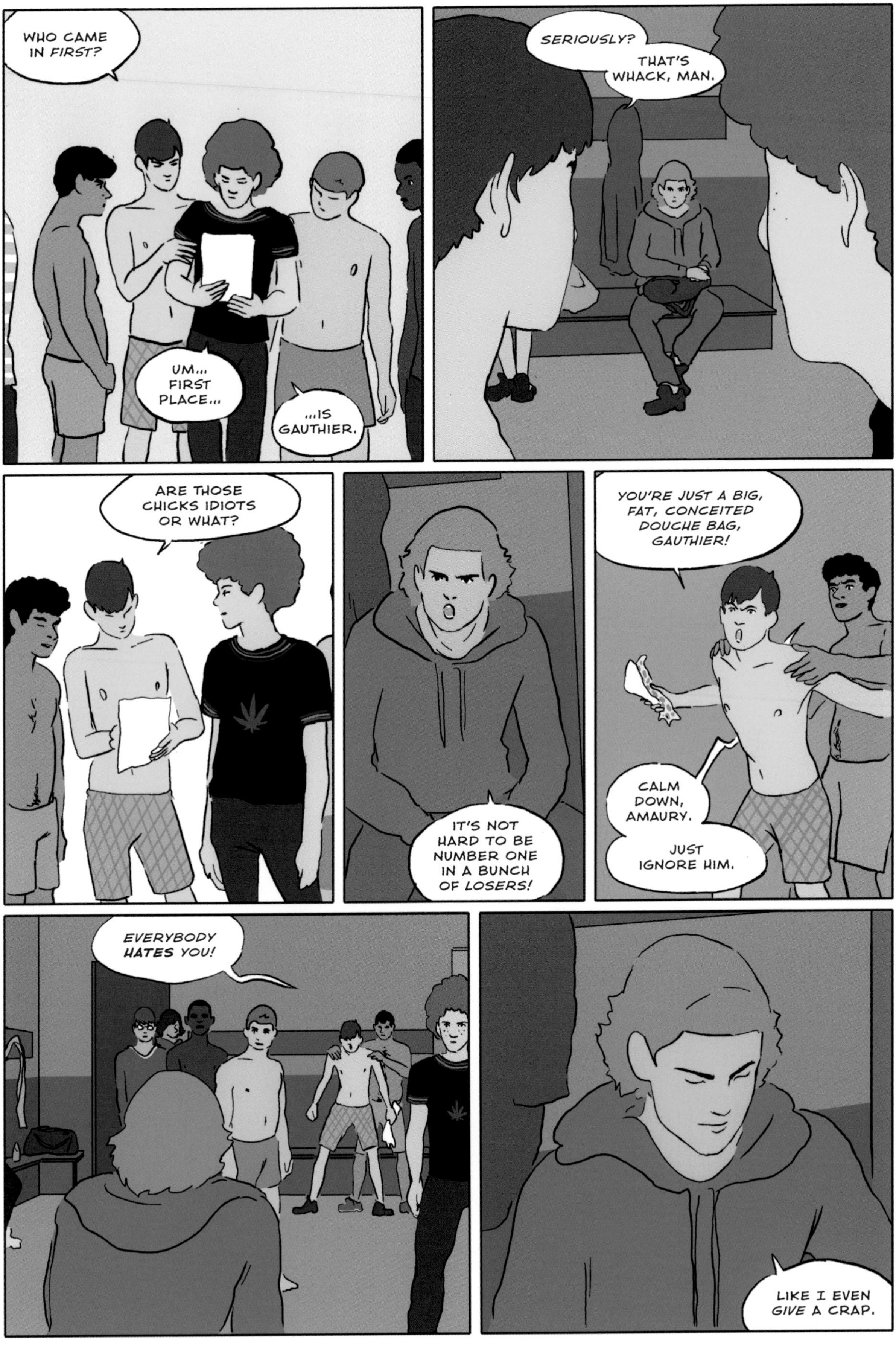

WHO CAME IN *FIRST?*
UM... FIRST PLACE...
...IS GAUTHIER.
SERIOUSLY?
THAT'S WHACK, MAN.
ARE THOSE CHICKS IDIOTS OR WHAT?
IT'S NOT HARD TO BE NUMBER ONE IN A BUNCH OF *LOSERS!*
YOU'RE JUST A BIG, FAT, CONCEITED DOUCHE BAG, GAUTHIER!
CALM DOWN, AMAURY.
JUST IGNORE HIM.
EVERYBODY ***HATES*** *YOU!*
LIKE I EVEN *GIVE* A CRAP.

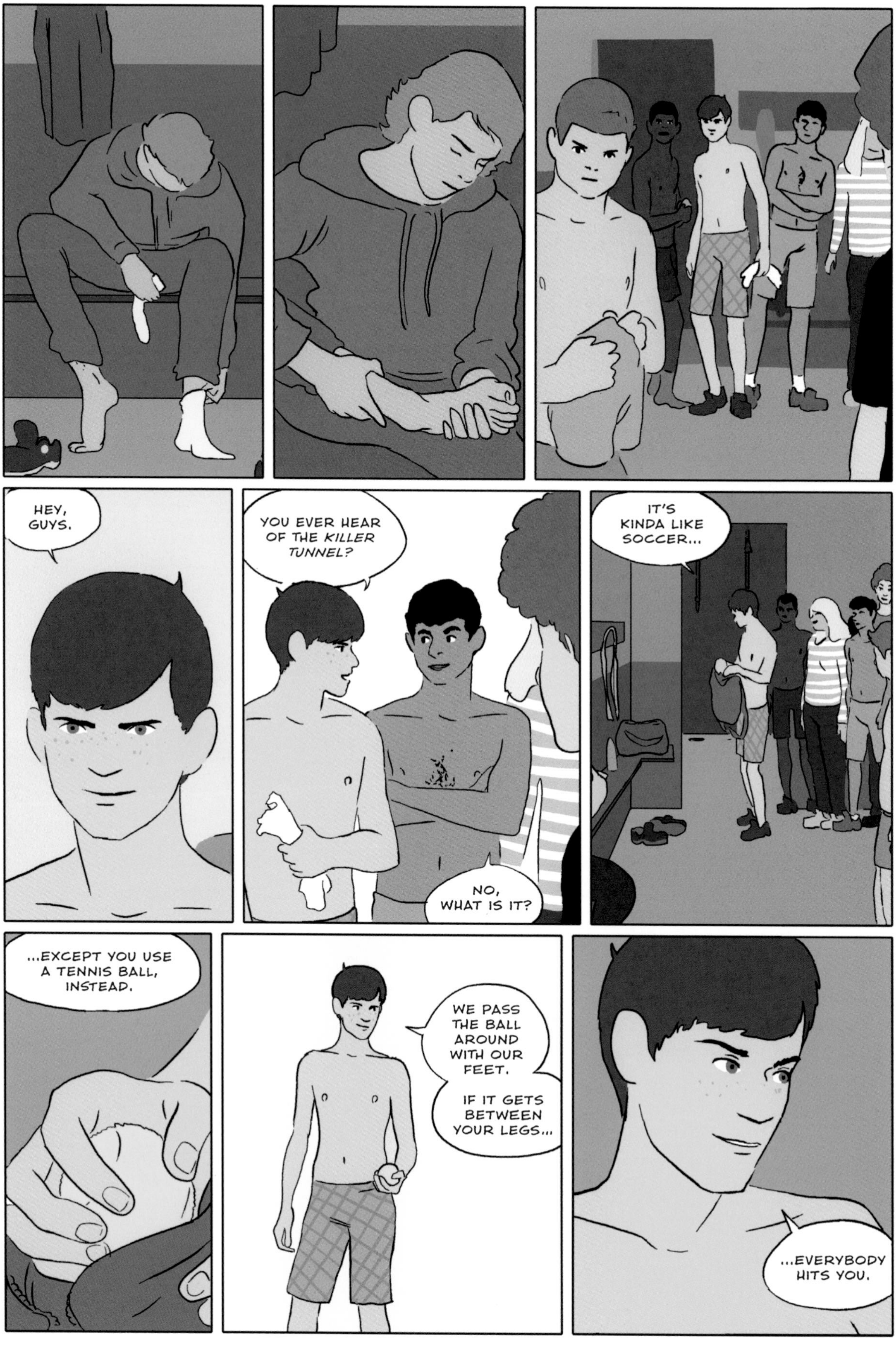
HEY, GUYS.
YOU EVER HEAR OF THE *KILLER TUNNEL?*
NO, WHAT IS IT?
IT'S KINDA LIKE SOCCER...
...EXCEPT YOU USE A TENNIS BALL, INSTEAD.
WE PASS THE BALL AROUND WITH OUR FEET.
IF IT GETS BETWEEN YOUR LEGS...
...EVERYBODY HITS YOU.

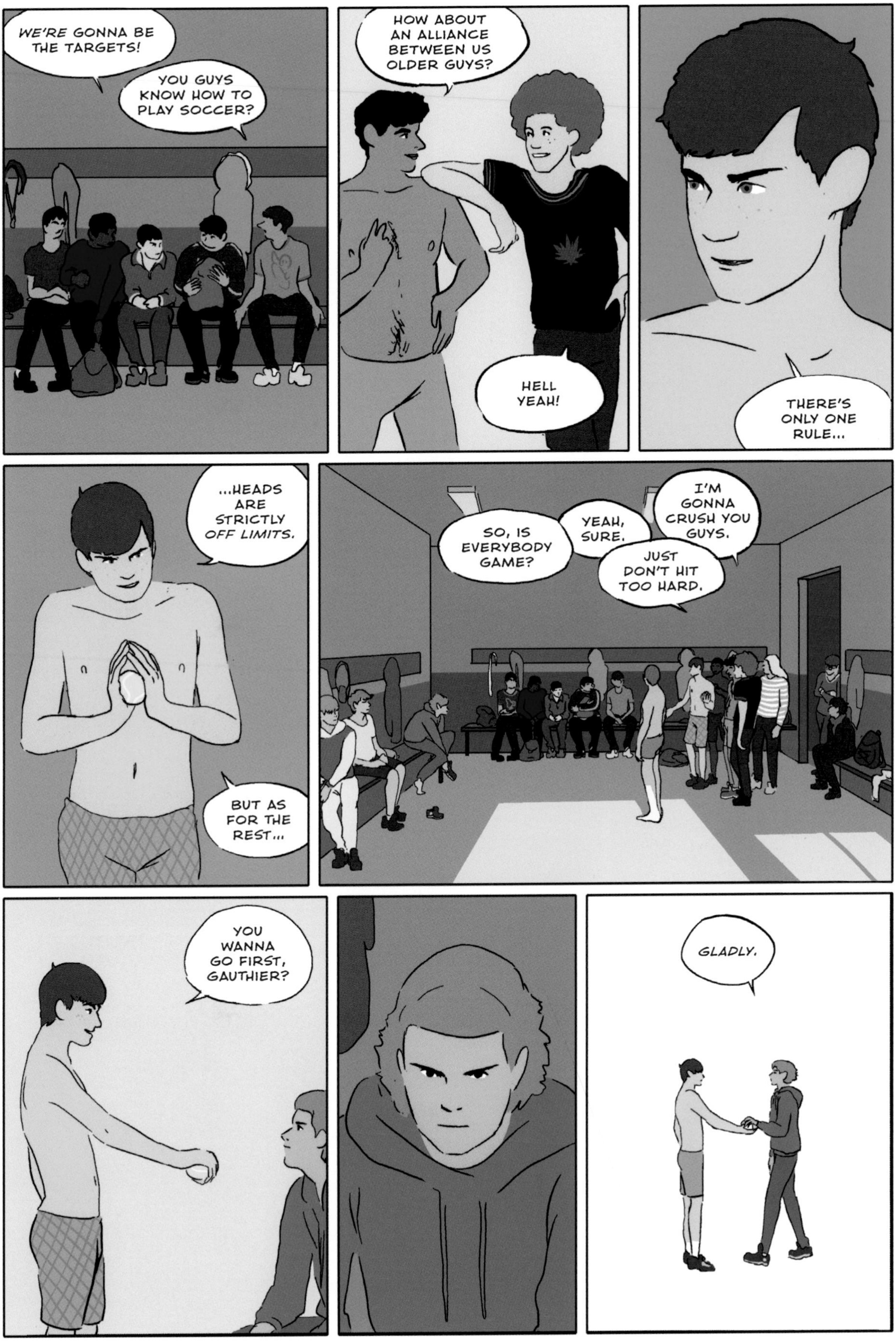

WE'RE GONNA BE THE TARGETS!
YOU GUYS KNOW HOW TO PLAY SOCCER?
HOW ABOUT AN ALLIANCE BETWEEN US OLDER GUYS?
HELL YEAH!
THERE'S ONLY ONE RULE...
...HEADS ARE STRICTLY OFF LIMITS.
BUT AS FOR THE REST...
SO, IS EVERYBODY GAME?
YEAH, SURE.
I'M GONNA CRUSH YOU GUYS.
JUST DON'T HIT TOO HARD.
YOU WANNA GO FIRST, GAUTHIER?
GLADLY.

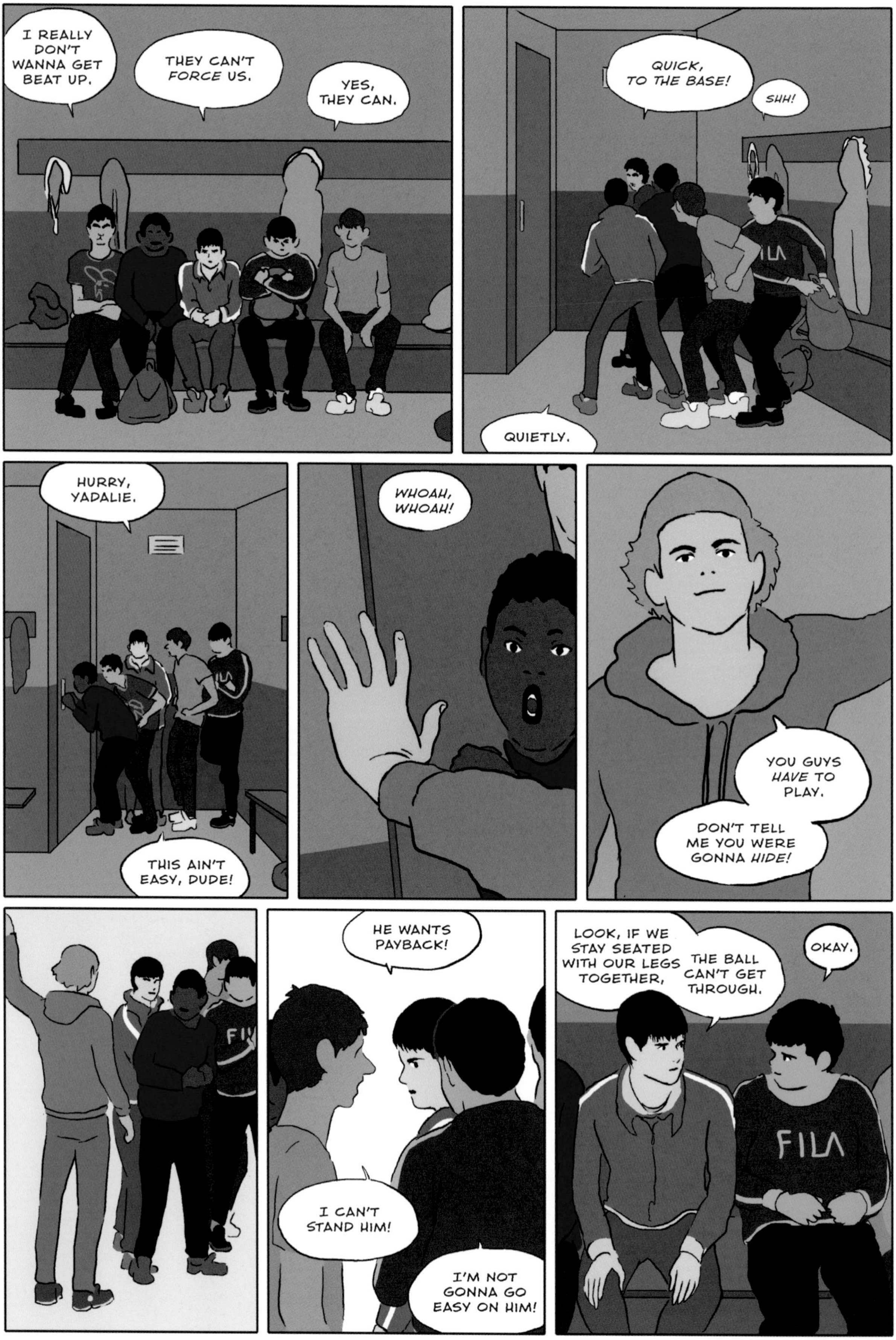
I REALLY DON'T WANNA GET BEAT UP.
THEY CAN'T *FORCE* US.
YES, THEY CAN.
QUICK, TO THE BASE!
SHH!
QUIETLY.
HURRY, YADALIE.
THIS AIN'T EASY, DUDE!
WHOAH, WHOAH!
YOU GUYS *HAVE* TO PLAY.
DON'T TELL ME YOU WERE GONNA *HIDE*!
HE WANTS PAYBACK!
I CAN'T STAND HIM!
I'M NOT GONNA GO EASY ON HIM!
LOOK, IF WE STAY SEATED WITH OUR LEGS TOGETHER,
THE BALL CAN'T GET THROUGH.
OKAY.
FILA

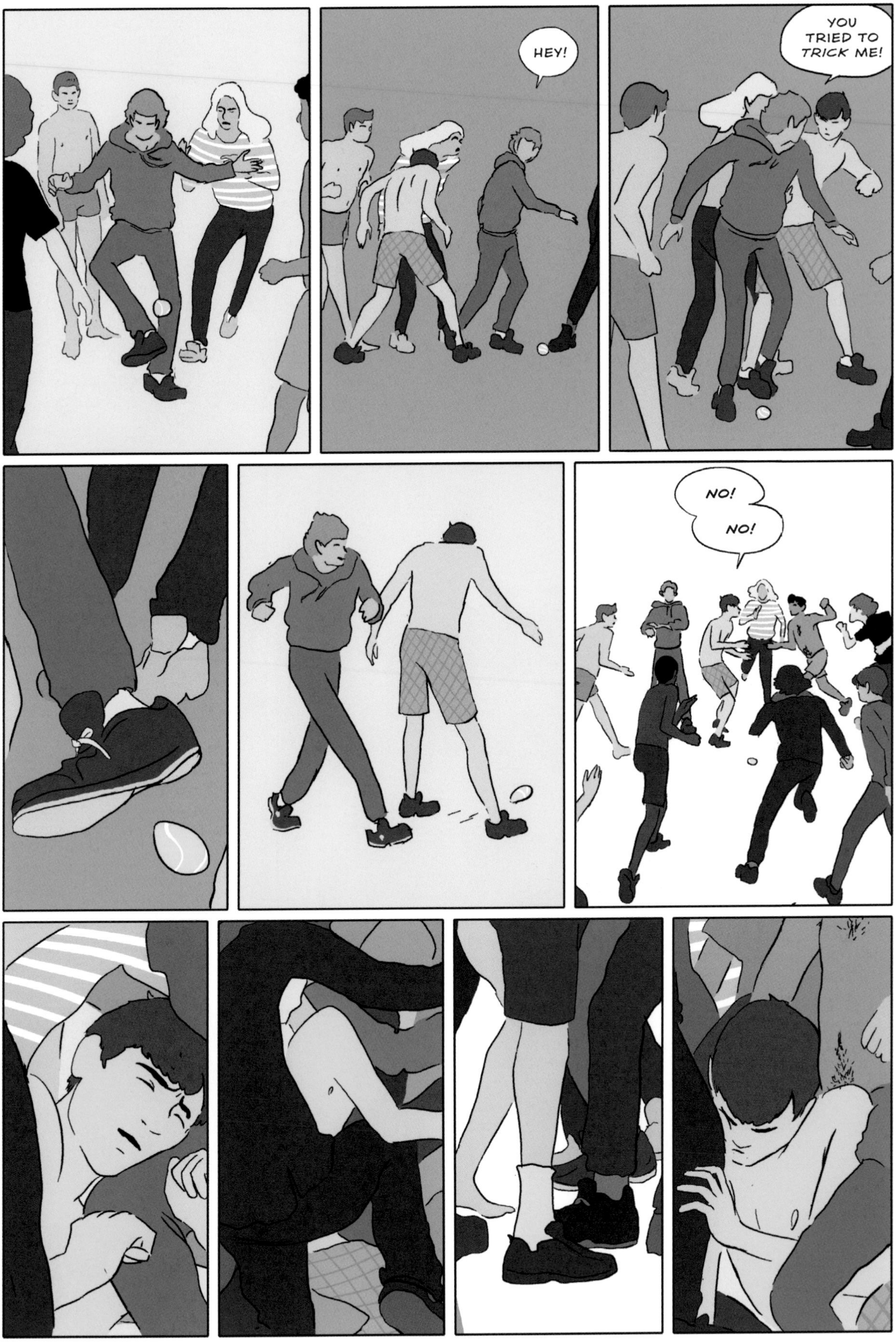
HEY!
YOU TRIED TO TRICK ME!
NO!
NO!

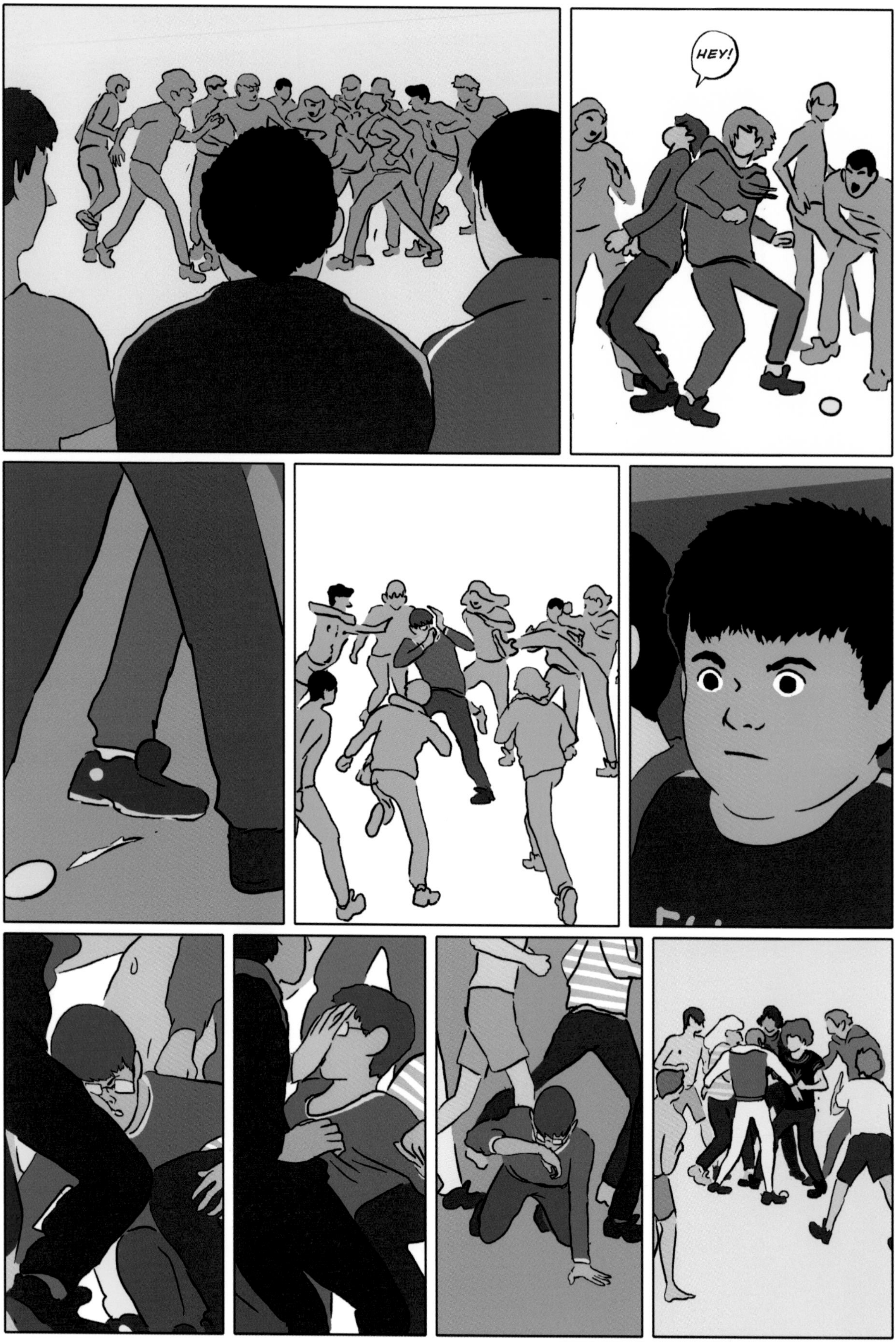
HEY!

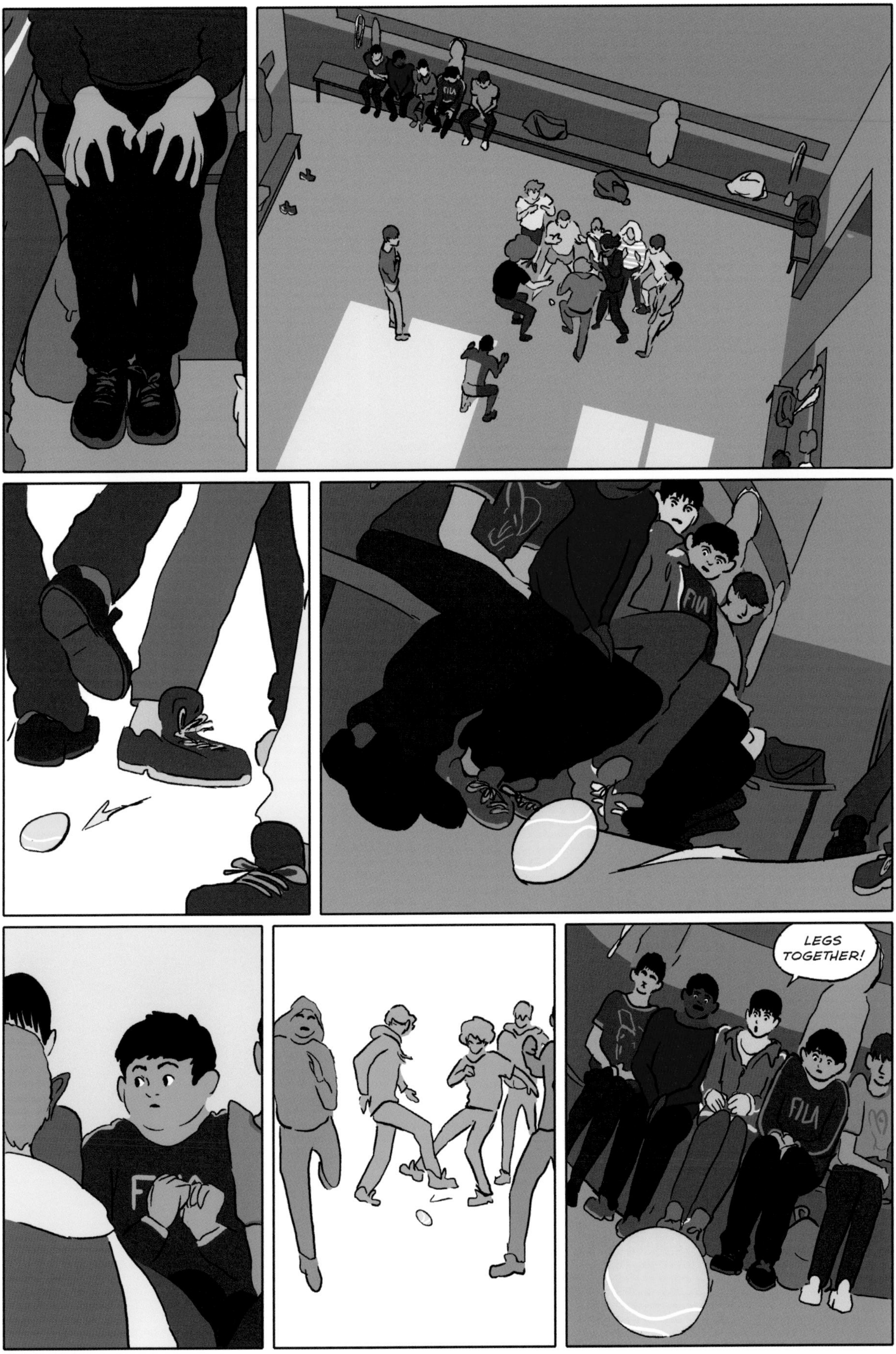
FILA
FILA
FILA
LEGS TOGETHER!
FILA

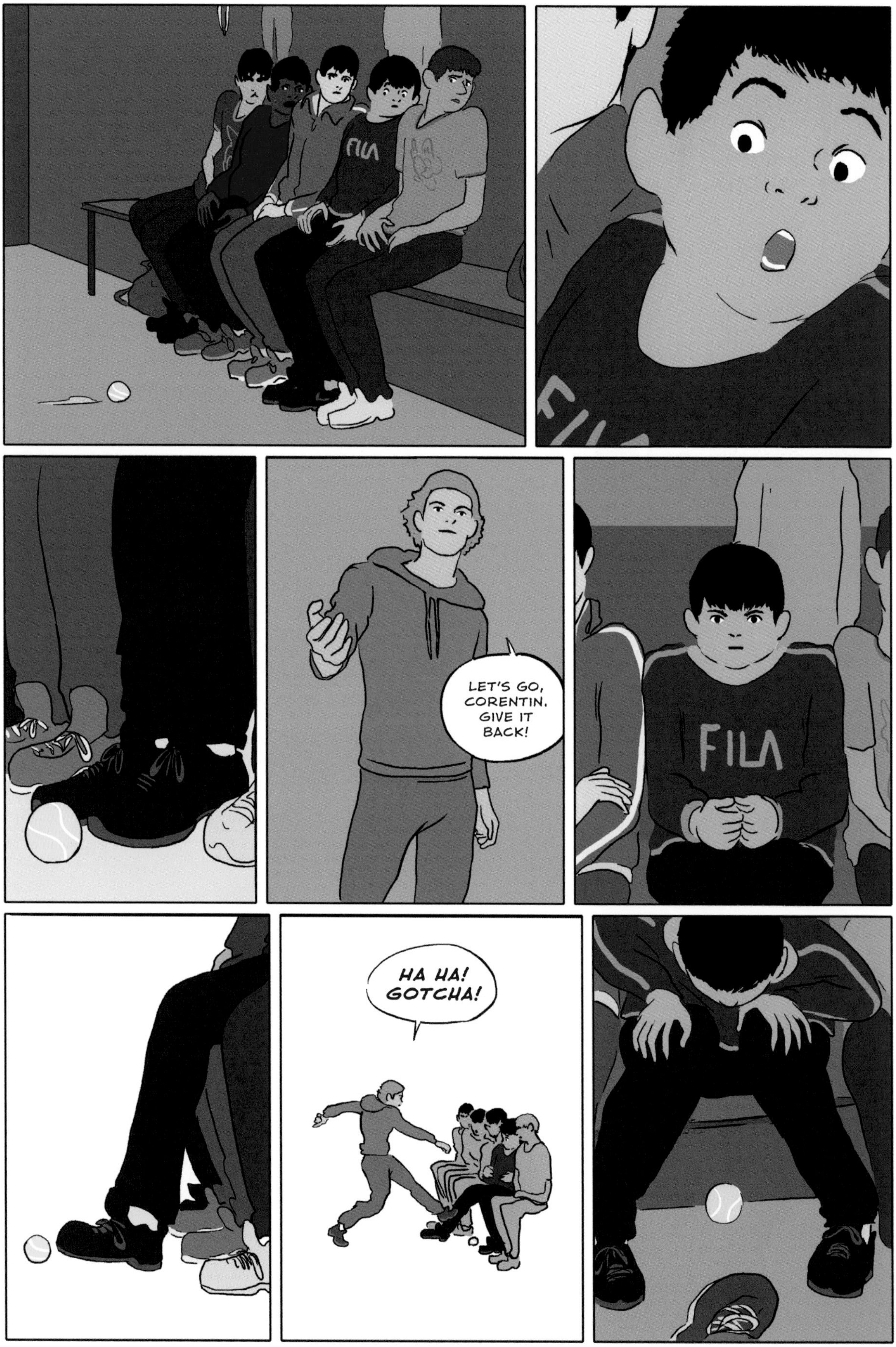
FILA
FILA
FILA
LET'S GO, CORENTIN. GIVE IT BACK!
HA HA! GOTCHA!

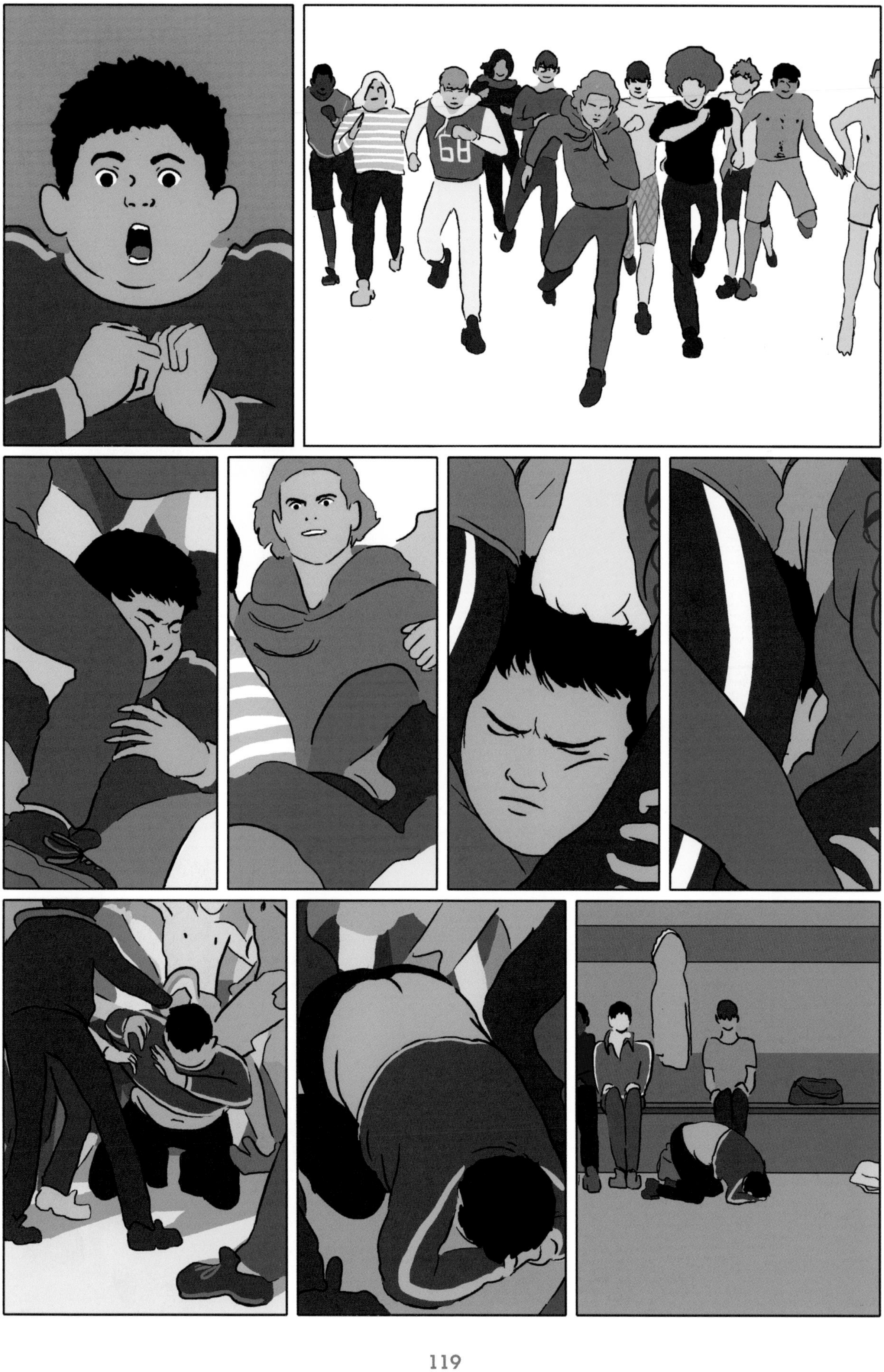

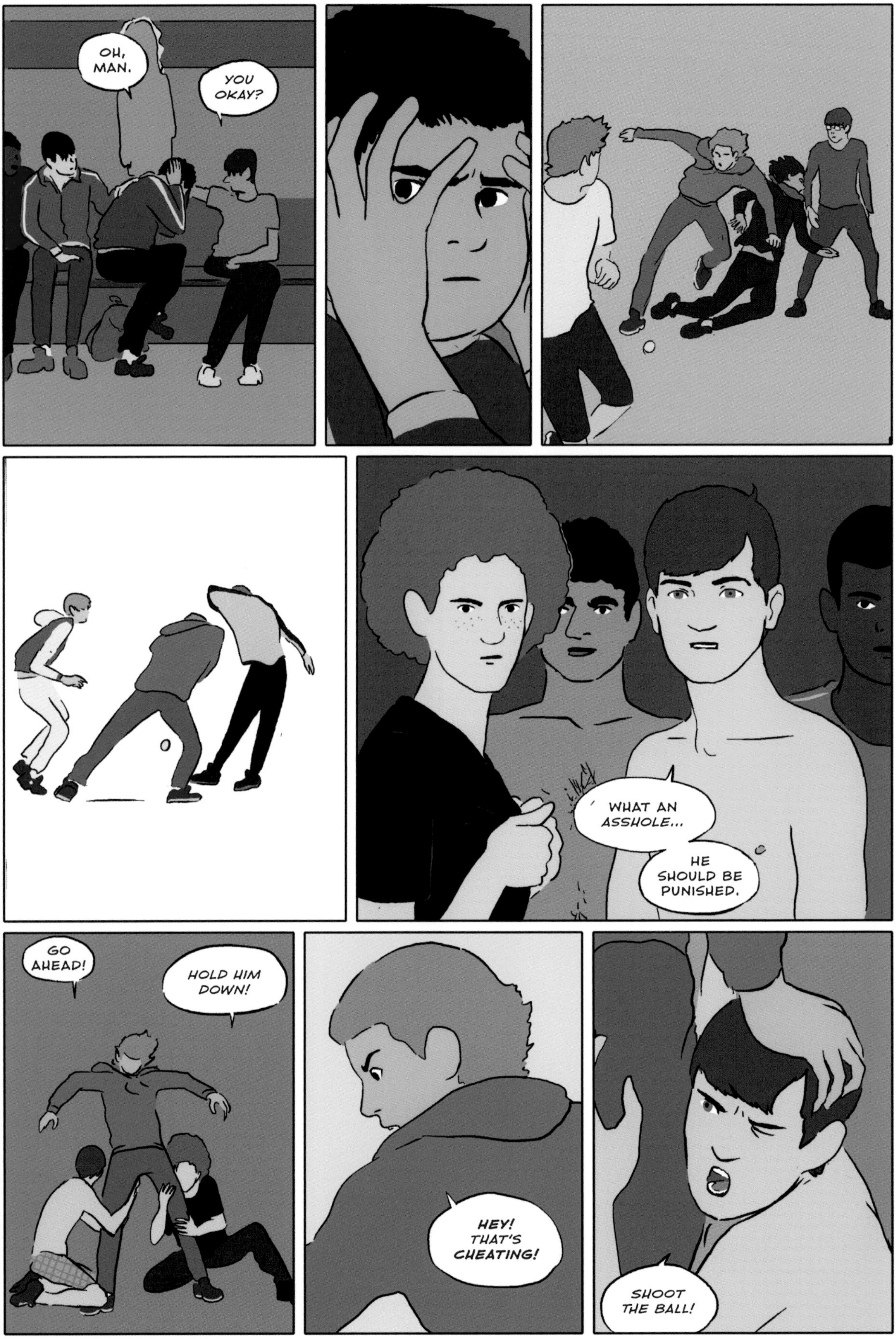
OH, MAN.
YOU OKAY?
WHAT AN ASSHOLE...
HE SHOULD BE PUNISHED.
GO AHEAD!
HOLD HIM DOWN!
HEY! THAT'S CHEATING!
SHOOT THE BALL!

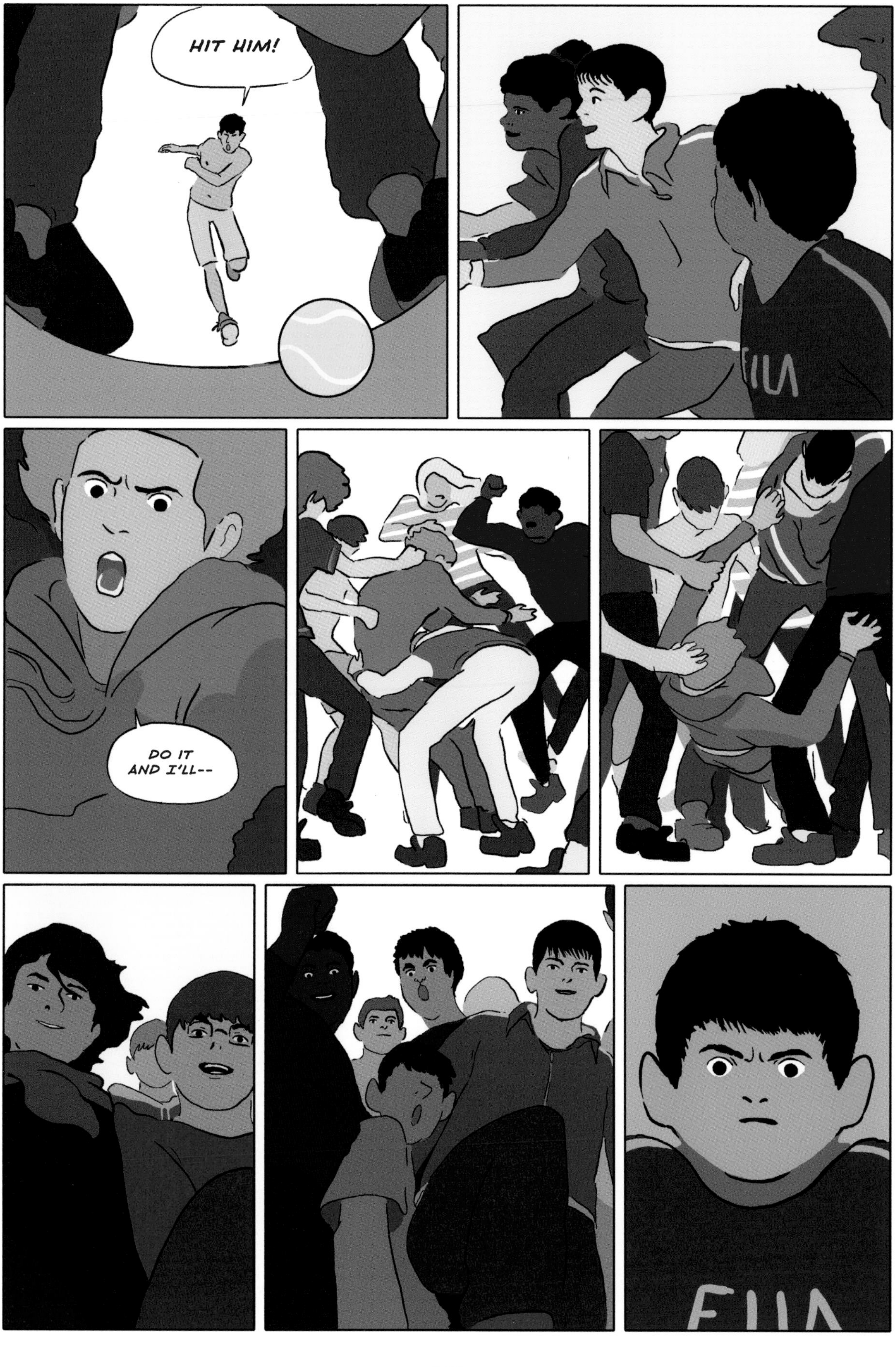
HIT HIM!
DO IT AND I'LL--
FILA
FILA

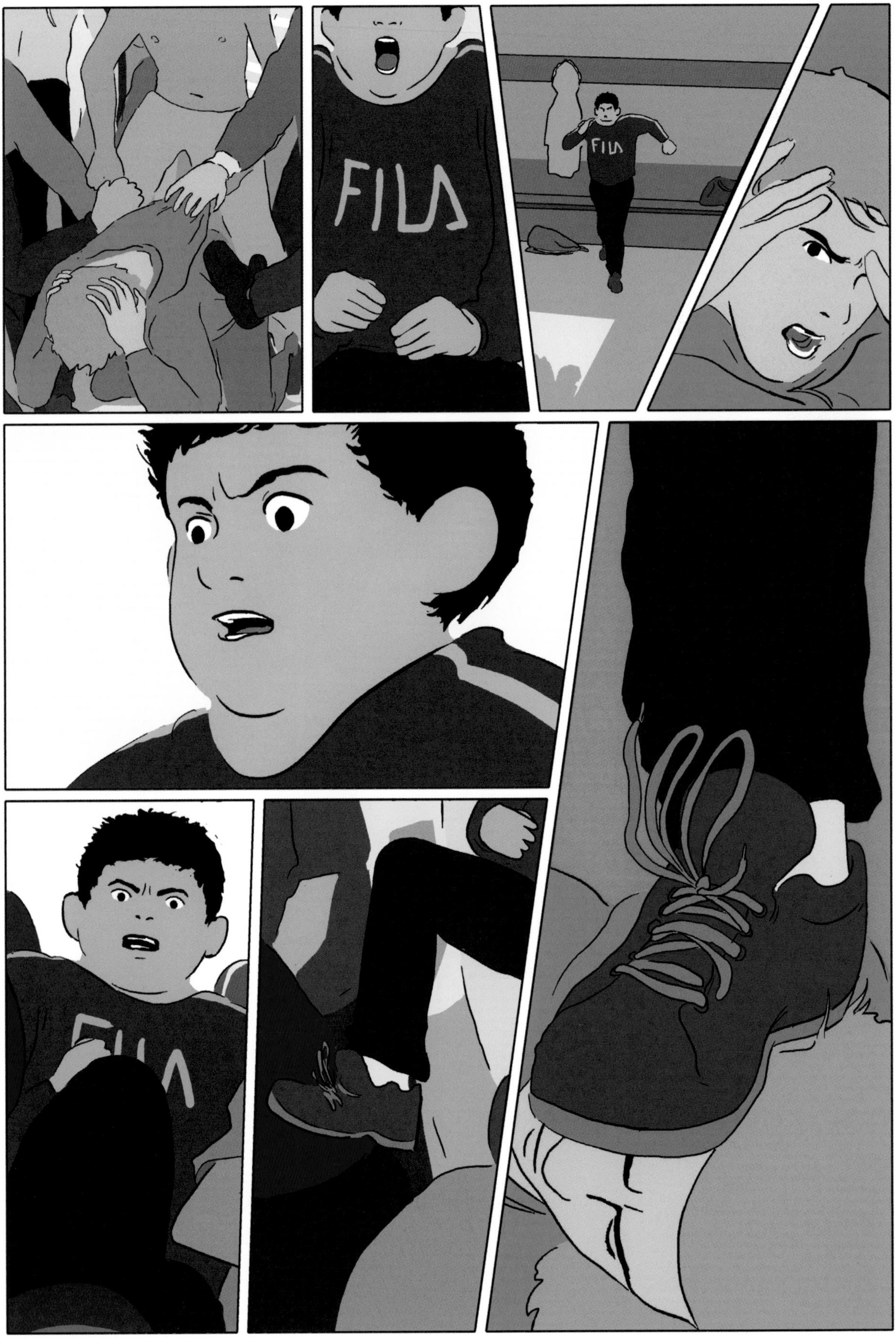
FILA

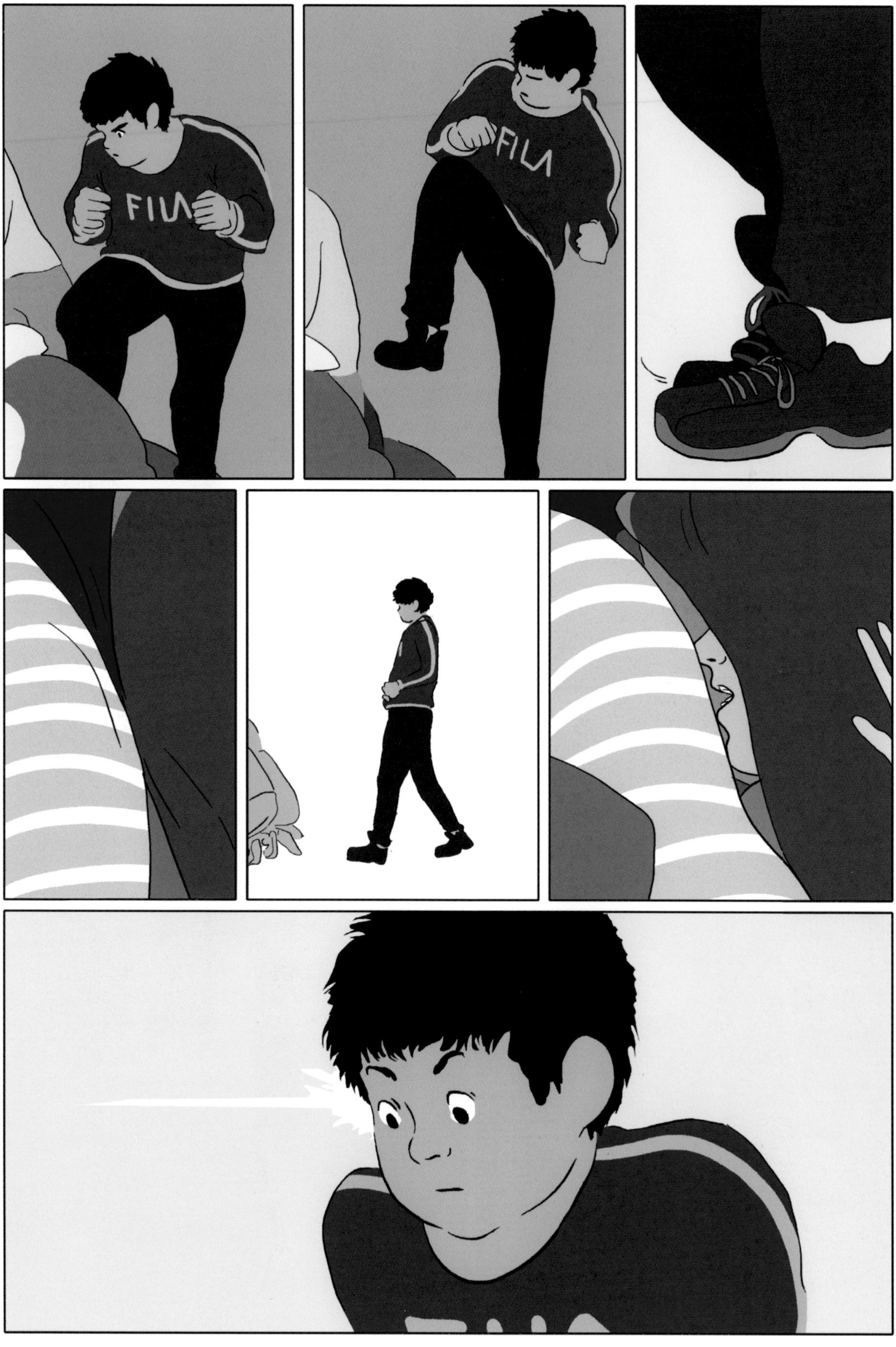
FILA
FILA

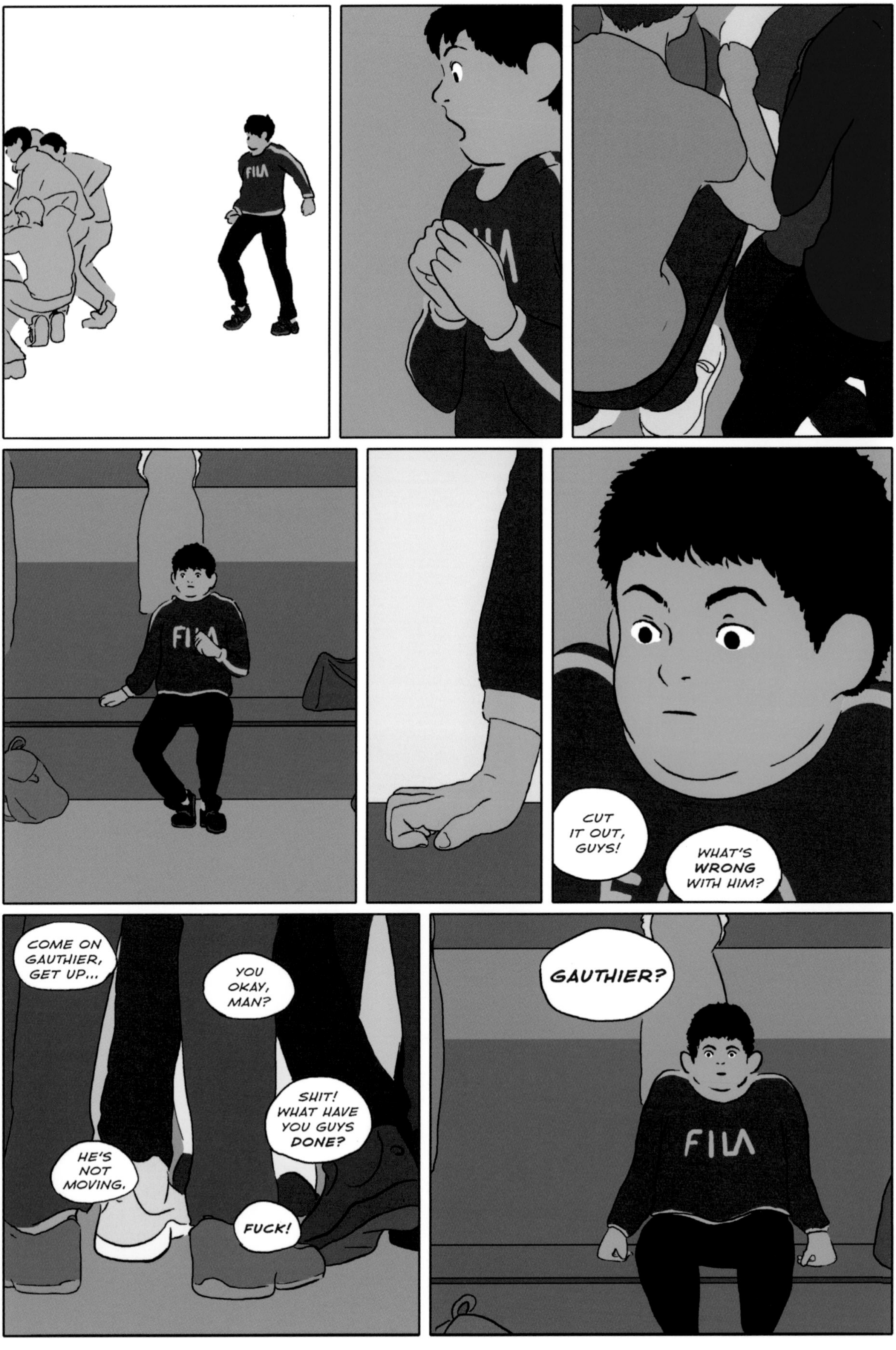
CUT IT OUT, GUYS!
WHAT'S WRONG WITH HIM?
COME ON GAUTHIER, GET UP...
YOU OKAY, MAN?
SHIT! WHAT HAVE YOU GUYS DONE?
HE'S NOT MOVING.
FUCK!
GAUTHIER?

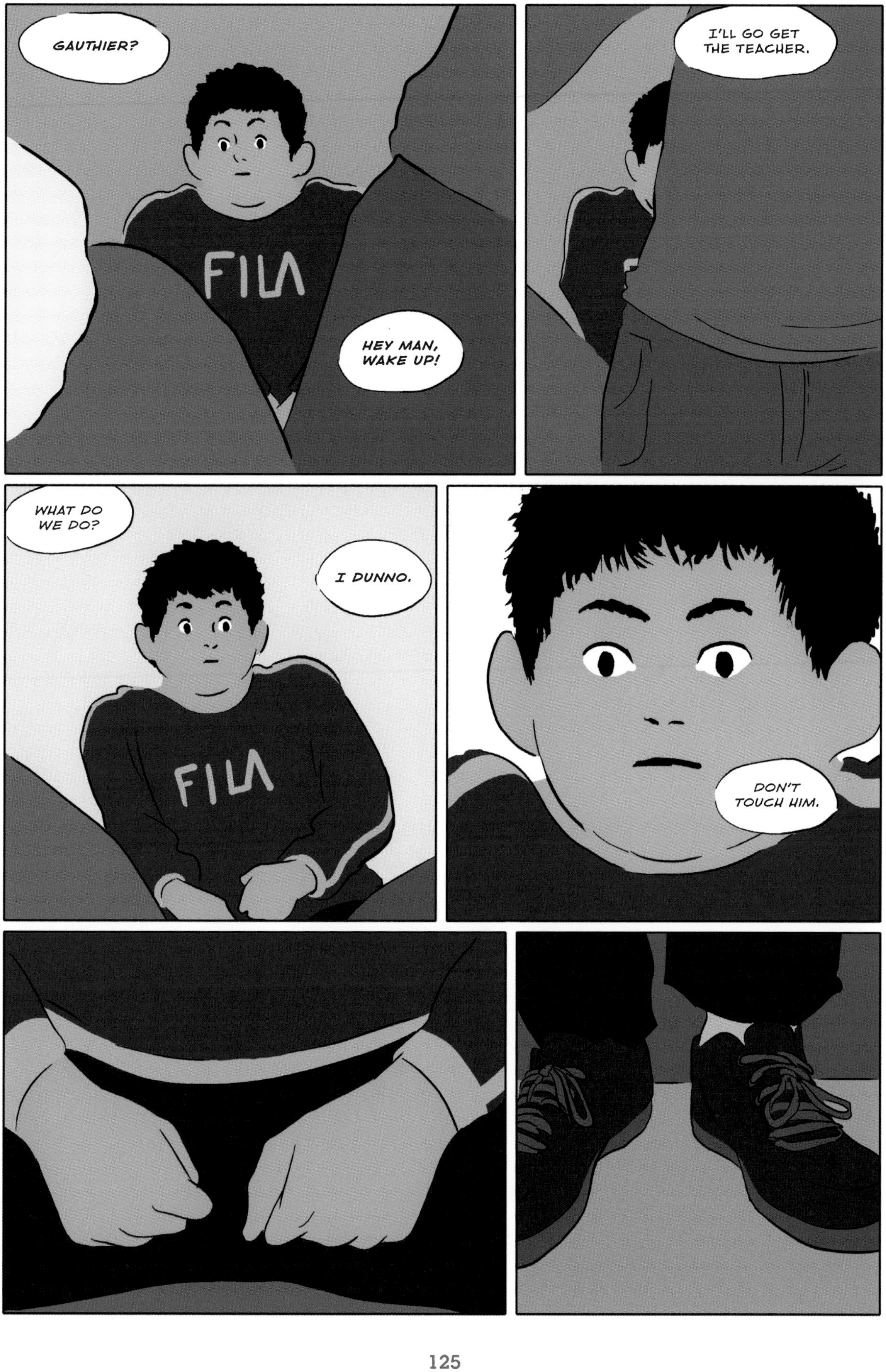
GAUTHIER?
HEY MAN, WAKE UP!
I'LL GO GET THE TEACHER.
WHAT DO WE DO?
I DUNNO.
DON'T TOUCH HIM.

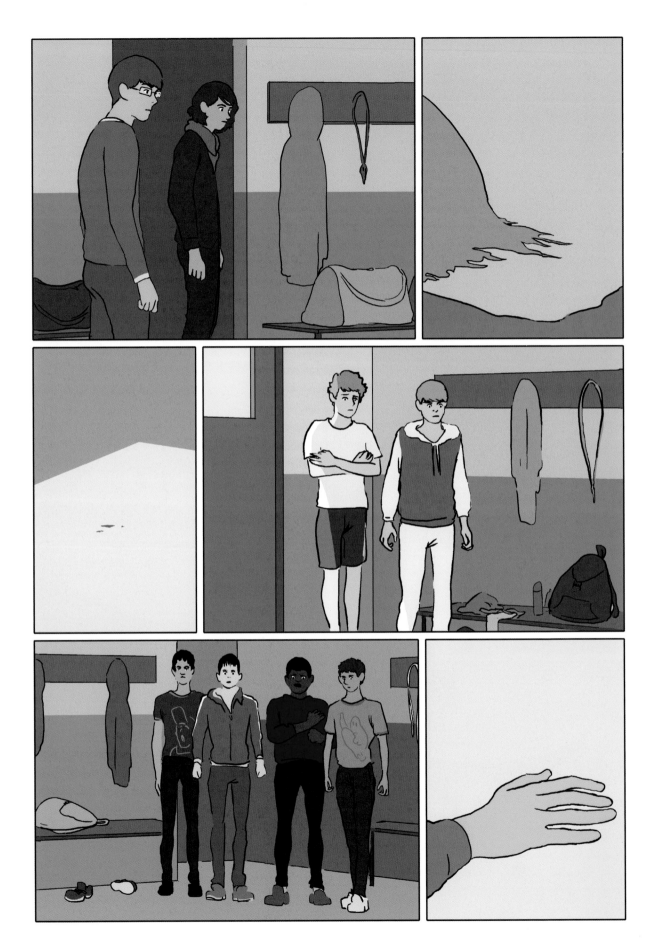

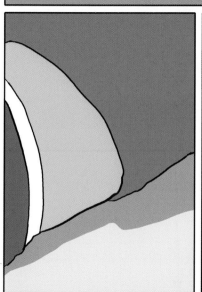

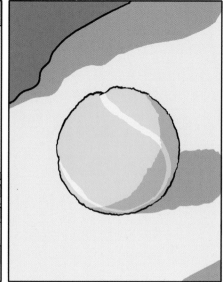

Bullying is unwanted, aggressive behavior
that involves a real or perceived power imbalance.
The behavior is repeated, or has the potential to be
repeated, over time. Both kids who are bullied and who
bully others may have serious, lasting problems.

Bullying can threaten students' physical and
emotional safety at school and can negatively impact
their ability to learn. The best way to address
bullying is to stop it before it starts.

StopBullying.gov provides information from
various government agencies on what bullying is,
what cyberbullying is, who is at risk, and how
you can prevent and respond to bullying.

StopBullying.gov
is a federal government website managed
by the U.S. Department of Health and Human Services
200 Independence Avenue, S.W. Washington, D.C. 20201
1-800-273-TALK (8255)